Maddie + Max

Dad, thank you for teaching me the magic of stories.
May you live forever in them. I miss you so much.

Maddie + Max

A Tale of Enduring Love

By Megan Effertz

Maddie + Max: A Tale of Enduring Love

Paperback ISBN: 978-1-955541-33-6
eBook ISBN: 978-1-955541-34-3
Hardcover ISBN: 978-1-955541-35-0
Library of Congress Number: 2023923685

Cover and Interior Design by Ann Aubitz
Published by FuzionPress

FuzionPress
1250 E 115th Street
Burnsville, MN 55337
612-781-2815
FuzionPress.com

PART 1
DREAM TETHERS SOULS

CHAPTER 1

"Maddie! Maddie, can you hear me?" Max shouts as he drops down onto his knees next to her. He puts two fingers on her throat, looking for a pulse. There is a faint one.

"Maddie! Maddie, wake up! I'm here," Max shouts at her. He wants to shake her, but he knows he can't move her. He gently puts his hand on her to let her know he's there and to check for breathing.

Maddie's eyes begin to flutter open.

"Maddie, stay with me. Don't go. You have to stay with me."

Maddie fades in and out, blood streaming down her face.

"You're going to be okay. Stay with me!"

Maddie's eyes slowly open. Max stops shouting. He lays down on the ground, placing his face in front of hers. He slides his hand from her back to her face, brushing her blood-stained blonde hair out of her eyes. As he does, their eyes lock in a stare just as they used to do. A small smile washes over Maddie's face, and Max smiles back, getting lost in the delicate moment.

"Help is on the way. Can you hear the sirens? Those are for you. You just have to stay with me, okay? Can you do that? Can you stay with me?" Max pleads with her, looking for a response.

Maddie smiles really big, like when they first met. "I've waited my whole life for you to stop me from running away," Maddie says faintly. "You never chase after me. You always let me go."

Max stares at her in silence, not knowing what to say. He knows it is true. Then a look of sadness comes over Maddie's face, and she says, "I have to go. My dad is waiting for me."

"No, no, no, Maddie. Stay with me," Max pleads.

"My dad needs me to come home," Maddie says as she starts to fade.

"Maddie, your dad can wait. I need you! Stay with me. You belong with me."

"I have to do what my dad says. I miss him so much."

"No, Maddie! Stay with me."

"I have to go."

"I love you, Maddie. Don't leave me. You can't leave me!"

"I love you."

Max doesn't know if she is talking to him or her dad. "Maddie! Please, stay with me, Maddie. I can't lose you again. Stay with me!"

Maddie doesn't move. Max's heart shatters as he is pulled off her. He reluctantly lets go and watches as the medics work on her, trying to force life back into her limp body. As he watches, he notices that the pool of blood under her head has circled out, around her blonde hair, almost looking like an angel's halo.

Max flashes back to the first day he met Maddie, when he saw that same halo framing her face, the moment he fell in love with her.

CHAPTER 2

It is one of those perfect Minnesota days when winter feels like it has finally melted away and anything is possible. With a fresh energy in the spring air, Maddie, Samantha, Max, and Ted step off the school bus and walk a couple of blocks toward a 1970s green rambler perched at the end of the cul-de-sac.

Ted unlocks his front door, and they pour into the silent, empty house. They know they have a couple of hours before his parents or sisters come home. The boys show the girls around the house and lead them downstairs. Off the basement, there is a three-season porch with a hot tub.

"There it is," Ted says as he points toward the tub. "I'll get it started. The bathrooms are that way." Ted points down a hallway covered in fake wood paneling and shag green carpet that tries to mimic the forest. A macramé owl hangs on the wall, watching them.

The girls run off to separate bathrooms to change. The boys change, slip into the tub, and turn on the bubbles so their bodies can't be seen beneath the water. The girls come back, covering themselves with bath towels.

Samantha wears a neon pink and yellow Body Glove bikini, her curly auburn hair pulled back in a scrunchie. She looks more like a nineteen-year-old MTV spring break contestant than the fourteen-year-old that she is. She is physically mature for her age and very self-aware of the power that gives her over the boys in her grade—and some of their older brothers too.

Maddie is in a yellow and black one-piece with a zipper down the front. She looks like a thirteen-year-old trying to look older. Her long blonde hair falls across her bare shoulders, framing her girlish smile and petite frame. Next to Samantha, she looks like a little sister, although they are the same age.

The girls drop their towels. Maddie quickly slips into the hot tub, joining the boys, while Samantha slowly lowers herself in so Max and Ted can get a good look before she disappears under the bubbles. Together in the tub, they all feel the thrill of adolescence—that feeling of being alone with the opposite sex for the first time, no parents around, not knowing what to expect next. As the water bubbles around them, they laugh awkwardly and avoid eye contact.

"Do you believe in soulmates?" Samantha asks the other teens, trying to be provocative.

"Totally. My grandparents are still madly in love after fifty years. The way my grandpa looks at my grandma melts my heart. I want that someday," Maddie replies.

"My aunt found her soulmate when she was our age and never got over him. It was tragic. She used to say to me, 'sometimes the heart has to endure love alone,'" Samantha shares.

Between Samantha and Maddie is Max. He is fourteen with an athletic build, black flowing hockey hair, and a face most girls find attractive, although he doesn't seem to notice.

"Did he die?" Max asks.

"No, why?"

"Because you said it was tragic."

"No, it was tragic because she spent all her life hung up on him. No guy is worth that. I've probably had more boyfriends than she has had."

Ted, the fourth hot tubber, also looks old for his age. At fourteen, he is already growing stubble and has thick wavy brown hair, like Patrick Demsey in *Can't Buy Me Love*, and could pass for nineteen like Samantha. He is bored with the conversation.

"I'll be your boyfriend," Ted interrupts, teasing Samantha and sliding closer to her.

"Shut up," she laughs but likes the attention as she fake pushes him away as an excuse to touch his chest.

"Soulmates are dumb anyways. Let's play Truth or Dare."

Their game is innocent enough to start but, as with any good game of Truth or Dare, it always escalates to a sexual nature, pushing the limits—especially with curious teens. When the dares turn a little more adult, Samantha teases the boys and Maddie quickly makes an excuse to stop playing to keep them out of trouble. The girls jump out of the hot tub and towel off, making their way to the bathroom to change so they can look like they just came from school when they leave.

Maddie notices Max's North Stars hat as he approaches the bathroom door while she is blow-drying her hair. She doesn't turn to talk to him; she can see him perfectly well in the mirror she's facing.

"Ted wants me to tell you to tell Samantha he thinks she's hot."

Over the blow dryer, she says, "Everyone thinks Samantha is hot. Should I tell her you think so, too?"

"Nah, she's not my type. I'm not into redheads."

It catches her attention. Everyone thinks Samantha is hot, and Maddie is used to being overlooked. She looks up from her hair into the mirror and catches his piercing blue eyes with hers. They stare at each other with the hum of the blow dryer filling the silence between them. He flashes a sweet, mischievous grin. She reciprocates the smile, not saying a word, eyes locked. The energy in the air crackles like lightning.

A loud popping sound breaks their trance as the lights go out. A scream from the other room echoes around them. They dash towards it.

It is Samantha, spooked by the sudden darkness. Ted flips a breaker and the lights come back on.

"Happens all the time when my sisters are both blow-drying their hair," Ted says without a care.

"We should go," Samantha instructs as she looks at Maddie, slightly embarrassed for screaming.

"Are you guys going downtown tonight?" Ted asks.

"Totally," Samantha says. "You guys going to be there?"

"Yep, see you there," Max says as he turns to Maddie to see if she is looking at him.

She is, and she quickly looks away, blushing slightly. They make plans to meet up and quickly say their goodbyes, then head out to beat Maddie's parents home.

♦ ♦ ♦

Downtown isn't what you would normally expect if you were in a big city. It is the main drag in a quaint lake town. It has a bar/liquor store the townies frequent, a Pizza Hut, a theater, and an ice cream shop on it, with the road ending at a boat launch leading into Lake Minnetonka. The rest of the strip is dotted with stores that sell art, clothes, gifts, and other local goods. The main crossroad extends from McDonald's, a mini-putt, and a few other popular local restaurants on one side to a beach, tennis courts, and a bandshell on the other side. A single phone booth marks the central meeting point in the area the kids call "downtown."

The local kids gather there on Friday and Saturday nights and hang out in the Pizza Hut parking lot, hopping between McDonald's, the theater, the ice cream shop, and walking to the beach to make out.

About forty teens mill around downtown that night with a buzz of chatter and laughter in the air. It's the first nice night of spring, and the energy is high with the anticipation of summer. Maddie is chatting with another girl from her class when Max walks up to them. She's dressed in a faded jean skirt, a navy Nautica t-shirt, white socks, and white Keds with a pair of Oakley's on her head like a headband.

"Hey!" Max interrupts. He's dressed in Girbaud jeans and a black No Fear t-shirt, and Air Jordans. He's drenched in Drakkar cologne, as are all the guys.

Maddie turns around and locks eyes with him again, and the biggest smile grows across her face.

He notices.

"Hi!" Maddie eagerly replies.

"What are you doing?" Max asks casually.

"Just hanging. You?"

"Same."

"Where's Ted?"

"I don't know. Where's Samantha?"

"I don't know. I was going to walk down to the beach and see if she's there. Maybe she's with Ted."

"Yeah, maybe."

"Want to come with me?"

"Sure."

Max and Maddie walk side by side toward the beach, chatting about nothing along the way. The beach area is quieter than normal—a rarity for the night.

They look in the secluded spots, but Ted and Samantha aren't there.

Not seeing their friends, Maddie and Max turn to head back. As they do, they catch each other's gaze again. Maddie sheepishly grins and breaks the stare by looking down at her feet. The sun dips below the edge of the lake, with only a bright pink glow reflecting off the water. The last of the sunlight casts a warm glow on her face and bounces off her Oakleys, creating a halo around her head. Max thinks she looks like an angel and can't turn away.

A street light flickers on, breaking the moment, and the halo is gone.

They finish turning around and start walking, drawn toward the buzz of excitement in the distance. Max slips his hand into Maddie's, and they walk the rest of the way back locked in silence. Not the awkward silence you might expect when two people don't know each other, but the way an old married couple sits in comfortable silence after knowing each other for a lifetime. They both sense a stillness and peace that is unusual for teens coming of age. Neither wants the moment or feeling to end, and they slow their pace to a leisurely stroll.

As they near the main road, they see the street is full of minivans with parents cruising the strip, looking for their kids. The minivans slow as they reach the stop sign, and kids quickly hop in the cars and slam the doors, so their parents can keep driving and they don't have to die of embarrassment from being seen getting picked up. Ironically, everyone is being picked up by their parents. No one can drive, and if you can, you're not hanging out downtown.

The crowd around the phone booth is dwindling as the taillights of the minivans fade away down the street. Maddie and Max spot Ted and Samantha and quickly drop hands before anyone notices. They walk up to the phone booth, and Ted and Samantha see them.

"Hey, kids!" Ted taunts. "What have you been up to?"

"Nothing, looking for you," Max replies.

"Whoa, sounds like you didn't get any!" Ted jibes.

"Hey, Samantha, there's my dad. Let's go," Maddie says, breaking up the banter and nodding toward the navy Chrysler minivan slowing in front of them.

Maddie and Samantha make their way toward the stop sign—a routine they've been doing for a year. As Maddie's dad stops, they slide the minivan door open, hop into the captain's chairs in the middle row, and quickly slide the door shut, not looking back at the boys—both because they don't want to be seen and because they don't want Maddie's dad to know they were talking to boys, although it is pretty obvious.

"You kids have fun tonight?" Maddie's dad quizzes.

"Yeah."

"Did you stay out of trouble?"

"Yeah."

"What did you do?"

"Nothing."

"You did nothing for four hours?"

"Yep."

Maddie's dad shakes his head, unconvinced.

"Where were you?" Samantha asks Maddie.

"I ran into Max, and we went looking for you and Ted."

"He's dumb, but his friend Tyler, he's cool. He's more my type. He plays drums and has an edge to him."

"Cool." Maddie isn't surprised. Samantha is constantly into new guys, and Maddie can't keep up. She doesn't even bother to try anymore.

"I love this song," Samantha shouts when "Kokomo" by the Beach Boys comes on the radio.

Maddie's dad turns it up. As they all sing along to the song. Maddie thinks about how Max held her hand. It's a moment she decides to keep to herself like a precious secret, not knowing it will be the first of many secrets she keeps about him.

CHAPTER 3

"Hey, Tyler wants us to pick up his friend, Chief, on the way to the band concert. He lives at the end of the street by the church," Samantha says as she finishes applying red lipstick to match her red polo shirt.

"Cool. Who's Chief?"

"I don't know, a hockey buddy or something."

"Ok. Ready? Let's go."

"I can't wait for school to be over and summer to start. I'm so bored with junior high," Samantha says as they walk toward the junior high. "I can't wait to be in college like my sisters."

"Two weeks! I'll miss walking to school. I don't want to take the stupid bus."

"You're lucky; I've been taking the bus forever."

"Do you know which house it is?"

"No, Tyler said he'd meet us by the church."

"Is that him?" Maddie asks as she points to a kid in a hockey jersey.

"Chief!" Samantha shouts.

"Hey!" Max says with a bit of a nervous laugh as he turns around and sees Maddie.

"Why do they call you Chief?" Samantha asks.

"Because I'm the boss at hockey," Max replies jokingly, but he's actually serious.

"Hi!" Maddie says excitedly.

"You should come watch me play sometime," he says casually to both girls.

"Let's go. I don't want to miss Tyler. He only gets to play the first half of the concert. The other drummer gets the second half," Samantha commands. "He's going to play me Bon Jovi."

The three of them walk toward the school. They can hear the band warming up as it echoes through the open cafeteria windows where they are set up to play. Minivans fill the parking lot as they arrive. The trio grabs seats in the back row.

When the band takes a break for intermission, Max, Samantha, and Maddie meet up with Tyler in the hall and they go outside. Samantha tags Tyler and yells, "You're it," taunting him to chase her. He does. Maddie and Max follow suit, running after Samantha. The four of them play chase across the parking lot, down the road, and end up on the hill in front of the church. Laughing and out of breath, they drop to the ground when they hear the band start again. Samantha deliberately made them miss the window to go back into the concert. No one cares, and they are happy to just be with each other outside on a perfect spring night.

Tyler looks at Samantha and grabs her. They start kissing in front of Max and Maddie.

Maddie and Max look at each other awkwardly.

Tyler sees the look. Like the instigator he is, he starts taunting the two to kiss. Tyler and Samantha can see the tension between Maddie and Max. They want to but neither moves.

"Chief, do it already. Kiss the girl," Tyler harasses.

"Yeah, do it!" Samantha encourages him.

Maddie looks up at Max, eyes locking. Time stands still as it did the first time they locked eyes in the bathroom at Ted's house.

Tyler breaks the moment shouting, "Kiss already!"

Max leans in. Maddie does too. Their lips touch. They lose themselves in the sweetest, most innocent kiss. Neither Samantha nor Tyler realizes they are witnessing Max and Maddie's first kiss. Not just with each other, but ever.

As Max leans in, Maddie can feel her heart beating in her chest. She wonders if he can hear it.

Max can't hear it, and even if he could, he's too nervous to notice. He hasn't stopped thinking about what it would be like to kiss Maddie since he met her, and now it is happening. His first kiss. His lips meet hers, and the taste of strawberry Chapstick surprises him. He pushes his lips harder on hers, wanting to taste every inch of her mouth.

She gives way to the kiss and melts a little. She can feel her body wanting to give out, but her lips cling to his, and she holds on. As his lips press harder on hers, she softens and opens her mouth slightly. She's surprised as his tongue slips into her mouth. Knowing how a French kiss works is different from actually experiencing it for the first time. She likes it, and she thinks he does too.

Max does like it and can't get enough of it. He forgets their friends are watching and reaches his hand behind Maddie's head to cup it so she doesn't fall away. They are in sync for their first kiss, as if they've been kissing for a million years.

The four of them spend the next hour laughing and intermittently kissing on the hill at the church. When they hear the concert wrapping up, Tyler heads back to the school to meet up with his parents. Max reluctantly heads home. Maddie and Samantha walk back to Maddie's house.

"Do you like him?"

"Yeah, he's funny and cute."

"He seems like he really likes you."

"You think so?"

"Totally! You should go out with him."

Maddie is beaming inside as she thinks about kissing Max. She can't wait to see him next week at school and hopefully kiss him again. It is all she thinks about over the weekend.

CHAPTER 4

The next two weeks of school fly by with tests to study for, papers to write, and, most importantly, making plans for the last day of school. In the halls, between classes, Tyler and Samantha can't keep their hands off each other. Maddie is a little jealous as she has to endure the PDA. She hasn't spoken to Max since the night of the concert and secretly wishes that was them.

The hallways are crowded and chaotic with kids going in both directions and suddenly stopping without notice at lockers. Maddie and Max see each other often in the hallways, but Max is always with his hockey buddies and Maddie with her friends, none of which know what happened. Only Samantha and Tyler know. Samantha is so consumed with herself, Maddie knows she won't bother saying anything to anyone else, and she thinks Tyler doesn't have an attention span long enough to remember. Max and Maddie walk by each other every day and smile but don't say anything. They both secretly think about kissing each other again.

One day Samantha sees Maddie smile at Max as he passes with his hockey crew. She asks, "Have you even talked to him at all since the concert?"

"No. We're always headed in the opposite direction or

with a bunch of people."

"Well, Tyler thinks he's into you," Samantha says as she retouches her bright pink lipstick in her locker mirror.

"He has a funny way of showing it," Maddie responds as Samantha shuts her locker door.

Samantha shrugs her shoulders and heads into class.

"Maybe we'll run into him tonight. Everyone's going downtown, right?" Maddie asks hopefully.

"Of course, it's the last day of school."

Downtown is packed with teens excited to be free from school, homework, and early morning schedules. The teenage crowd is like an outdoor concert but without the band. People aimlessly walk around chatting and bursting with joy in anticipation of the entertainment.

Maddie and Samantha are in the thick of the crowd. Samantha is waiting to be seen while Maddie scans the crowd for Max.

"Yo! Girls!" Tyler shouts from across the parking lot.

"There you are hot stuff!" Samantha says loudly so everyone can hear.

Samantha saunters up to Tyler and kisses him. Maddie follows her.

"Is Max here?"

"Chief? No. I think he's at home. His dad wanted him to do something to prep for hockey camp this summer."

"On the last day of school?"

"Yeah, his dad is pretty intense about hockey. Makes him practice all the time. Wants him to make varsity as a freshman," Tyler explains. "He's been pushing him since we could walk.

Kind of relentless about it, if you ask me."

"Wow, is he that good?"

"He's really good, but his dad doesn't think so, or if he does, he sure doesn't show it. He's making him go away to a bunch of different camps this summer. Probably won't see much of him. Too bad. I think he's into you." Tyler says flippantly as he leans in for another kiss from Samantha.

Maddie looks bummed, but then someone runs up to her and yells, "Tag you're it," and she takes off running. She forgets about him for the night and enjoys the freedom and excitement of the last day of junior high. Summer is here.

♦ ♦ ♦

"Dad, can't I go for a little bit? It's the last day of school. I want to see my friends," Max begs.

"I spent a lot of money getting you into this camp. I'm not going to have you half asleep at practice because you played all night with your little friends. You can see them later," Max's dad snaps.

"But Dad, everyone is there."

"I said, you can see them later. Go practice your stick handling if you're bored. Lord knows you need the practice."

Max heads outside and shoots tennis balls against the garage door in frustration, leaving dark marks on the pristine beige paint. He knows he'll hear about it later, but he doesn't care. He doesn't want to go to hockey camp. He just wants to be a normal teenager and hang with his friends on the last day of school. He also wants to see Maddie and maybe sneak another kiss while no one is watching.

Max thinks about how he has been avoiding Maddie for the last couple of weeks but really wanted to see her tonight downtown. He doesn't know what to say to her. He likes her, but he knows his dad would never let him have a girlfriend. His dad says girls are distracting and his hockey is too important. *Well, what about my happiness?* he thinks. *Hockey used to make me happy, but maybe something else could, like Maddie.*

He thinks about how he felt kissing her soft lips that tasted like strawberry. He wants to feel that way again, lost in a kiss, not stuck in a never-ending fight with his dad. He slaps the tennis ball hard in frustration against the garage door, and it bounces back quickly, hitting him in the stomach, snapping him out of his thoughts.

CHAPTER 5

At the start of the summer, Maddie really misses Max. Samantha can tell and tries to distract her with other boys. Maddie isn't very interested in the other boys and thinks about Max a lot, hoping to run into him, not knowing when he'll be back from hockey camp. As the days go by, Maddie's thoughts of Max fade, and she gets occupied with dance class, getting a tan and having the most fun possible before school starts. She eventually forgets about Max and enjoys the long days and short nights of summer with her friends.

Max spends his summer at various hockey camps. As the summer passes, he thinks less about Maddie and more about the upcoming hockey tryouts. He knows he has to be at the top of his game to make varsity as a freshman. It's a long shot, but if anyone has a chance, it's him. His dad has been grooming him since he was first on skates at three years old.

Max works hard all summer and shows vast improvement in his stick-handling skills. He's even surprised by how much he's grown over the summer—not just in skills but in height and muscle mass as well. He's gained a few inches and thirty pounds of muscle putting him at six feet one inch and one hundred and seventy pounds, giving him an even better shot at varsity. At the start of the summer, Max thought about kissing Maddie a lot, but eventually, those thoughts faded as he focused on drills and pushed her aside. Maybe his dad was right about girls being a distraction, he thinks. He has to be better than the rest of the guys. He doesn't have time for distractions.

As the summer comes to an end, he knows he's improved. Even though he didn't get to see his school friends, he saw his hockey friends, and best of all, he got a break from his dad hounding him all summer. He's a little sad to be going home and knows the pressure of tryouts is going to be intense, hanging over him all fall. He has a bit of fear about how intense his dad is going to be until tryouts are over, but he knows he worked hard and has the best shot he possibly can to make the team.

CHAPTER 6

On the first day of high school, the halls are bustling with four hundred new and confused freshmen trying to figure out where to go. The sophomores snicker as the freshmen walk by, looking at their maps and intermittently staring up at the numbers over the doors. The sophomores reminisce with each other about what it was like on their first day of school but don't offer any help. The first warning bell rings, and kids start filing into classrooms.

Maddie barely finds her classroom on time and walks into the room as the last bell rings, signaling classes are starting. There are twenty desks lined up, five chairs wide and four chairs deep—most of them already taken. She does a quick scan of the room and doesn't see any of her friends. As she is about to sit down, the teacher instructs everyone to stand up so she can seat them alphabetically. *So much for more freedom in high school,* she thinks. *It feels more like kindergarten, being told where to sit.* After the teacher finishes reading off names and everyone is seated, Maddie finds herself next to a girl named McKenna.

McKenna has a pretty, girl-next-door look, with long thick brown hair, brown eyes, and pure Scandinavian skin like Joey from Dawson's Creek.

"Hi!" Maddie cheerfully says.

"Hi, I'm McKenna."

"I'm Maddie. Did you get lost getting here? This school is so big compared to the junior high."

"No, I came to school last week and figured out the route to all of my classes. I live by a bunch of high schoolers, and they gave me the idea."

"Smart. I didn't know you could do that. What other classes do you have?"

McKenna shows her schedule to Maddie.

"Sweet. We have the next couple of classes together. Can I follow you?"

"Sure."

Maddie and McKenna spend the first half of the day together. McKenna points out where Maddie should go for her other classes as they walk between classes. They meet up again at the end of the day as Maddie is looking for her bus.

"You were a lifesaver today, McKenna. Thanks for showing me around. I don't think I would have made it if it weren't for you."

"No problem. It was nice to meet you. I'll see you tomorrow. Have fun on the bus. I live over there, so I get to walk home," McKenna says as she points to the houses about a half-mile away.

"Nice, I used to get to do that. I DO NOT want to ride the bus. Soooo lame," Maddie calls out in fake agony. "See ya tomorrow."

Maddie gets on the bus. It's pretty full already. She looks around for an open seat. An older girl she recognizes from dance shouts at her.

"You can sit with me in the back," Amber yells.

Maddie makes her way to the back to sit down. When she gets there, she sees Max sitting in the seat across from Amber. She almost doesn't recognize him, he's changed so much physically, until she sees his piercing blue eyes look at her.

"Hi," Max says.

"Hi."

"How was your summer?"

"Fun. How was yours? I didn't see you at all. Did you leave town all summer or something?"

"Yeah. I was at hockey camps for most of it, and when I was in town, I was at the rink practicing."

"Wow, don't you get tired of it?"

"Not really. It's peaceful on the ice, but I do miss my friends."

"You play hockey. What do you mean it's peaceful? Don't you just hit people into boards and fight?"

"I don't know, I just get in the zone and forget about everything else," changing the subject, he asks, "what are you doing after school?"

"I'm going for a run."

"Where are you running to?"

"I don't know. I just run."

"You could run to my house."

Maddie blushes as the thought of kissing him flashes across her mind. She brushes the thought away and replies, "Okay, maybe?"

The bus stops at his street, and Amber, the girl she is sitting with, and Max get off the bus with a few other kids. Amber says, "See ya tomorrow, Maddie."

Max smiles and asks, "See ya later?"

Maddie smiles and shrugs her shoulders.

Amber teases Max as they walk from their stop to their neighboring houses.

"She's cute. Do you like her?"

"Stop, no, of course not."

"Yes, you do. You like Maddie," Amber taunts. She's been Max's neighbor for years, and he's like a little brother to her. "I think she likes you too. She blushed when she sat down with me and saw you. You should go for it."

"You know my dad is strict about girls. I can't."

"He doesn't have to know," Amber shouts as she walks into her house.

Max thinks about kissing Maddie as if it were yesterday. He hopes she decides to come over.

Maddie gets off the bus a few stops later and walks to her house with a skip in her step.

She punches the keypad on the garage door to open it and lets herself in. Her family won't be home for an hour. She heads to her bedroom to find the perfect outfit for running. She picks bright pink spandex biker shorts, blue nylon Umbro shorts, and an oversized, inside-out grey sweatshirt. She laces up her Nike running shoes with a big blue swoosh on the side and heads out the door with her Walkman. Maddie clicks play on the Walkman, puts the headphones over her ears, and hears "Welcome to the Jungle" playing. She looks both ways, trying to decide which direction to run before heading towards the church.

When she gets to the church, she looks at the spot where she had her first kiss. Then she looks down the road where the bus dropped Max off. She runs towards the house she thinks is his, not quite sure.

Max's neighborhood is much like Maddie's. She thinks his house is a blue two-story home with a carefully maintained yard and a hockey net in the driveway. Situated at the end of the cul-de-sac, the home is the kind you'd see on a coffee commercial with a happy family inside. Little does she know, that's far from the reality that exists behind the front door. She's super nervous as she walks up to the house. Before she can ring the bell, Max sees her and opens the door.

"Hi. You came," Max says a little too eagerly.

"Yeah, I guess I did. Wasn't sure I would," Maddie responds shyly.

"What made you change your mind?"

Maddie looks back at the church, shrugs her shoulders and says, "I don't know." Then looking down, "Cute dog."

"Thanks. I'm surprised he's not barking at you. He barks at everyone. He must like you."

Maddie leans over and pets the dog, "Good boy. I like you too."

Max walks outside and shuts the door behind him.

"Want to go for a walk?" he asks, holding out his hand.

Maddie nervously says, "Sure," as she wipes her hand on her sweatshirt before sliding it into his. She gets the same rush of feelings she did the first night he held her hand and wonders why he couldn't do this while they were in school last year.

They wander down the road towards the church, chatting

about nothing. When they get there, the parking lot is empty. They sit down on a grassy hill under a hollowed-out old tree, chatting and nervously plucking grass from the ground, avoiding each other's eyes.

Eventually, they look up from the grass and lock eyes.

"Remember what we did the last time we were here?" Max asks with his mischievous grin.

"Yeah, that was my first kiss. Kind of hard to forget," Maddie says, blushing.

"Have you kissed anyone since?" Max asks, avoiding the fact it was his first kiss, too.

"No. You?"

"No. The guys at hockey camp didn't do it for me."

They both laugh and then fall into an awkward silence. Then Max leans in for a kiss and wraps his arms around her pulling her close. Maddie feels small, but safe, next to his large muscular body. Like only teenagers do, they passionately kiss for what seems like hours. They are interrupted by a car pulling up and parking right in front of them. The church pastor gets out. Embarrassed, they quickly jump up. The pastor smiles at them and walks into the church.

"I gotta go," Max says abruptly, worried someone might tell his dad what he was doing today.

"Um, okay, I probably should too before my parents wonder what happened to me," Maddie says, a little surprised.

Maddie and Max take off in separate directions, thinking about kissing and wishing they had more time together.

CHAPTER 7

Over the next couple of months, Maddie sits with Amber on the bus ride home. Amber can tell that Maddie and Max are into each other and encourages it. She talks Max up a lot to Maddie. Although Maddie pretends not to be interested, she loves hearing stories about him. Max constantly cracks jokes to try to divert Maddie's attention; he hates being talked about. Some days, Maddie announces she's going running, and Max extends an invitation for her to stop by on her run. Other days, Max initiates and asks Maddie where she's running that day. They see each other about two to three times a week after school when they don't have other plans, practice, or too much homework. After a while, it becomes a bit of a routine, with Maddie picking out the cutest running outfit she can and jogging the mile to Max's house so she doesn't work up a big sweat before seeing him. They often go to their spot at the church under the tree unless there's a church activity taking place, and then they walk over to the old abandoned railroad tracks that split their two neighborhoods. It's always secluded there after school, with woods on each side of the tracks shielding it from the neighbors' windows and curious eyes.

Still shy with each other every time they meet, they start

with playful banter as Maddie waits for Max to kiss her. Once the kissing starts, the talking stops until it's time to head home. They spend most of September and October this way, never able to get enough time to kiss and dying with anticipation of when they'll meet again.

As fall starts to fade into winter, the weather makes it harder to meet up. Between the cold weather and Max preparing for hockey tryouts, the only time they get to see each other is on the bus ride home. Max's sister brings him to school in the mornings; she's a senior and has a parking pass but has theater after school and can't bring him home.

Luckily, Maddie has her own telephone line at her house and knows they probably won't be able to keep their secret rendezvous up much longer. She writes her private number on a slip of paper and hands it to him before he gets off the bus. "Call me when you want. I have my own line, so you can call whenever."

"Cool," Max says, relieved. He's really into her and knows their meetup time is coming to an end and didn't know how to keep it going once hockey starts.

♦ ♦ ♦

Maddie is in her room watching a big old tube TV with a pop-up VCR sitting on top. Her phone rings. It's a black Swatch Watch phone, which she answers on the first ring.

"Hey, what are you doing?" Max asks on the other end of the line.

"Wishing I could run. My dad said I can't run outside

anymore, too cold and I could get hypothermia."

"I'll keep you warm."

"I know that's what I was thinking, but I can't tell him that," Maddie says, picturing it in her mind.

"Have you told anyone?"

"No, have you?"

"No."

"It's kind of fun having a secret."

"Yeah, it's like something just for us."

"Do you think anyone knows?"

"You mean besides the pastor?"

They both laugh.

"So embarrassing, but really, do you?"

"No, it's not like we're ever in school together. That school is so big we never run into each other."

"I know. I can't believe we don't have one class together. At least we get to see each other on the bus."

"Not for long. I just found out I made the hockey team. Practice starts next week after school. I won't be on the bus anymore."

"Congratulations! That's so awesome. I'm so happy for you, but sad for me. You're the only good thing about that bus ride. I can't believe you made varsity."

"You'll survive. You've got Amber. Actually, I only made JV. Come to my games?"

"That's still good, though, as a freshman, right? I've never been to a hockey game. I'll ask my friends if they want to go."

"I gotta go. My dad is yelling for me. He's not going to be happy I made JV. Bye."

"Bye," Maddie says to the ringtone.

Max runs down the stairs from his room to the kitchen, where his dad is waiting for him. He's excited Maddie said she'd come to his games but only gets to enjoy the moment for a second.

"Well? What did you hear about the team?"

"I tried my hardest, Dad. I really did," Max says, with his eyes staring at the ground.

"What's that mean, Max? Did you make the team or not?" Max's dad demands.

"I only made JV. I'm sorry," Max says, ashamed.

"What do you mean, you only made JV? What happened at tryouts? Did you take your eye off the prize? We've been training you for this forever. How did you not make the team?"

"I don't know, Dad. I tried my hardest. I'm the only freshman that made JV. No freshman or sophomores made varsity. They have a good team that's been playing together for a long time."

"I'm calling the coach tomorrow. This isn't acceptable."

"Please don't, Dad. That's only going to make it worse. He can't change the team now. Maybe somebody will get hurt, and I'll get a chance to play up this season."

"I'll be talking to the coach. I want to know what you did wrong that you didn't make the team. I spent a lot of money on you with the expectation that you'd be on varsity this year. Go to your room and do your homework. You're going to need to get good grades if you want a shot at college now."

Max is crushed. He knew his dad would be disappointed, but he had hoped that he'd still be at least a little excited that

Max made JV. The hockey program at his school is really competitive, and making varsity as a freshman was always a long shot. Everyone else was impressed he made JV with the stiff competition. Knowing he let his dad down steals any chance for him to enjoy the fact that he at least made the JV team. He knows he's going to have to spend all season being the best on the team if he has any chance of making his dad proud.

CHAPTER 8

"Your brother plays hockey, doesn't he?" Maddie asks.

"Yes, I live in the stupid rink," McKenna shares.

"Do you ever go to the high school games?"

"Yeah, my brother practices before them and likes to stay and watch. Why, you want to go?"

"I've never been to a game. It could be fun."

"Come with me. I could use a friend at the rink. It gets so boring."

"Okay, let me know when the first one is. I'm excited to go to my first game."

"Great, you can come over to my house and ride with us after school."

The first game of the season is at the home rink and the ice is full of JV hockey players warming up. There is a crisp smell of ice that has been freshly groomed by the Zamboni. The sounds of sticks hitting pucks and ricocheting off the boards hang in the cold air.

"Watch out!" McKenna shouts as a puck flies at them. "You've got to pay attention, or you could get hit. Sometimes the boys flip them out on purpose, but most of the time it's just a wild puck."

Maddie looks out on the rink. Max skates by the glass and taps it with his stick; he knows she is there. She smiles to herself. That puck was meant for her. She leans down, picks it up, and slides it into her coat pocket.

McKenna watches Max as he holds Maddie's gaze.

"Don't even bother dating a hockey boy. Hockey comes first, especially if they are good. It's 24/7 hockey. They don't have time for anything else. Look at my brother. He eats, sleeps, and breathes hockey."

McKenna and Maddie watch the JV and varsity games together. McKenna explains the game so Maddie can understand. She's interested in learning, but mostly she just wants to watch Max skate. She looks for him after the JV game, but the coach has the team watching together so they can learn from the varsity game.

♦ ♦ ♦

"Hello?" Maddie answers on the first ring.

"Hi!" Max replies.

"Been awhile."

"Yeah, between hockey and homework, I don't have much free time. But I think about you all the time."

"Yeah. I knew you'd call today."

"Were you dreaming about me again?"

"Yep."

"You know they say when you dream about someone, your souls get tangled. The more you dream, the stronger the tether becomes between the two."

"I believe it. When I dream about you, I honestly feel like we're together in those dreams. It feels so real to me, like our souls are dancing while we're asleep. Do you think we're soulmates?"

"Maybe. What are you doing?" Max changes the subject.

"Watching our show, *Jenny Jones*."

"What's the show about today?"

"Turn it on. It's about long-lost lovers reuniting."

"Maddie, I bet we'll be on that show someday."

"What? What do you mean?"

"You'll be the one that got away, and I'll have to find you."

"You can always find me in my dreams, Max."

Max groans.

Maddie gets serious. "You have to officially date me before you can say you lost me. Maybe someday you'll make an honest woman out of me, and I'll be your actual girlfriend, not just your secret."

"If only I had the time," Max says, when he really means a different dad.

"What's time have to do with it?" Maddie asks, taking a chance. She's been wanting to make their relationship official.

"You deserve someone who can devote more time to you," Max explains. "I can't take you on real dates because I'm always at hockey games or practice, or off at camps."

"I understand that, but a lot of guys who play hockey have girlfriends. Don't you want me to be your girlfriend?" Maddie pushes some more.

"Honestly, I think what we have right now is better. Just you and me. It's special. Something no one else has or knows about. I want to hold on to this secret as long as I can. Once other people know, they'll have opinions and mess things up. Don't you think what we have is special?"

"Well, yeah. I mean, when you put it that way, it makes me want to keep it a secret forever. But then you can't go on *Jenny Jones* to find me. The whole world would know about us then," Maddie teases.

CHAPTER 9

"Thanks for coming to all these games. You know you don't have to," McKenna says.

"I like them. Plus, it's fun to hang out," Maddie says. "I can't believe the season is almost over."

"First, I had to go because of my brother, and now I'm stuck here because of my boyfriend. I'm never getting out of this rink. We should get you a hockey boy if you're going to be here all the time too."

"I thought you said hockey boys don't have time for girlfriends."

"Ugh, they don't, and they smell too. How did I end up with a hockey boyfriend? I spend too much time in this stupid rink. Who do you like?"

Maddie shakes her head. "No one."

"No one? Come on. There has to be someone. I've known you for almost a year now, and you never talk about boys you like. Don't you want a boyfriend?"

"With dance and school, there isn't much time for boys."

"There is always time for boys. You're missing out."

The sound of a stick hitting the glass in front of them breaks them from their conversation.

"So annoying. We know you're there, Chief. Why does he do that every game? It's like he's saying, 'Look at me. I made JV as a freshman, and no one else did,'" McKenna mimics.

Maddie smiles and shrugs her shoulders.

"You should date him. I don't think he's ever had a girlfriend," McKenna says, inspired.

"Hi, ladies," Tyler says, in a way that makes them think he's up to no good.

"Hi, Tyler. What do you want?" McKenna asks, sounding annoyed.

"I like your idea, McKenna. Chief hasn't had a girlfriend and should date Maddie," Tyler replies.

"What, oh God, no. I was just kidding," McKenna says, trying to take it back.

"You know, I recall a time when those two had a thing," Tyler says, grinning at Maddie.

McKenna looks at Maddie.

"What?!" McKenna shouts loudly. The crowd turns to look at her to make sure everything is okay.

"When?" Maddie asks, startled, looking at Tyler with wide eyes pleading not to say anything.

"You know what I'm talking about," Tyler presses.

Maddie shakes her head. "No, no, that was junior high. I don't even remember it."

Tyler looks at Maddie and then turns to McKenna and says, "Max and Maddie made out at the church last year during the spring band concert."

"Whatever, Tyler. It didn't mean anything," Maddie insists.

"I haven't seen him interested in a girl since then."

"I have," Maddie insists.

"Who? I am sure I would know if he liked a girl."

"Sure, he's with her every day after school."

"He's at hockey. What are you saying? Is he seeing the ticket lady?" he laughs as he thinks about it.

"The ice is his mistress," Maddie says. "Look at him out there."

"Whatever, you can't make out with the ice," Tyler says as he rolls his eyes and walks away.

McKenna looks at Maddie. "It's you!"

Maddie looks around. "What?!"

"It's you. He likes you. It makes sense. You are always here with me. You never show interest in other boys, and you watch him like a hawk on the ice, and he's always tapping on the stupid glass." McKenna concludes.

Maddie shakes her head trying to dismiss it.

"It is. Tell me it isn't," McKenna demands.

Maddie shakes her head no again.

"You can't say it. Tell me. Tell me everything."

"Shh. I don't want anyone to know."

Tyler pretends like he isn't listening and yells something at the ice. His mind is working out this secret and how he's going to catch Max in it.

Behind Tyler, a few rows back, is Max's dad who also started listening when McKenna shouted. Max did the one thing he told him not to do. He got distracted by a girl.

♦ ♦ ♦

"Something to Talk About" is playing when Max's dad turns the car radio off and asks, "Is there something you want to tell me?"

"Yeah, did you see me make the game-winning goal? I've been working hard on that shot at practice," Max says proudly.

Max's dad asks again, "Anyone you want to tell me about?"

"I have no idea what you're getting at," Max sneers at his dad. He's feeling hurt that he had a great game, and his dad is getting on his case again.

"There was a little blonde girl talking to your buddy Tyler tonight," Max's dad says.

"So?" Max replies.

"Do you know her?" Max's dad asks.

"I didn't see him talking to anyone. I was focused on the game. I'm always focused on the game when I'm out there. You taught me that," Max defensively replies.

"Well, Tyler seems to think there might be something going on between you two. He even said you kissed her last year at a band concert."

Max goes white. He knows he's in trouble. He searches for an explanation.

"Oh, her," he blurts out. "She's no one. One of Tyler's old girlfriend's friends."

"Did you kiss her last year?"

"No, well, yes, I mean, I guess," Max says, unsurely. "She actually kissed me after Tyler and his girlfriend were daring us. It was stupid. I didn't even talk to her after that."

"You know during hockey, no girls. You need to stay focused. She's probably the reason you didn't make varsity. Don't let her or Tyler distract you."

"I know. I am focused. Did you see me tonight?" Max asks, looking for some validation from his dad.

"Yeah, I saw you score some goals for the JV team. I didn't see you score any on varsity."

Max tries so hard on the ice to make his dad proud, but it never seems to be good enough. Max loves being on the ice, out of his head and in the game. It's the only place he feels sure of himself. Off the ice, he feels like he can't do anything right. His dad criticizes him on everything. He is even beginning to make him feel bad about hockey since this is the first year he didn't make the team his dad expected him to. Playing hockey is an escape, but it is beginning to feel like a prison.

What Max doesn't know is that he was actually good enough to make varsity. The coach told his dad and assumed he would pass the news on to Max. The coach wanted to develop Max and give his other players time they earned over the years on varsity. He also said having Max on JV would let him shine and push his other players, especially with his growth spurt, while on varsity, he wouldn't get a ton of ice time. Max's dad argued with the coach's logic but wasn't able to change his mind, so he took it out on Max. Max is the star player on the JV team but listening to his dad, it sounds like he is the worst player ever to play high school hockey.

His dad moved to Minnesota from Canada to play hockey in college and was quite good but had to stop playing when he got his girlfriend, now wife, pregnant with his daughter. Not having come from money and no family around to help, he reluctantly quit playing to work and support his new family. He still blames his wife for ending his hockey career and isn't about to let Max make the same mistakes with some girl. He pushes Max as a way to fulfill the dream he missed out on, not realizing how much he's taking away from his son.

Late that night, Max sneaks a call to Maddie.

"Hello," Maddie answers.

"What were you and Tyler talking about at the game? My dad knows we kissed and asked if something was going on with us," Max says, frustrated.

"McKenna said I should date you, and Tyler overheard and chimed in. I blew it off like it was a bad idea, and then Tyler outed us and told McKenna about our first kiss. McKenna about lost her mind that I didn't tell her, but I acted like it didn't even matter and that it was so junior high anyways. Your dad must have overheard."

"What else did you guys say?"

"Nothing! McKenna kept pushing me about you, and I said you were in love with hockey."

"Good."

"What?" Maddie asks, a little hurt. "Does it really matter if our best friends find out about us? I mean, we've been sneaking around for almost the whole school year. Wouldn't it be nice to stop hiding?"

"No, I like it this way," Max objects, not telling her about his dad.

"It was fun at first, but honestly, it's getting a little old. It'd be nice to be like the other girlfriends and cheer loudly for you, kiss you good luck before a game. Don't you want that?"

"No, I don't need that kind of distraction before a game. It's bad enough I'm on JV. I have to work my ass off so I make varsity next year. I can't fail again."

"Is that what I am to you? A distraction?" Maddie asks, now really hurt.

"No, I didn't mean that. You wouldn't understand," Max says, frustrated. He wants to tell her why but doesn't.

"Try me."

"I gotta go," Max hangs up as he hears his dad coming.

Maddie is crushed. She thought they had a precious secret between them, but felt in that moment maybe she was just a secret and not precious at all. Maybe he was embarrassed by her.

"Max, who were you talking to?"

"No one."

"I think we should take the phone out of your room until hockey season is over. Give it to me,"

"God, Dad, I was just getting help with homework," he shouts in frustration, not wanting to end the call with Maddie the way he did.

"Don't talk to me that way, son. Give me the phone. You can have it back when the season is over. If you need help with your homework, you can ask me."

♦ ♦ ♦

Over the next week, Maddie anxiously waits to hear from Max after school, but he doesn't call. She begins to wonder why they have to be a secret. She really did like having a secret with Max. There was a bit of a thrill—would he call, or wouldn't he? When would they meet up again? Would anyone find out? But after almost an entire school year, she thought it would be nice to tell her friends, especially McKenna.

McKenna had a boyfriend who played JV hockey with Max. They had met over the years at the rink and were friendly. When she became a freshman, he started making excuses to call her brother and eventually just called her. Somewhere along the way, they started "going out." They kiss before every game and talk about the game afterward. Maddie wants that with Max.

"Hey, I don't think I'm going to make it to the game tonight," Maddie says to McKenna in class.

"What's up?" McKenna asks.

"I'm just not feeling quite right," Maddie says, using it as an excuse. Really, she felt bad because Max hadn't called her since the last game, and she didn't know what that meant. She felt dumb going to the game if she was a distraction.

"Bummer, it is so much more fun when you are there. I hope you feel better."

"Me too. It's probably nothing. I'm sure I'll be better by the next one."

That night Max skates around the rink during warm-ups as he always does. He was hoping to catch a glimpse of Maddie before the game but doesn't see her. Finally, he sees McKenna talking to a blonde girl he assumes is Maddie. He skates over and taps the glass with his stick. When they turn around and look at him, he realizes it isn't Maddie; it's another girl he doesn't recognize. His gaze trails back to McKenna as he skates away, wondering why Maddie isn't there.

He has an awful game. He is distracted by Maddie not being there. Where was she? He knows he can't call her after the game because his dad took his phone. He decides to run into McKenna and find out where Maddie was. After the game, he chats up McKenna's boyfriend in the locker room and walks out with him. McKenna greets them both.

"Hey, guys," she says softly. "Tough loss tonight."

"Yeah, we just couldn't get it together," McKenna's boyfriend says, looking at Max. "Dude, you were way off tonight. Did you lose your lucky charm or something?"

"Something like that," Max says and looks at McKenna. "No sidekick tonight?"

"Maddie?" McKenna asks, intrigued.

"Yeah, you two are always together. Did you get in a fight or something?" he inquires, hopeful.

"God, no, she's the best," McKenna says. "I wish she was here. It was so boring watching my brother's game without her. She said she didn't feel well, but she seemed fine to me."

"She's probably sick of you two making out after the games," he jokes as he punches her boyfriend in the arm. "I gotta go; my dad is waiting. See ya!"

"See ya, Chief. We'll get 'em next time," McKenna's boyfriend Tommy says.

As Max walks away, McKenna looks at her boyfriend and asks, "Do you two normally chat?"

"No, not really," he says. "But I mean he had a really bad game. He was probably just trying to buy some time."

"Time for what?"

"Time before he has to get in the car with his dad."

"Why would he want that?"

"His dad is really intense when it comes to hockey. Rumor has it he tore into the coach after Chief didn't make varsity."

"What, why? He's a freshman. He's lucky he made the JV team," she says, annoyed. Max was good, but she didn't know what all the fuss was about.

"Chief has been training for varsity since he could skate; everyone knows that," Tommy says. "It was never an option to be on JV. His dad has very high expectations of him. Why do you think Chief is so good? His dad pushes him non-stop. He is brutal on a good night. I can't even imagine what tonight will have in store for him."

"Brutal how?"

"He breaks down every play and tells him everything he did wrong. He makes him practice every day, working on whatever mistake he made. And that's beyond normal practice. We played on a few teams together over the years, and even when we were little, his dad pushed him more than normal parents."

"Poor guy," McKenna says as she looks at him leave the rink with his head down. She had no idea.

"Let's go," he says and breaks her out of her thoughts.

The next day in class, McKenna asks how Maddie is feeling.

"Much better," Maddie says. "Must have just been a 24-hour thing. How was the game?"

"They lost. It wasn't good. Max was really off his game,"

McKenna says, purposely so she can watch Maddie's reaction.

"Oh, that's too bad," Maddie says, trying not to show any emotion, but her secret betrays her as she looks a little pleased.

"Did you just smile a little?" McKenna asks.

"No, why would I do that?" Maddie says defensively. She did smile a little. She is happy he had a bad game. She had a bad night, missing being with her friend and watching him on the ice. It was normally the highlight of her week. He hadn't called her since the last game, and she is hurt.

"Yes, you did."

"I don't know what you're talking about."

"Out with it."

"Out with what?"

"What is going on with you two?"

"With who?" Maddie tries to deflect. She knows McKenna is onto her.

"With you and Max."

Maddie's eyes drop to the ground. She shrugs her shoulders. "I don't know." When she looks up, McKenna can see her fight back tears.

"I knew it. You like him."

Maddie just looks at her, and a single tear rolls down her cheek. She brushes it away with the back of her hand.

"I did. I do," Maddie pauses. "But I don't think he likes me."

"After school, you are going to tell me everything," McKenna says. "My house, no excuses."

"Okay," Maddie says, pulling herself together as class starts.

After school, Maddie and McKenna walk to McKenna's house. They grab a snack and sit on the couch.

"I want to know everything!"

Maddie takes a bite of her chips and queso, thinking about where to start. When she's done chewing, she begins, "Tyler wasn't lying. We did make out at the band concert last year, but it wasn't like he made it sound. It was sweet. We had met a few weeks before and had an instant connection and hung out downtown. We walked around and held hands and just were with each other. It was so comfortable, like we'd known each other forever. We didn't talk after that, and I blew it off. Then Samantha and I were going to see Tyler—he was going out with her back then—at the band concert, and we had to pick up his friend Chief on the way. I didn't know Chief was Max. My stomach had butterflies when I saw him. I was so happy. After the first half of the concert, we were all hanging out on the hill at the church, and they dared us to kiss. And we did. It was my first kiss, and a long, slow one. I'll never forget it. Then that was it. We didn't talk or see each other all summer. He went off to hockey camp. I moved on but thought about him a lot, hoping to run into him somewhere."

"And…there has to be more than that for you to cry and for him to have the worst game of his life. Then what?"

"Okay, but if I tell you, you are sworn to secrecy."

"Oh, this is going to be good, isn't it?"

"Promise!"

"Promise!"

"Max and I have had a secret fling going on."

McKenna's eyes grow wide, and she says, "I knew it, I

knew it. How much of a fling are we talking about, huh?"

"No, not like that," Maddie says as she blushes. "It's sweet."

"Do tell."

"We ended up riding the same bus at the beginning of the school year. He asked me one day what I was doing after school. I told him I was going running, and he told me to run to his house, so I did," Maddie starts. "Then one thing led to another, and we were meeting up at the church or the tracks a few times a week after school. We would just kiss and kiss and kiss. It felt like hours, but it was never that long because he always had to get home before his parents got home from work."

"And…"

"Then hockey started up, and we didn't really see each other anymore. He'd call me when he could, but it was always right after school or late at night. He was at hockey or practicing all the time. Just like you said, hockey boys don't have time for a girlfriend. The only time we really would see each other would be at the games. Thank God we met or I don't know if I ever would have seen him this year. We don't have any classes together, and I never see him in the halls."

"So, what happened that you didn't come to the game last night?"

"I think we got in a fight, but I don't know. He was upset that his dad overheard us talking to Tyler about the band concert. I said, 'So what if our friends find out? Wouldn't it be nice?' and he said no, he liked it the way it was. I told him it was getting old, sneaking around, and it would be nice if I could cheer for him at the games like a real girlfriend. He told me he didn't need that kind of distraction, and then he had to go, and I haven't talked to him since."

"He had a really bad game last night. I've been watching him play for a long time, and I've never seen him do so bad. It has to be because of you."

"Well, if it was, you'd think he'd call, wouldn't you?"

"I don't know. Tommy said his dad is pretty hard on him after games and that it was probably going to be brutal last night. Maybe that's why he wants to keep you a secret?"

"Maybe, but he's never said anything about his dad to me. We just watch *Jenny Jones* together over the phone and talk about stuff. Sometimes he practices his jokes on me. He's really a clever guy and so funny. We can seriously talk about nothing forever. We never run out of things to say. I miss talking to him."

"Will you come to the next game with me and see what happens? It's the last one of the season. I'm guessing he wouldn't want you to miss it."

"Okay."

That afternoon after hockey practice, the coach asks Max to hang back. As the other boys head to the locker room, the coach talks to Max.

"You okay?"

"Yeah, why Coach?"

"You were really off yesterday."

"Yeah, I'm sorry about that. I don't know why. I promise I'll get it together before the next game. My dad has me focused on drills, so I won't screw up next week."

"Everything okay at home, Max?"

"Yeah, why Coach?"

"Max, it's not a secret how much your dad expects out of you. He was pretty upset with me when you didn't make varsity, even after I told him why."

"You mean because I wasn't good enough."

"No, you were good enough. I told him that. I didn't put you on varsity because you wouldn't have gotten enough playing time with the other guys, and I didn't want you to miss ice time. You've got the next three years to be on varsity. This year I wanted you to shine and help lead the team to a great season. You're a natural leader, you are dedicated, and you have so much passion for the sport. You wouldn't have gotten to play like you are if I'd put you on varsity, and that wouldn't have been fair to you. Your dad told you that, didn't he?"

"No, he told me I was a failure and that I had to try harder to make the team."

"Max, you are far from a failure. You are one of the best kids I've ever coached," he reassures Max. "That's why I'm concerned about you. What happened?"

Max doesn't know what to think or feel at that moment. He just found out after the worst game of his hockey career that he was good enough to make varsity and his dad knew it and never told him. He knows he can't say anything after his performance last night on the ice because his dad will throw it back in his face. It was bad enough, listening to him tell him how bad he was last night and how if he plays like that again, he's never going to make varsity. He's also hurt that his coach didn't tell him himself. That he made that decision for him and never thought about how it would affect him. But most of all, he wants to tell Maddie that he was good enough after all, but he knows he blew that too.

Shutting down all of his emotions, he says, "Just an off game, Coach. I was distracted. I won't let it happen again. Can I go? My dad is waiting."

"Sure. But I want you to know you can talk to me about anything. Okay?"

"I know, Coach. Thanks." He starts to skate away and then turns and asks, "Do I still have a shot at varsity next year, or did I blow it last night?"

"Max, play like you normally do next week and don't blow tryouts, and you're on the team. We're going to need you."

"Thanks, Coach!" He says as he heads towards the locker room.

He thinks to himself, Okay, I gotta get my head back in the game, and I still have a shot. I can do this. No distractions. He pushes the thought of Maddie out of his mind.

♦ ♦ ♦

The next week, Maddie goes to the game with McKenna.

"I'm glad you are here."

"Me too. I am probably overthinking things. I can't wait to see him tonight."

Max skates around the rink during warm-ups. Tonight, he doesn't tap the glass like he normally does. He sees Maddie and it gives him a boost of confidence but pushes her out of his mind as he skates by her. He has to focus. He has to have a perfect game tonight.

As warm-ups end, Maddie's heart sinks. *It's over*, she thinks to herself. McKenna notices too but doesn't say anything. Max is on fire that night with a hat trick and an assist. The crowd is wild watching him play. Maddie is excited for him but keeps herself in check. She's heartbroken inside and keeps wondering why he didn't acknowledge her. She thinks his last game must have just had an off night and it had nothing to do with her.

After the game, Max is so happy. He redeemed himself from last week and reclaimed his title as Chief. Best of all, Maddie was there to see it.

McKenna's boyfriend Tommy says, "Hey Chief, you must have found your good luck charm, hell of a game buddy." The other players echo the sentiments.

Max is beaming with pride inside. A feeling he doesn't get often. He decides he's going to sneak a phone call to Maddie tonight. He deserves to talk to her after how hard he worked.

As he leaves the locker room, he sees Maddie talking with McKenna and Tommy.

"Chief! What a game tonight!" Tyler says as he walks up to him and pats him on the back. As they walk by the girls, he adds, "Girls, did you see my boy tonight?"

Max looks at Maddie. Maddie looks down, feeling hurt that he's been ignoring her. Max is about to say something and pauses when he sees his dad and keeps on walking. Maddie's heart bursts. McKenna can feel it in her silence.

"We should probably get going. I've got a test I need to study for," McKenna says to Tommy and Maddie.

"Cool," Tommy says and leans over and kisses her. "I'll see

you tomorrow."

McKenna and Maddie walk in silence for a moment. McKenna breaks it, "I'm sorry."

"Don't be," Maddie says. "At least I know I didn't really matter to him. He was just passing the time. Better I find out now."

"He's a jerk," McKenna says, trying to make Maddie feel better.

"Yeah," she weakly agrees, and a tear rolls down her cheek that she wipes away.

Max gets in the car with his dad and is lost in thought about why Maddie looked down when he and Tyler walked by. *Maybe I shouldn't call her,* he thinks. *She didn't seem like she wanted to talk to me, and she did skip the game last week. Maybe I blew it after all.*

"Good game tonight," Max's dad says to him.

"What?" Max snaps out of his thoughts.

"You did good tonight. That's the kind of playing I expect to see all the time. It's that kind of playing that gets you on varsity."

That last comment stings, knowing what the coach told him about not making varsity. *I play like that all the time,* Max thinks. *Maybe not as many goals like tonight, but with the same skill and passion. Why is he praising me tonight?* He forgets about Maddie for now and enjoys the rare moment his dad is proud of him.

"Can I have my phone back?" Max asks. "Hockey season is over."

"Not just yet. Not talking to whoever you've been talking

to seems to have improved your game. Let's make sure you make varsity, and then you can have it back."

"But Dad, Coach said if I got my head back in the game tonight, I'd make the team next year," Max pleads.

"What about tryouts?"

"Well, yeah, I can't blow tryouts either."

"Then don't blow tryouts, and you can have your phone back."

And the moment is gone. His dad once again shows how little he believes in his abilities. He can feel the anger and frustration rising in him. He had a great game. He wants to be able to call Maddie, but at the same time, he doesn't know if she wants him to call her, and the only person he wants to talk to about his problems is her. He has so many emotions swirling around inside of him he feels like he is going to explode.

"What if I don't play?"

"What do you mean, what if you don't play? That's not an option!"

"You can't make me."

"If you are under my roof, you do what I say."

"If I don't make the team, you can't make me play."

"Don't test me, son," Max's dad threatens.

Max knows not to push it any further. He's seen his mom test his dad before, and it doesn't end well. But he wants to. He hates his dad in this moment. He's stolen all the joy of the game from him, and now he's keeping him from any chance with Maddie too. Max drops his head. "I'm sorry, sir," he mutters in defeat.

Max doesn't call Maddie that night. He pushed his dad too

far already to take the chance, and he doesn't think she wants to hear from him anyway, he reasons. He sulks in his room instead, staring at the posters of Mario Lemieux and Mike Modano. He thinks, *one day, I'll be like them, and then I can do whatever I want. I won't have to listen to my dad anymore.*

His dad is still fired up about his threat not to play hockey next year. To show him who's in charge, Max's dad signs him up for another summer of hockey camps, ensuring he'll have no free time for girls or other distractions.

When Max finds out, he's a little relieved. He doesn't know if he can bear knowing why Maddie didn't talk to him at the last game. He assumes he blew it with her and would rather not have to see her this summer. He knows he won't see her in school, and if he remembers right, Amber says they are taking a different bus now to get to dance class after school. He should be able to avoid Maddie for the rest of the school year, and he does.

McKenna and Maddie still hang out, even though hockey season is over. They don't see each other as much since McKenna's boyfriend has more time for her now, and Maddie is busy with dance. One day, after school, they are hanging out chatting.

"Have you heard from Max at all?"

"No, have you?"

"No, but Tommy is going to one of the hockey camps he'll be at this summer. Do you want me to ask him to ask about you?"

"No, it's clear he doesn't want to talk to me anymore. If he did, he would have called by now," Maddie says. "I just can't believe it just ended, and I never talked to him again."

"It is weird. I would have sworn it was you that made him play like crap that day. But then he came back and had an amazing game and totally blew you off."

"Yeah, thanks for the reminder."

"I didn't mean it like that. It just doesn't make sense. You snuck around for a year, and it sounds like he was really into you, and then boom, nothing."

"I don't get it either, but I can take a hint."

"Have you ever thought about calling him?"

"And say what? Remember how you called me a distraction, and then stopped talking to me, and had your best game ever?"

"Yeah, I guess, what would you say?"

"It's okay. He was a distraction for me too. I've really been focusing on my dance. I want to make dance line next year. I don't have time for him anyway. Tryouts are at the end of the year, and if I make it, I'll be practicing all summer. They do summer boot camp to make sure we are conditioned for the season. My friend Samantha is on it this year, and she says it is all-consuming."

Maddie spends the next few weeks going to dance class or running. When she runs, she goes the opposite way of the church to avoid any accidental meet-ups. She thinks about Max a lot while she runs but tries her hardest to push him out of her brain. She keeps turning it over in her head. *Did I miss something, or was he really just using me? But using me for what? All we did was kiss and talk on the phone. Why did he just stop talking to me when I suggested we "go out"?* She can't figure it out and it's driving her mad, so she promises herself to stop thinking about him—and she does.

She focuses on dance and practices the tryout routine for dance line over and over in her basement room. Her aunt was a Rockette. Maddie grew up hearing her aunt's stories and has wanted to be on dance line since then. She is determined to make the team this year.

During the week of tryouts, girls are taught the routine that they will perform for the final day of tryouts. The week starts with about a hundred girls. Girls slowly drop out as they struggle to learn the routine. One Saturday, Maddie spends the day at tryouts. There are about sixty girls trying out for twenty-four spots. More than half will go home disappointed like she did last year. During the final day of tryouts, girls are placed into large groups and they perform the routine together. From those groups, some girls are dismissed and the remaining girls get put into smaller groups to perform again. Same process: some girls get dismissed after that performance. The remaining girls are asked then to perform the routine individually so the coach can really focus on technique and stamina. After all of the performances, the remaining girls wait in the gym for their names to be called. Maddie waits to hear her name. After twenty other girls' names are called, she is beginning to give up hope of hearing hers. Then, she finally hears her name called. Inside she is bursting with joy and relief, but on the outside, she keeps it together because after three more names are called, there are going to be a bunch of sad girls. She knows; she's been there before and remembers how bad it hurts after working so hard. After the other girls leave, the new dance line team celebrates together. Maddie is so happy. A few of her friends are on the line, including her friend Samantha. She can't wait to tell her parents. For a split second she wants to call Max and tell him—then she pushes that idea out of her mind.

Maddie spends the summer running the track at the high school with the rest of the dance line girls in the mornings for conditioning and then they go into the gym for a couple of hours, learning steps and new routines. Their first performance will be for the homecoming pep fest and then the homecoming football game, which will be a practice for the upcoming competition season. Their performance is choreographed to Van Halen's "Dreams."

Chapter 10

As sophomore year starts, Maddie remembers her first day of high school and takes care to point the freshmen in the right direction to class. She's excited for a new year and open to the possibilities it will bring. She makes it through her first day of classes and is thankful that Max isn't in any of them. There is a cute boy named Jake in her English class, and they strike up a quick friendship. He calls her often for help with homework. The only homework they have is reading a book, so she knows he's making an excuse to talk to her, and she likes it. Maddie likes the idea of a new guy and one that doesn't play hockey. Jake is a skier, and it doesn't seem that practice and meets are as time-consuming as hockey. After a month of getting to know each other, Jake asks Maddie to the homecoming dance. She's excited. This will be her first real date, and Jake is one of the older kids in class, like Max, and has his license, so their parents won't need to drive them.

Maddie spends the next week dress shopping with girlfriends when she's not at dance practice. They go to the local mall and shop the department stores and boutique shops for the perfect dress. After trying on what feels like a hundred dresses, Maddie picks an off-the-shoulder, short, form-fitting purple sequin dress with a big bow across the front. One of her girlfriends chooses a fuchsia satin and black velvet dress, another one chooses a teal satin dress with matching sequins with big puffy shoulders. They are all excited about their dresses and talk about how they are going to do their hair and what they'll do before the dance.

The day before the dance is the homecoming pep fest and that night the football game. More importantly, though, it is her debut on the high school dance line team. This is a big week for Maddie. When homecoming arrives, Maddie is ready. Her team is dressed in short white Lycra dresses with blue sequins across one arm and chest wrapping around their waists. They have on white tights, white Keds, and their hair is pulled back in a French braid fitted with a white sailor's cap with a blue sequin star on top. Maddie is the shortest one on the dance line, which means she is on the end of the line. The line has all the tall girls in the middle, and on each side of the line, it spans out from tallest to shortest. Being an "end" is extra hard work as Maddie has to keep the whole line straight and not let it sway as they are kicking. It also means she's either first on or last off as the dancers enter and leave the performance floor. Today, Maddie is first on and leads the line out into the gym surrounded by students in the bleachers on all sides. There are four sets of bleachers, and each class sits together. When all of the girls are lined up in a straight line across the gym floor, Maddie finds herself staring into her class's bleachers section. She scans the crowd before the music starts, and her eyes land on Max.

Max is staring at her. He didn't know that she made the team but had wondered and was happy for her. He can't take his eyes off of her and when she finds him in the crowd, they lock eyes. Maddie's nerves for her first performance get replaced with a mix of emotions when she sees Max. At first, she is giddy as she hasn't seen him since the last hockey game. Then it turns to hurt that she hasn't talked to him since before the game, which quickly evolves into anger that he is clouding her thoughts when she's about to perform.

The music starts. The dance line girls all slap their arms to the sides, making a loud clap that echoes in the gym. This breaks Maddie's thoughts, and the adrenaline kicks in, and she goes into dance mode. For the next four minutes and twenty seconds, her body is on autopilot, performing the routine, hitting every beat. Although she is focused on her routine, she looks for him every time she faces the crowd. He doesn't take his eyes off of her, and she thinks, *Maybe, he did like me.*

That night at the game, she dances centered on the 50-yard line on the football field. Maddie scans the crowd once again and finds Max in the stands with his hockey buddies. He's looking at her again and watches her the whole time. She's happy that he does.

The next day, she gets her hair done with a few friends for the homecoming dance. The hairdresser puts her long blonde hair in an updo high on top of her head and rats her bangs as big as possible. Her mom does her makeup, transforming her from a young girl into a young adult.

She puts on her dress after her makeup is done. The purple eyeshadow brings out her blue eyes, and the bright pink lipstick highlights her full lips. She looks stunning, not like the cute blonde girl she's used to seeing in the mirror. She wonders what Max would think if he saw her now. Then she pushes the thought of him out of her mind and thinks about Jake.

Maddie and her friends are going in different groups since Jake has ski practice at a faraway ski hill that day. Maddie finds it funny that of all the days he'd have this, it'd be on the day of the dance. Once again, sports are getting in the way. But she doesn't care; she's excited to be going on a real date. Jake and Maddie decide to go to dinner at the Metropolitan just outside of downtown Minneapolis. That's where most of her friends are going, and she hopes to see them before they finish dinner since they'll be late. She feels like a grown-up as she waits for him to arrive.

Jake pulls into her driveway, gets out of the car, and rings the front doorbell. Her dad answers the door to check him out. When she walks up to the door to greet him, she's surprised and a little confused to see him in khakis and a nice long sleeve polo shirt and not a suit.

"We're going to the dance tonight, right?" Maddie asks.

"Yeah, of course," Jake says confidently. "You look great."

She's still confused why he isn't dressed up but doesn't ask because she doesn't want to make him feel bad. Her parents take the obligatory photos and tell them to be safe and home by 11 p.m. Normally her curfew is 10 p.m., but they gave her a special exception since it is a school dance and the dance ends at 10 p.m.

"Love you," she says to her parents as she leaves the house.

They hop in Jake's car and start driving.

"Where are we going to dinner?" Maddie asks as he turns the opposite direction she was expecting to go.

"The Metropolitan."

"Isn't that the other way?"

"Yeah, but we have to pick someone up."

"Who?" she asks, confused again as she didn't think they were going with another couple.

"Chief."

"What?" her heart sinks. She cannot bear to sit through a night with him on a date with another girl.

As they get closer to his house, she is trying to think of an excuse to go home. But she can't think of any that wouldn't be too obvious. She takes a deep breath as they pull into Max's driveway.

Max walks out the front door in khakis and a polo too. He sees Maddie and stops. Jake honks the horn and says, "Let's go, Chief."

Max looks at Maddie, and his stomach does a flip. He's never seen her look so beautiful. He almost doesn't recognize her, but when their eyes meet, she can't hold back her smile, and they both can't deny they still have strong feelings for each other. He smiles back and takes a deep breath as he walks past her car door and hops in the back.

"Get in. We're going to be late."

"Who else are we getting?"

"No one, why?"

"Isn't Max bringing a date?" Maddie asks and looks in the passenger mirror at him when she does.

"No, we just decided he should come with us right before I picked you up," Jake explains. That's the reason Jake isn't in a suit. They decided to wear khakis since Max didn't have a suit ready to wear. But they don't tell Maddie that.

Maddie really doesn't know what to think, but she is happy that she doesn't have to watch him with another girl. She feels a little awkward she's on a date with two people, and then she begins to wonder if she is actually on a date at all.

When they get to the restaurant, she sees a big group of her friends that are just finishing up dinner. As the trio waits to get seated, Maddie excuses herself to go say "hi" to her friends before they leave.

"So, do you have two dates?" Samantha asks. Samantha is going to homecoming with a senior and looks absolutely gorgeous in a skin-tight red mini sequin dress.

"I guess?" Maddie responds.

"Good for you."

"What do I do?"

"What do you mean?"

"I didn't know Max was coming. Jake just picked him up on the way."

"Funny how his friends are always bringing him along to see you. Do you think it is a coincidence?" Before Maddie can answer, she continues, "Who cares, just have fun. See where the night goes. That's what I am going to do. Live like Madonna would!" Samantha gives her a telling wink and leaves.

Maddie goes back to the boys, and they get seated at their table. They all laugh at Max's jokes while they eat. After dinner, it's time to go to the dance. Jake is going to drop Max off, and Maddie doesn't want to see him go.

"What if we skipped the dance?" Maddie asks spontaneously.

"You'd want to do that? You're all dressed up," Jake says.

"Sure, why not. I already got the pictures and saw my friends. Plus, you're not really dressed for the dance."

They all burst out laughing.

"Okay, let's keep the night going, Max, you in?"

"Sure, I don't have hockey for once tomorrow."

The trio drives around for much of the night, being silly, listening to music, and telling stories. When they run out of places to drive, Max invites them over. He knows his parents will be going to bed soon. They all go to Max's house. Max's parents greet them and say it's okay to watch TV for an hour, and they head to bed. Max's dad doesn't recognize Maddie as the blonde girl from the hockey games and assumes she is with Jake, who always seems to have a new girl with him whenever he sees him.

Maddie sits on the couch. Max's dog jumps up next to her. Max sits on the other side. Jake looks around and chooses an armchair. He's annoyed that Max sat on the couch. Maddie and Max start flirting, and it is clear to Jake he is suddenly the third wheel.

Without thinking, Jake says, "I have to get home for an early practice."

Maddie is caught off guard and pleads, "My curfew isn't for another hour. I don't want to go home yet. Can we stay a little longer?"

Jake, really annoyed now, says, "I have to be up early. Can you get yourself home?"

Maddie looks at Max and then back at Jake and says, "Yes."

Jake is surprised and disappointed. He expected her to say

no, and then he would have had the next hour to spend with her alone in the car. He leaves, and Maddie doesn't even think twice that her date just left her at another boy's house with no way home. Her heart is racing in her chest that she gets to be alone with Max in his house for the first time.

As the door shuts behind Jake, Maddie looks at Max and gently nudges the dog to the floor. Max moves across the couch and puts his hand on the back of her head and pulls her face close to his. Her body melts into his athletic frame. Their blood is pumping as they make up for lost time. Kissing slowly at first but working themselves into a frenzy. It's the first time they've been alone in a house, on a couch, and they take full advantage of it. They press their bodies against each other as they move from an upright position to being stretched out across the couch with Max lying heavy on top of Maddie. Maddie can feel the excitement surging through her body. She can feel it in Max too as he presses against her. She's still in her dress, and Max takes a chance, running his hand up her bare leg. She doesn't stop him. As he reaches her silky panties, he suddenly jerks his head back and looks her in the eyes. He seems startled and excuses himself quickly. Maddie doesn't know what happened. He comes back a few minutes later, shirt untucked and acting strange. She looks at him curiously, wondering if he is going to keep kissing her. Just then his mom yells down the stairs.

"Max, I think it's time for your friends to go home."

"Okay, Mom. They are just leaving."

Max reaches for Maddie's hand to help her up and ushers her out. He's in a hurry. Her heart is still pumping, and she doesn't understand why he's pushing her out so quickly. The next thing she knows she's outside in the dark, holding her heels, standing barefoot in a dress. The night air is cool on her heated skin. Her head starts to clear, and she thinks to herself, *How am I going to get home?* She starts walking down the dimly lit street toward home.

It's only a mile, and I've run it a thousand times, she thinks. Then she hears something in the distance, and her imagination kicks in. *Oh God, I'm going to get kidnapped tonight, and no one is going to know where to look for me.*

She picks up her pace a bit. She thinks about how if there is a murderer on the railroad tracks, she has to cross, she won't have a chance without shoes on. The tracks are full of rocks, and she won't be able to run. Her heart starts pounding but not the way it did a few moments ago. She starts to jog and decides to take a shortcut through the woods. As she runs through the woods, her hair starts to fall out of its updo, and it hits branches as she ducks beneath trees. When she gets to her street, her mind starts to settle down. She reaches up and touches her hair and then brushes herself off. How is she going to explain the mess? She slips her shoes back on and walks up the driveway, pulling out the rest of the bobby pins and leaves from her hair. She can see the TV flickering in the dark in the living room. Her dad waited up for her.

Maddie slips in the front door and yells, "Hi, Dad," as she runs to the bathroom.

Her dad yells after her, "Come and say hi to your old dad. I waited up for you."

"I will; I have to go to the bathroom, I'll be right there."

While she's in the bathroom, she picks the rest of the leaves out of her hair and brushes it back into a ponytail. Then she washes off her face and heads to her bedroom to change clothes.

When she comes back, her dad asks, "Why didn't I see headlights when you got home?"

Maddie lies, "Jake was going to be late for curfew, so I said to drop me off at the corner so he didn't have to turn around."

Maddie's dad looks at her disapprovingly and says, "You deserve to be dropped at the door. He's not good enough for you." Her dad shakes his head and continues, "Don't let boys treat you poorly."

If he only knew how she had treated Jake that night. He'd probably say, "Boys deserve to be treated better. You're better than that." Then she thought about Max and wondered what he would say about how he ushered her out the door into darkness so fast.

Maddie sits with her dad for a bit watching *Saturday Night Live*. She's so excited about what just happened she can't stop thinking about it and tells her dad she's tired and heads to bed. When she gets to her room, her mind is reliving the evening. She thinks, *Max does like me? Why did he come? Did he ask Jake, does Jake know? Why was Jake so mad when he left?* Her mind was still racing when she falls asleep that night, thinking about Max.

The next day she tells McKenna what happened, and McKenna is shocked.

"So, are you going to keep talking to Jake, or are you back with Max?"

"I don't know. I really liked Jake, but I thought it was over with Max. Jake was kind of mad when he left, so that might not be an option anyway."

"Wow, I just can't believe it. You guys don't talk for six months, and then he watches you dance and crashes your date. How did that happen anyway?"

"I have no idea why Jake brought him with or how that happened. But I'm glad that it did," Maddie replies.

"Have you talked to him yet?"

"Yeah, he called me this morning to make sure I got home okay. He couldn't talk long, but that is a good sign."

"Wow, I don't even know what to say. You have to tell me everything," McKenna urges.

"I will. I promise. I'm not going to keep it a secret from you this time."

♦ ♦ ♦

Maddie and Max resume their secret fling with the exception of McKenna knowing. Maddie tells Max it is a deal-breaker if she can't tell McKenna. Max agrees not wanting to screw things up again. Maddie doesn't push Max on being his girlfriend. She's content with the way things are. He goes to all of her performances and watches her from the crowd. She looks out into the audience and always finds him, and it makes her smile bigger and brighter knowing he is watching.

Max makes varsity with ease, and so does McKenna's boyfriend, Tommy. The girls go to all of the games. Max skates with more passion knowing she is there watching. Max's dad relaxes a bit and even shows a sense of pride with Max on varsity. At the games, Tyler watches Maddie watch Max and gets a sneaking suspicion something is going on. Tyler occasionally will make a comment to Maddie and McKenna, but they blow it off, not giving him the answers he is looking for. When he confronts Max, Max simply tells him he doesn't have time for a girlfriend and reminds him how much his dad would kill him if he did.

The summer between sophomore and junior year gets more physically intense between Maddie and Max. Max has his driver's license, and the two of them have a little more freedom and privacy. One night, Max picks Maddie up, and they drive around. Eventually, they end up in their favorite church parking lot. After an intense make-out session, while they are putting their shirts back on, Maddie says, "I think Tyler is beginning to suspect us."

"Yeah, he's said something to me too, but I blew it off."

"Do you think we should just tell him so he stops asking questions?"

"No!"

Maddie is taken aback. She wasn't expecting that answer from him. They've been getting really close, seeing each other more often, and talking on the phone on a regular basis. She doesn't understand why he wants to be so secretive.

Before she gets a chance to ask, a car turns into the parking lot and drives towards them with its bright lights shining into their eyes. Luckily, they are fully clothed. As they are trying to figure out who it is, a cop gets out of the car and walks up to the window, shining a flashlight on them and in the back seat of the car. He knocks on the window with the flashlight. Max rolls down the window.

"What are you kids doing here?"

"Nothing, officer, just talking."

"This is private property, you know."

"Oh, I didn't realize we couldn't be here. This is my church."

"Hmm, and you, miss, is this your church too?" the cop asks as he flashes his light into the back seat again.

"No, sir, it's not. Max was just telling me how great it was and swung by to show it to me."

"What's in the bag?"

"My hockey bag?"

"Is that the bag in the back seat?" the cop says, a little sarcastically.

"Yeah, that's my hockey stuff."

"Anything else?"

"No, just my skates, breezers, gloves, like I said, hockey stuff."

"You got hockey sticks back there too?"

"Yeah, a couple."

"You know I could consider that a weapon and search your car. What would I find if I did that?'

"A weapon, hockey sticks?"

"That's what I said, son. Now answer the question – what else would I find?"

"Nothing, sir. I play on the high school varsity team and am working on advancing my hockey career. I'm not going to do anything stupid to mess it up," Max says very seriously.

"You play varsity? You look a little young."

"He's the only sophomore on the team," Maddie chimes in, trying to break the tension. "He's really good."

The cop's demeanor shifts once he knows Max is on varsity. Top athletes get lots of breaks in this town. "It's getting kind of late. You kids should get home. You shouldn't be hanging out in a church parking lot."

"Yes, sir."

The cop walks away, and Max starts the car.

As the cop pulls out of the parking lot, Max says, "I'm going to be a cop someday."

"Why? He was such a jerk."

"They aren't all jerks. He didn't have to harass us like that. What are we doing? Sitting in a church parking lot. He doesn't need to intimidate us, saying he could search the car for having weapons, they are hockey sticks. Half the town has hockey sticks in their car right now," Max says angrily. "It's guys like him that give the rest of the cops a bad rap."

"How do you know that's what you want to do?" Maddie pauses for a second. "Wait, I thought you wanted to be a professional hockey player."

"No. That's what my dad wants. I've had to deal with them before."

"Hockey players?"

"Cops."

"What? Why?" Maddie asks, surprised.

"I don't want to talk about it," Max says as he drives out of the parking lot.

"Okay," Maddie says, letting it drop. "My dad is in the Army, and every time he has to leave on a mission, I'm scared he won't come home. I can't imagine being married to a cop and worrying every day that he won't come home, too."

"It's different than going to war. Cops help people."

"My dad helps people too. He's not just going overseas and blowing people up. He's helping the little guys stand up to the bad guys," Maddie says defensively.

"I didn't mean it like that. I meant cops are out helping people every day. It's not like in the movies, where it seems like they are in harm's way fighting the mob or something."

"I don't know, I'd still worry. Sometimes they have to go up against the bad guys too," Maddie says as Max pulls into her cul-de-sac to drop her off. "Did I tell you my dad has to go to war again? He's headed to Bosnia soon. He'll be gone all of next year."

"I'm sorry, that sucks. I know how close you two are," Max says, thinking he wouldn't mind if his dad left for a year.

"Thanks, goodnight," Maddie says as she shuts the passenger door. She looks up at the house, TV light flickering; her dad waited up for her again. This time, instead of running to the bathroom to avoid him, she walks into the TV room and sits down next to him to watch *Saturday Night Live*. It's a weekly tradition she's going to miss when he's away.

♦ ♦ ♦

The next day, Maddie watches football with her dad as he shines his boots and packs his rucksack. She can smell the polish in the air. The sound of the brush against his boot is rhythmic. It's a moment she's experienced a hundred times before, a ritual her dad undertakes before leaving. She likes spending the time with him, knowing he'll be gone soon, so she tries to soak in every moment just in case he doesn't come back.

"Do you have to go?"

"Yes, sweetie, I have to go."

"But I don't want you to."

"I know, honey, but I have to. They need me."

"I know, but I need you too."

Her dad continues brushing his boot with polish while staring at the TV.

"They need me more right now. I'll be home soon enough."

It's the same conversation they've had since she was a little girl. He said it to her every time he left her family behind. He said it more recently when he left to fight in the Gulf War. She assumed it wouldn't be the last time either. She hoped he'd come home okay, and if he did, she knew, he'd be off again soon.

CHAPTER 11

Maddie's dad leaves for his tour in Bosnia, and Maddie knows it is going to be hard on her whole family. She's always been close with her dad. She's going to miss him. He's the kind of dad that says "I love you" every chance he gets and gives great big hugs and kisses. He lets both his kids know how proud of them he is, always pushing them to be their best but never criticizing them as long as they try their hardest. He encourages them through praise and teaches by example, always using conversation to share a lesson. He and her mom open their home to all of their kids' friends and treat them all like their own kids. Many of Maddie's and her brother's friends like to hang out at their house because he and her mom give them the attention and praise they don't get in their own homes. It's fun and easygoing at Maddie's home with him around. She knows with her dad gone there will be a void that she'll miss more than she can possibly understand.

Between hockey practice, dance, and Maddie helping her mom with her little brother, Maddie and Max don't get much time to connect. Junior year is turning out to be a really hard year for Maddie. She can't wait for it to be over and her dad to come home.

Her dance line coach is a perfectionist and drills the girls harder than they have ever been drilled before. They are headed to state for the first time in four years, and the coach wants them to be perfect to win. She's the type of coach that doesn't use praise to bring the best out in the girls but instead criticizes every mistake. She makes the weaker dancers do the routines over and over while the stronger dancers watch.

Maddie has been the victim of these extra practices lately as her mind has been wandering with the stress at home without her dad around. Her mom is struggling with Maddie's independence, and her younger brother is developing an attitude. Without her dad around to keep the balance, there is a lot more bickering at home. It's been a year without praise or positive reinforcement on many fronts, and it's taking a toll on Maddie.

Needing something good in her life to happen, Maddie pushes Max again about going public. Max resists again. Every time she brings it up, he shuts down and doesn't want to talk about it. Lacking positive reinforcement in her life, she begins to doubt herself. She wonders if Max is just embarrassed of her because she's not cool enough, or pretty enough, or skinny enough. Although they talk all the time and he is clearly into her physically, the feeling grows that he is hiding her because he's embarrassed to be with her.

Max hasn't shared the real reason why. He's not embarrassed of her; he's embarrassed that his dad won't let him have a girlfriend and he can't stand up to him. He doesn't want Maddie to know what his relationship is like with his dad. He watches what she has with her dad and thinks she'll think less of him because his dad doesn't love and respect him like her dad does her. Max's dad makes him feel bad all the time. Maddie is the only one that makes him feel good, and he doesn't want to give her a reason to doubt his worth. So, he avoids it.

Toward the end of junior year, Maddie is desperate for something, but she doesn't know what. She feels so bad about herself and wants to fill the void. The void that is missing is attention, but she's too young to understand that. She ends up filling that void in other ways.

One Tuesday after school in March, Maddie and Max both find themselves with no practice and no commitments. It's been a while since they've had a chunk of time to be together, alone. Max has a car that day and offers to drive Maddie home after school. She's so excited to spend time with him she can't concentrate in class. She keeps looking at the minute hand on the clock above the door. It feels like eternity for it to get to three o'clock. When it finally does and the bell rings, she bolts to his car. She can't get there fast enough.

Max is already there. He left class a few minutes early so they could beat the parking lot traffic. That's what he tells Maddie, but really, he didn't want anyone to see them leaving school together. They drive around for a while until they eventually find themselves at their favorite place, the church parking lot. It gets dark early, and they know they are safe for a while in the cover of darkness. On the radio, "Rebel Yell" is playing. The music creeps into Maddie's body and she starts moving seductively looking at Max. Maddie, desperate for something, maneuvers herself on top of Max. She kisses him so deeply, like she is trying to consume him. Max senses that something is different today. He pushes her back a little and holds her face as he looks at her.

"Are you okay?"

"Yeah, I just love this song," she says, leaning forward to kiss him more.

"You seem off."

"I've just missed you. I want you," she says, implying something more. "Do you want me?"

"What do you mean?"

"You know what I mean," she says and starts kissing him again.

They kiss passionately as they pull each other's clothes off. They find themselves naked, wrapped in a knot of body parts in the back seat of the car. Maddie runs her hands over Max's muscles and then pulls Max's hips towards her; she wants him to fill the void she is feeling.

"Are you sure?"

"Yes, I need you."

And a few minutes later, they are done. Max isn't sure what just happened, and Maddie still feels empty. In the moment, it felt right, but now that it is over, she can't shake the feeling that she needs something more. Something is missing, and she just doesn't feel like herself anymore.

"Could you imagine if the pastor saw us now?" Max makes a joke to lighten the mood.

Maddie laughs at the image and replies, "Or the cop? I wonder what he'd say about that weapon."

"Probably arrest me for having such a big weapon."

They both laugh and get dressed again.

"You sure you are okay? You seem off lately."

"Yeah, I'm fine. This year is just really hard. I feel like I could break at any moment. I love dancing, but my coach rides me so hard. I feel like a failure. She just picks and picks."

"I know the feeling," Max says.

"Really, it seems like your coach loves you. He rides you too?"

"Not my coach, my dad," Max opens up in a rare moment.

"Your dad? What could he possibly pick on you for? You're the youngest person to make varsity in the school. You're having a killer year, and you're getting scouted."

"Nothing is ever good enough. It doesn't matter how well I play or what team I make, he always thinks I should do better. So, I keep trying," Max shares, being the most vulnerable he's ever been with Maddie.

"I'm sorry, I had no idea, Max. Why haven't you said anything?"

"I'd rather spend my time being happy with you than dwelling on that. Plus, I didn't think you'd understand. You and your dad are so close."

"I get it. You can tell me anything. I'm always here for you," Maddie says, missing her dad at that moment.

"Thanks, I know," Max says and leans in to kiss her.

"I think you are good enough," Maddie says with a mischievous grin on her face. "In fact, I think you are so good, we should do it again."

"Oh yeah? Should we go for a hat trick?" Max asks, jumping on top of her.

CHAPTER 12

Prom is approaching, and it's all that most girls are talking about. Not Maddie; she wasn't thinking about it at all because she'll be at the state dance line competition the same weekend as prom. This time, her sports are getting in the way of the biggest social event of the year.

During history class, a group of girls sitting next to Maddie start talking about their prom plans. One of the girls lists off all the couples, and Maddie hears Max's name. Her face turns red; the heat in her cheeks rises up through her ears. She holds back the tears welling in her eyes. *Max was going with another girl to prom? Two months after they had secretly lost their virginity together, he asked another girl to prom?* Her head spinning with thoughts, she keeps thinking, *Not my Max.*

The girls look at her and ask if she is okay. No, she isn't okay; she's in shock.

To confirm it's her Max, she asks, "Chief is going to prom with Nancy?"

"Yeah, he asked her earlier today."

"Oh, I didn't know they were even talking. Huh."

"Are you okay?"

"You know, I don't think so. It must have been something

I ate in the cafeteria. I gotta go."

Maddie grabs her books as she flees class and runs to the bathroom. Locking herself in the stall, she breaks down sobbing. *After all that we have shared, how could he do that? And not even tell me?* She knew they didn't have a commitment, but she also thought they had something. Her mind is reeling. Devastated, she manages to pull herself together as the bell rings and classes let out. As she leaves the bathroom, she runs into him. He looks at her and can see she has been crying.

"Are you okay?"

"Fuck you!"

Max is stunned and confused. His friends are too.

"Dude, do you know her? Why did she just yell that at you?"

Tyler is there too and watches how Max reacts. He expects him to chase after Maddie. Max doesn't reply, and he doesn't follow her either. He just stands there and watches her go.

Neither Maddie nor Max reaches out after school. They are both hurt.

Maddie is devastated. She feels like a truck has run over her heart and then backed up and ran over it again. She cannot wrap her mind around the fact that Max, her Max, is going to prom with someone else. *How could he? How could he spend all this time with me? How could he share a special bond with me, losing our innocence together, and then just go to prom with another random girl? How? How could he betray me like that?* She screams into her pillow a gut-wrenching wail, like someone has just run over her dog. Her screaming turns into weeping, which turns into hyperventilating.

When she was a kid and her emotions would get the best of her, she'd hyperventilate. Her dad would say, "Honey, just breathe." She can hear him saying that to her now, even though he is halfway across the world fighting in a war. That makes her miss her dad even more, and she cries herself to sleep.

♦ ♦ ♦

The next day she tells McKenna what she heard.

"No! I'm going to kill him!"

"My heart is broken. How could he? He didn't even have enough decency to tell me. I had to find out in history class."

"What did he say when you confronted him?"

"I haven't talked to him since I found out, other than shouting 'Fuck you' to his face in the hallway. Ironic, right? I literally never see him at school, and then when I do, it's after I've been sobbing in the girls' bathroom. How pathetic am I?"

"You're not pathetic. You guys have something, but he's an asshole!"

"I don't even care. I'm never going to talk to him again. I'm dumb for wasting almost all of high school on him. He can fuck off! I hate him."

After an hour of hashing it out with McKenna, Maddie moves from devastated to angry. She is burying her feelings. She is good at that. She has had to watch her dad go off to war too many times not to learn how to push the sadness way deep down inside. She knows how to focus her mind on something else and throw her thoughts and energy into it. She has a state dance line competition coming up, so she knows she can lose herself in practice. She spends the next few weeks turning up the music and burning off her feelings. She dances until she collapses and can fall asleep at night.

Max learns from McKenna's boyfriend Tommy why Maddie is so mad.

"Dude, seriously dumb move taking Nancy to prom. Maddie is a wreck, and McKenna is pissed at me for it," Tommy says to Max. "You're going to ruin our prom."

"She knows?" Max asks, ashamed.

"Yeah, she found out in class the other day. You didn't even tell her?"

"I was going to after school that day, but she yelled 'Fuck you' to my face. What was I supposed to do?"

"Not ask Nancy to prom."

"I didn't. She was just standing there after school in the hall by the lockers, and so was I. Tyler was talking to his girlfriend, who is friends with Nancy. Tyler was like Max isn't seeing anyone; you two should go together, and she said yeah, okay. What was I supposed to say?"

"Um, say I don't want to go."

"Yeah, I guess that would have worked. They just kept talking and the girls were so excited. We're just going as friends, and Maddie has state that weekend anyway."

"But you're with Maddie," Tommy reminds him. "And what about your dad's rule of no girls?"

"No, I'm not," Max says defensively, thinking about what his dad is going to say about prom. "He'll probably forbid me from going, and then this won't even be a big deal. That's why I didn't say anything."

"Whatever, dude. You blew that one. She's a good girl, and she puts up with your moody shit," he snaps back. "If you're going to go, you should be going with Maddie, McKenna and me."

Max feels really bad. He knows he screwed up and just wants to explain. But honestly, how could she forgive him? He tries to call a couple of times, but she doesn't answer because she's usually at McKenna's house or dance practice. Max doesn't leave a message. He is afraid to know if she will call back or not.

Maddie is heartbroken. Her dad is overseas, fighting a war; her coach is pushing her to her breaking point; her mom has no time or energy for her, and the boy she's wasted all of school with is going to prom with someone else. She channels all that negative emotion into her dancing. Before prom, the school holds another pep fest where the dance line performs their state competition routine for one last practice. Like every other time she performs, she scans the crowd for Max's face. This time when she finds it, it doesn't bring a smile; it fuels her pain, which she funnels into every kick, every move, making her performance explosive.

Maddie and her team spend the weekend at state. She uses the energy to be the best she can be. Although they don't win, they do take fourth. Dressed in red, white, and blue dresses, they perform a stunning tribute to the troops overseas, which makes her even sadder that her dad isn't there to see it.

That weekend, Max reluctantly goes to prom. He was hoping his dad would have forbidden it so he'd have an excuse to cancel, but he was super cool about it and even told him how great of a season he had that year. His dad was oddly happy recently. He didn't know why, but didn't think much about it either. Maybe it was because he was invited to talk to some colleges about playing hockey for them after being scouted all year? He did think about skipping prom and watching Maddie at state, but he decided not to after seeing her face at the pep fest. Her intensity was not the sweet Maddie he was used to. It scared him. *How badly had he hurt her?*

The following week, Maddie has to endure seeing the photos and hearing the stories of prom in history class. She is absolutely heartbroken and doesn't have dance to focus on anymore. The empty feeling is back, bigger than before. She can feel the anger filling it, burning her cheeks and imagines them turning bright red as the girls are flipping through photos. *That should have been her. He should have taken her.* The mix of anger, sadness, and rejection claw at her insides and make her feel like she is going to vomit. Once again, she ran out of class and found herself sobbing in the girls' bathroom. This time she knew better than to leave when it was time for the next class. She waits until everyone switches classes and then walks to her locker, packs up her bags, and leaves school. She walks home, lost in thought. As she walks by the church, she begins sobbing uncontrollably again. She looks down towards the end of the street at his house. Maddie starts yelling at him even though he is nowhere near. No one was, the street was empty, and Maddie fills it with the sounds of her heartbreak.

♦ ♦ ♦

Over the next few weeks, Max picks up the phone every day to call Maddie. He dials her number, but before he pushes the last button, he always hesitates and hangs up. Maddie made him feel good. She laughs at his jokes, listens to his stories, and never makes him feel stupid. He loves talking to her about nothing. She is like the ice to him. He gets lost in her, escaping reality. He has never told her about how hard he really has it at home. Just the little he shared the night they lost their virginity together. She is a bubble for him to escape to, and he selfishly keeps her away from his family and friends so he can live in a different world with her. Max misses talking to Maddie and lets the perceived rejection consume him. He knows he was the one in the wrong but is used to being rejected by his dad and assumes it'll be the same with Maddie. What he doesn't understand is that she desperately wants him to call her and explain why he did it. She is drawn to him even though he crushed her.

The night before he leaves for the summer for more hockey camps and college visits, he almost leaves a message for Maddie. He wants to share that all of his hard work is about to pay off, and when it does, things will be different if she can forgive him.

CHAPTER 13

Max has a great summer at hockey camps and at the end of summer is invited for an official tour at the University of Michigan to talk about his hockey future.

"Thanks for taking the time to visit this weekend," Steven says. Steven is the head hockey coach at the University of Michigan.

"Thanks for having us," Max's dad replies. "The campus is beautiful and the facilities are top notch. We've enjoyed our visit."

"I'm glad you enjoyed it. It's important for families to be comfortable with where their kids will be going. I know Max is pretty used to the rink after all of the time he's spent here at hockey camps."

"The camps are certainly worth the money I've spent to get him here today."

"You should be proud of your son. Not many boys get this opportunity. As you know, we've been scouting him for the last few years. He has consistently impressed us and he's grown into a very strong hockey player. He's got the size and the speed we're looking for and we want him to play for us after he graduates. Max, would you like to be part of our team?"

"You're not the only ones," Max's dad says before Max can respond.

"Here's the thing. Most of our players spend time in the USHL playing Juniors for at least a season before they join our team, or really any NCAA D1 team. The experience will make him a stronger player and get him ready for the competition he'll experience at the college level."

"Sure, I know, I played Juniors in Canada before I played in college."

"Great, so you know how valuable it can be."

"Yes, as you know he's attended many of the USHL camps to get ready to play at a D1 school. A few of the other colleges have been scouting him there too."

"Yes, I've heard. That's why we asked you here today. We want Max to commit to Michigan and have arranged a spot for him on a Juniors team if he's ready to take the next step."

"Is that an official offer?"

"Yes, contingent on him agreeing to play Juniors."

"When does the offer expire?"

"I know Max is talking to other schools but these spots on Juniors fill up fast. I can give you forty-eight hours to make a decision. If it's a yes, we'll get the details in writing." Looking at Max, Steven says, "Max, we want you to be part of the Michigan hockey family. I know it's hard to leave school your senior year but I promise playing Juniors will set you up for success when you come to play with us. You'll develop skills playing against stronger competition than you'll ever see playing at the high school level. I know you've gone to all of the camps and played against these guys over the summer but playing on the team is way different then playing at camps. You'll be surprised at how much your skills improve. Do you think that is something you want to do? Do you want to be part of our family?"

"Yes, sir," Max says without hesitation. "When would I have to leave home?"

"Pretty much immediately. They'll set you up with a billet family and get you practicing with the team ASAP. Anyone would jump at this chance."

"But Max isn't anyone," Max's dad says. "Thank you for the offer. We'll get back to you in the next couple of days and let you know what we decide."

"Please do. Max if you have any questions reach out to me or our team captain. This needs to be your decision. This is your future and it needs to be right for you."

"Yes, sir. I understand."

"Like I said, we'll get back to you."

♦ ♦ ♦

"Dad, I'm surprised you didn't let me accept on the spot. I thought this is what we've been working for, what do you want to think about? Max says from the back seat of the car as they merge on to the highway to head back to Minnesota.

"Are you kidding me? I'm not thinking about it, you're going. I just didn't commit you on the spot because I didn't want you to look desperate."

The words cut deep and once again his dad manages to steal the joy from the moment. The sting makes him think of Maddie. He doesn't want to leave before he can fix things with her.

"What if I don't want to miss my senior year?"

"Son, we've worked hard for this. You haven't worked out every day, played every game, and spent my money on all these hockey camps to be a quitter now. You are going to commit as soon as we get home."

"Then why didn't you just let me say yes while we were there?"

"I wanted him to think you had other prospects even though you don't. If you were any good, the other colleges would have made an offer by now," Max's dad says, cutting him down and dashing any hope he had of staying home.

"Honey, Max is good. He just got asked to commit to Michigan. That's a big deal," Max's mom says, sticking up for him. "You don't know that the other colleges won't make him an offer. Michigan just moved faster."

"You're too easy on him. It's what makes him weak."

"Someone has to show him some empathy. All you do is push him. He's still a kid and he needs some encouragement too. I think he deserves it. Look at all he has accomplished. You should tell him you're proud of him." His mom turns to the back seat and looks at him. "Max, you are good, or we wouldn't be here now. Enjoy this moment of being asked and we'll talk about it more at home."

Max's dad grabs her collar, looks directly at her, and says, "I warned you! This is not up for discussion. I've worked hard to get Max to where he is. I've spent a lot of money to give him this opportunity. He is going and you're not going to blow it like you did for me. That is final!"

"Dad! Look out!" Max's sister shouts from the back seat.

Sick of his dad bullying his mom, Max unbuckles his seat belt to pull his dad's hand off her. His arm is still under the seat belt when his sister shouts, he looks forward seeing debris falling from a truck bouncing before them. Max's dad swerves to avoid the debris, losing control and flipping the car. Max is flung forward, but his arm twists in his seat belt and he is wrenched backward. The belt saves him from being ejected, but it breaks his arm and wrecks his back muscles. When the car lands on its roof, Max hits his head and loses consciousness. When Max awakes, he's in a hospital in Michigan, his mom and sister sitting at the end of the bed.

"What happened?" Max asks in a lot of pain.

"He's awake!" his sister yells to his dad, who is pacing the halls.

"We were in an accident," his mom says. "You didn't have your seat belt on and you got thrown around. We're lucky you're still with us."

Max doesn't remember the accident or the fight.

"Where are we?"

"We're still in Michigan," his dad says, walking into the hospital room.

"Why are we in Michigan?" Max asks, his short-term memory foggy due to his concussion.

"We were picking you up from hockey camp and meeting with the coach," Max's dad says. "He wants you to commit to the University of Michigan."

"That's cool," Max says, as a wave of pain washes over his body. He winces when it does.

"Are you okay?" Max's mom asks.

"I hurt."

"You should have just done what you were told, and we wouldn't be here," his dad says.

"What?" Max asks, confused.

"You were lipping off about committing, and it distracted me," Max's dad says.

Max doesn't remember the conversation.

"I'm sorry, sir," Max instinctively responds.

"You should be. You ruined your chances of playing for a good school," Max's dad says.

"What?" Max says, still confused. "Why am I here? Why do I hurt so bad? Did I get hit in hockey?"

"No, dear, we were in a car accident. A truck lost its load, your father swerved to miss it, the car lost control, and we flipped over," his mom says.

"If you both weren't arguing with me, I would have seen it, and we'd be home by now, and Max would still have a future," Max's dad says.

Max looks at his mom to explain.

"Max, you have a severe concussion, a broken arm, and some pulled, maybe torn muscles in your back and shoulder. You have a long road of recovery ahead of you."

"Can I still play hockey?"

"We don't know for sure, but you likely can't play Juniors."

"Why not?"

"You need time to recover and heal. Juniors is a lot faster and rougher, and you could end up getting hurt worse than you are now if you take a bad hit."

"I've taken plenty of bad hits and have been fine," he says, looking at his dad.

"Max, your body is broken. It's going to take eight or more weeks for your arm and shoulder to heal, and we're not sure how bad your back is yet."

Max thinks for a minute and struggles to do the math.

"It'll be close, but I can still do it. I can get better if I work really hard."

"They aren't going to hold a spot for you on Juniors. You'll be lucky if you can still play varsity this year. Looks like you got your wish. You won't be leaving your senior year, but don't think that means you can spend time with Maddie," Max's dad says and leaves the room.

Max looks at his mom with a question on his face.

"You've been saying the name Maddie in your sleep. Do you have a girlfriend?" Max's mom asks.

"No, I don't have a girlfriend. Remember, no girls during hockey."

Max is crushed. He's given up so much to become an elite hockey player. He missed every summer, parties, just getting to be a carefree kid, and Maddie. *Now it's over, just like that*? He doesn't believe it and vows he's going to work hard and get back to where he was.

The next few weeks are terrible for Max. He's in a lot of pain as his body fights to heal. His dad is worse than ever, blaming Max for the accident. His mom tries to defend him but knows his dad is on the verge of blowing and treads lightly. On particularly bad days, Max's dad reminds Max what he thinks of him. Really, it is what he thinks of himself and is projecting onto Max. He says things like, "You've got nothing now.

Hockey was all you had to offer, and now it's gone. You are worthless."

When Max insists, he's going to get better and train harder than he has ever trained before, he's met with more anger from his dad.

"You'll never be good enough. You were barely good enough when you were healthy. No one is ever going to want you."

Max knows his dad is talking about colleges, but it makes him think of Maddie. He misses her and wants to talk to her, but what does he have to offer her now? He thinks his dad is right. He's not good enough for her. The one thing he was good at is gone now, and he's going to have to use all of his energy to fight to get back to where he was. He thinks, *Once I get better, I'll get Maddie back, somehow.*

CHAPTER 14

School starts and Max shows up with his arm in a sling. The story of his accident spreads quickly between classes, and Maddie hears about it. She's still hurt about prom and never hearing from Max, but now she has mixed emotions. *How could he not tell me about the accident? What does that mean for his hockey career? Is he okay?* She hurts because of him and for him, and she doesn't know what to do with all of those feelings.

Between her dad being away for almost a year, her coach pushing and criticizing too much, and Max cutting her out of his life, she is lost. Maddie quit dance at the end of last year and stopped doing other things she loved. She went through the motions with her friends. She went to a lot of parties over the summer with Samantha, discovering drinking. She learned that alcohol makes her feel happy and free. It helps quiet her mind, filling the emptiness like nothing else does. With alcohol, she sheds the feeling of rejection, transforming from a little girl into a wild one who gets the attention she craves so badly.

By homecoming of senior year, Maddie has cast off all commitments and is determined to just have fun and drink whenever she gets the chance. She can't bear to repeat her junior year, which nearly ate her alive.

McKenna is going to homecoming with Tommy and some other friends, and Samantha is off at a college party with her sisters for the weekend. Since none of her other girlfriends are dating anyone seriously, they decide to get dressed up, go out to dinner, and then have a hotel party instead of going to the dance.

All the girls gather at Maddie's house to get ready. Her mom does all their makeup like she did for the other dances. Her mom has already done her makeup, and Maddie is packing a bag to stay out overnight. She brings her bag up to the front door so it is ready when it is time to leave.

"What's that?" Maddie's dad asks.

"It's my bag for tonight?"

"For what?"

"It's my PJs and stuff to stay out overnight."

"Whose house are you staying at?"

"We're not, we got a suite. It's a girl's night; we're all staying there."

"No, you're not. You are seventeen years old. You don't need to stay at a hotel. You can come home at 11 p.m."

"Dad, I'm turning eighteen this month. All my friends are going. It's not a big deal. This way, we get to stay up all night and no one's parents have to yell at us to keep it down. We've done it before."

"I don't care. No daughter of mine is staying at a hotel unsupervised."

"That's not fair! You don't get to come home and start barking orders like we're your soldiers. Mom said it was okay. All of my friends are here getting ready, and I've already paid my share. I'm going."

"Don't you talk to me that way. I am still your father, and I say what goes."

"What's going on out here?" Maddie's mom interrupts.

"Dad says I can't stay out tonight, and I have to be home at 11 p.m. Tell him it's okay."

"Honey, calm down. We can talk about this."

"No, I don't want to talk about this. We already talked about this, and you said I could go. It's not fair," Maddie says, fighting back tears of frustration.

"She's seventeen. She's not staying out all night. There's no good reason. She can come home when the night is over," Maddie's dad says to her mom. "Nothing good happens after midnight."

"No good reason? We've been planning this for weeks. I'm the one who has coordinated everything and now I can't go?"

"You can go; you just can't stay out."

"It's not fair!"

"I'll tell you what isn't fair. Being gone for a year fighting a war to come home to a daughter that doesn't have any respect for her father. What happened to the little girl I left a year ago? Where is she?"

Tears well up in Maddie's eyes. She turns toward the front door and opens it. She runs out the door in her dress and high heels and starts running down the driveway. Her dress is a spaghetti-strap, short, fitted, velvet dress with diamond trim across the top. There is a large silky bow tied in the middle with a small slit in the back. As she runs down the driveway, she hears a tear in her dress. Her stride is too long for how tight the dress is, and the slit in the back begins to rip. She gets to the bottom of the driveway and bursts into tears. She thinks, great, now my dress is ruined, and my makeup will be too. She doesn't know where she is going but walks briskly down her street. She is overwhelmed with emotion since she was looking forward to some fun tonight and can't bear to fight with her dad. She missed him while he was gone, and it hurts to hear him ask where she went. The little girl he knew before he left is gone, disappearing in his absence.

Maddie's dad pulls up behind her in the same minivan that he has picked her up in for years. "Where are you going?"

"I don't know," she says, wiping the tears from her eyes so he can't see that she has been crying. Having no sleeves on her dress makes it hard, and as she pulls her hand away from her face, she sees a smear of black mascara across it. She thinks there's no way he isn't going to notice she's crying. She keeps trying to dry her eyes, though.

"Get in."

"No," Maddie says as she keeps walking.

"Get in. If you want to go out tonight, you have to talk to me like an adult. You want me to treat you like one, then act like one."

Maddie stops in her tracks. She realizes that she doesn't know where she is going or what point she is trying to prove if she keeps going.

"Fine," she says as she gets into the front seat.

"Listen, honey, this is hard on me. You've grown up a lot while I've been away. You and your mother have created new rules, and I'm not up to speed on them. You have to cut me a break. You are my little girl, and I love you. My job is to protect you. I don't want anything bad to happen to you," Maddie's dad explains.

That makes Maddie cry even more. She is so frustrated and doesn't know how to process her emotions. Is he mad at her, or does he love her, she wonders.

"What bad thing do you think is going to happen with a bunch of girls staying in a hotel room together? There are like ten of us."

"I was a kid once too, and I know from my experience kids don't always make the best choices. But as your mother pointed out, you'll be at college next year, and it is better to let you start learning this while we are close by than to let you go off to college without learning to be independent."

"So, does that mean I can stay out tonight?"

"I'd still prefer that you come home, but yes."

Maddie feels conflicted. She wants to stay out with her friends, but she also doesn't want to let her dad down. It is always hard when he returns from war and adjusts to family life again. He's shaking off his command-and-control style he has to operate in to survive, and she's growing up and is used to being trusted to make her own decisions.

"Daddy, I really want to go. We won't get into any trouble, I promise."

"It's up to you, honey. I trust you to make good decisions."

They pull into the garage, get out, and go inside. The rest of the girls are ready to go. Maddie's mom is taking pictures. She turns to them and says, "Smile." Maddie is so mad at her mom for wanting to take a picture while she and her dad are still in a fight. Her dad leans in and puts his arm around her. Maddie gives a half-smile, wondering how bad her makeup looks. She then excuses herself to the bathroom to touch herself up. When she comes out, everyone is headed out to the cars to go out for the night.

She looks out at them and back at her parents.

"I'm sorry," she says and gives them both a big hug and kiss. "Goodnight. I'll see you in the morning."

"Have fun," her mom says cheerily.

"No drinking, no drugs, no boys," her dad says. He says that to her on a regular basis. It's his mantra ever since she became a teen.

"Okay," Maddie calls out as she walks out the door and shuts it behind her.

Maddie and her girlfriends head out to dinner and afterward to the hotel. They open up the suite and throw their bags in the master bedroom. As they change into their party clothes, there is a knock at the door.

A handful of boys who didn't go to homecoming walk in, carrying cases of beer and a bottle of whiskey. The girls turn up the music on the boombox that has a CD player on top.

"Let's get this party started!"

The teens crack open beers. Maddie, still upset about the fight with her dad, skips the beer and heads straight for the whiskey. She pours some in the hotel glass and drops a few ice cubes from the ice bucket into the cup. She looks around and finds a can of Coca-Cola, opens it, and pours it in. She waits while the Coke fizzes to the top and then drops back down. She pours a splash more into the glass. She's reliving the fight with her dad in her head as she stands alone at the bar. She's wondering if she should have stayed home. He did just get back from war a couple of weeks ago. She misses watching movies with him and the rest of her family on the couch. Next weekend, she thinks to herself. She takes a sip of her drink. She shakes her head, trying to shake the memory of the fight out.

Everyone else is dancing in the living room. She heads out there to join them. The beers are flowing. She's drinking the whiskey faster than she should. She can't seem to shake the feeling from the fight, so she keeps drinking to make it go away.

More teens start showing up as the night goes on. At about 10:00 p.m. Maddie is completely drunk when Max walks through the hotel door. She sees him and feels unresolved feelings racing in. She's had too much to drink to keep them back. Coupled with the fight she had with her dad, she starts crying while dancing. One of her friends notices and pulls her into the bedroom.

"Are you okay?" Jessica asks.

"No."

"What's wrong?"

"I got in a fight with my dad. Wait, you were there; you heard it," Maddie says with a slight slur.

"Yeah, that was awkward. But you made up, right?"

"I guess, but I still feel bad, like I let him down for growing up while he was gone," Maddie says and starts crying again.

"Maybe you should stop drinking."

"I don't want to stop drinking," Maddie says. She wipes the tears from her face this time with a sleeve from the back of her shirt.

"How about if we get you changed into your pajamas?"

Maddie has a habit of doing what she's told when she's been drinking and obliges. As she is changing, she realizes she has brought Max's old hockey sweatpants as her PJ bottoms. She got the pants during one of their rendezvous when it got cold, and he offered them to her to keep warm. She turns them inside out before she puts them on. You can still see the outline of his name and the number eighteen printed on her upper right thigh. She thinks she's hiding it. Jessica laughs to herself, realizing that she wants to hide it from Max, who is in the other room.

"Don't worry, he won't see," Jessica says. "Why do you have them anyway?"

"Who won't see what?" Maddie asks, confused.

"Max won't see the pants. You can go to sleep, and he will never know."

"Why is Max here? He sucks."

"It's a party."

"I want another drink," Maddie says as she gets up to make herself another one.

"I don't think you should do that. You've had enough."

"No, I want another."

Maddie pushes by Jessica and walks into the living room and past everyone to the bar. She starts to pour herself a drink. Another friend tells her not to have another. She feels like it's her dad telling her what she can't do again.

"I can have another drink if I want to," as she finishes pouring one. She walks back through the living room and grabs the boombox on her way to the bedroom. She slams the bedroom door and crawls into bed with the boombox. She starts playing sad country songs and turns up the sound. The crowd just stares at the door, wondering what just happened.

"Maddie and her dad got in a big fight tonight and she's upset about it. I'll go talk to her and get our music back," Jessica explains.

"I'll come with," Max says. "Let me help."

"Good luck with that. She's in rare form tonight. She just needs to go to sleep."

Max has been looking for a reason to talk to Maddie, and a fight with a dad is his expertise.

Jessica and Max walk into the bedroom. Maddie looks at Max and picks up her drink and takes a big gulp.

"No, not you," she says, pointing at Max.

"Maddie, can I have the music back? People want to dance," Jessica asks.

"Fine!" Maddie says and pushes the boombox toward the end of the bed. The CD skips as she does it.

Jessica grabs the boombox and quickly walks out while Max distracts Maddie.

"How are you?"

"Fine!"

"Nice pants."

Maddie rolls her eyes.

"I heard you got in a fight with your dad tonight," Max prompts.

Maddie nods her head up and down, a tear rolls down her cheek.

"When did he get home?"

"Couple of weeks ago," Maddie says softly, trying to hold back the tears.

"How's it going?"

"It's hard. We're still adjusting. Things changed while he was gone this time."

"Like what?"

Maddie stares at Max for a few seconds, thinking about how to answer the question.

"I'm not his little girl anymore," Maddie says and starts to sob.

Maddie knows her dad would be so disappointed in her if he knew what had happened since she met Max. And here she is sitting, spilling her guts to him. She thinks she should have stayed home tonight. *What's one party versus letting your dad down who's been putting his life at risk for the last year?*

A couple stumbles into the bedroom looking for some privacy.

"Hey, do you want to get out of here for a bit?" Max asks Maddie and extends his hand to her.

She nods her head yes. Max grabs her white Keds from the floor and helps her put them on. He grabs her hand and leads her through the party. As he passes Jessica, he lets her know he's taking her to get some air to sober up.

Max walks Maddie to his car parked in the parking lot. He doesn't drive anywhere because he's had a couple of beers. Instead, they sit and talk.

"It'll get easier once you can drive," Max says, referring to the fight.

"What do you mean?"

"When my dad and I fight, I always leave and go for a long drive afterward. It helps me clear my head."

Maddie is drunk, and it takes a while to register what he is saying. She wants to ask him about fighting with his dad. Before she can, he changes the subject.

"I've missed you. I've wanted to talk to you."

"About what?"

"Just wanted to see how you are doing. It's been a long time since we've talked."

"Yeah, because you went to prom with Nancy," Maddie reminds him, too drunk to filter what she says.

"I'm sorry about that. I didn't mean to hurt you."

"Well, you did."

Maddie starts to cry again as the emotional wound rips open. She thinks, *I really should have stayed home.* She's not normally one to cry, and tonight she can't seem to shut it off. *Damn whiskey, no more of that stuff.*

Max looks at her and feels all of her hurt. He wants to take it away but doesn't know how. She's staring at him now, lost in his blue eyes, waiting for him to do just that. He wipes the tears from her face with his sleeve. When her face is dry, and she's stopped crying, he kisses her.

"I'm sorry," he says and kisses her again. "I'm so sorry, Maddie. I've missed you so much. I never meant to hurt you." He can't stop kissing her.

As his words sink in, she leans into his kisses. The next thing she knows, Max is on top of her in the passenger seat. He pulls the lever on the side of her seat, and the seat reclines. He's lying on top of her, kissing her. She's missed him too. Missed his kisses, his touch, the weight of his body on hers, but she's still mad at him and confused with her feelings. Her brain is slow to process everything that is happening, but she doesn't resist.

As she's soaking in his kisses and trying to figure out what's going on and why this is happening—a minute ago, she was just crying about her dad, and he was talking about long drives—he pulls the string that is holding his sweatpants tight around her waist. The pants loosen, and he slips them down around her knees. She reaches down for them to pull them back up but can't find them. He unzips his pants and presses himself against her. She stops kissing him when she is suddenly surprised, feeling him inside her. Her eyes go wide open, looking into his and he quickly pulls himself off of her.

Maddie is more confused than ever. She reaches down and pulls his sweatpants back up and fumbles, trying to tie them. He zips himself up and helps her finish tying his pants.

She's no longer crying or angry at him or sad about her dad. She is just confused about what happened in the parking lot. *Did Max and I just have sex? Why did that happen? How did that happen?* He was just consoling her about her fight with her dad. *Why does he have to drive after fights with his dad—how often do they fight?* Maddie is so confused, and her normally fast mind is not keeping up with all of her thoughts.

"We should get you back. Your friends are probably looking for you," Max says, breaking her train of thought.

Maddie nods her head yes again, still trying to process what just happened.

Max opens the passenger door and holds out his hand to Maddie. He walks her back to the hotel room. Jessica looks at them when they walk in. Maddie isn't crying, and she is calm.

"I'm going to put her to bed," Max says to Jessica.

"She okay?"

"Yeah, she's good now."

Maddie thinks to herself, *Am I? I don't really feel anything now.*

Max brings her back to the bed she was in before. The other couple is gone. He tucks her into bed and kisses her on the forehead. She just looks at him, still confused. He smiles and doesn't know what to say. He hadn't planned on that happening either and feels guilty considering her state. He doesn't know what came over him but just knows he wanted to take the pain away and go back to how it used to be. He backs out of the room as they stare at each other, not saying a word. He turns off the light and pulls the door shut behind him. Maddie falls instantly asleep.

Max didn't mean to take advantage of her. He meant what he said, that he misses her and wanted to talk, but that wasn't what he expected. He starts beating himself up over it and thinks he's ruined it again. He sits watch over the bedroom door for the rest of the party. He doesn't let anyone in until the rest of the girls want to go to sleep.

Max calls Maddie the next day to check on her.

"How ya feeling?"

"I've been better. I should have stayed home like my dad said."

"Yeah, you were in rare form."

"Thanks for taking care of me."

"I'm glad I got to see you. I wish it had been under better circumstances."

"I'm glad I saw you too, but it's all a little fuzzy. Did we?" Maddie trails off.

"Um, yeah," Max says hesitantly. "I'm sorry, I don't know what came over me."

"It's all a blur to me. Did you put me to bed?"

"Yeah, and I watched over the door all night to make sure no one disturbed you."

"Well, isn't that sweet of you?"

"You seemed like you needed to be alone."

"I'm not sure what I needed. I'm just so confused."

"Well, it was good to see you."

Not sure if he wants to end the conversation or not, Maddie replies, "Yeah, well thanks for everything." She didn't mean to say it the way she did. It came out sarcastic and somewhat final. She wishes she could pull the words back, but they just sit there in the air.

Max doesn't know what to make of it and defaults to thinking she is mad and rejecting him again, so he says, "Anytime. See ya around."

"See ya?" she responds, confused, and hears him hang up the phone abruptly.

Neither of them knows what to make of that conversation. Max called with the intention of resuming their relationship where they left off. Maddie, already confused about the night before, is now more confused. *Why did he take care of me and then call to be like "see ya around"? Don't I mean more to him than a casual screw?*

Maddie and Max don't speak again for a while. As the days go on, Maddie is still running from the hurt. She looks forward to the weekends when she and her girlfriends go to parties and dance the night away in a drunken blur.

Max has no idea what's going on with Maddie. He's too busy trying to get back to his previous level of hockey. He still isn't sure if he'll be able to play varsity his senior year, as he isn't getting the strength back as quickly as he'd hoped. He can skate well, but he just isn't as quick with the stick as he needs to be. His coach is also concerned about him taking a bad hit. Ultimately, his coach makes the hard decision to cut him, so he can play rec hockey and have the ice time to get fast again.

A lot of the guys he played hockey with growing up are on the team, including his buddy, Tyler. Most of the team are classmates that didn't make varsity but still love playing. They are happy to have him join the team and promise to have his back. The team is a fun group and has a good fan club who just want to have some fun. Maddie included. She swore off watching the varsity games last year after prom.

When hockey season starts up that winter, Maddie goes to the games and the after parties that follow. After a few games, Maddie's friends can tell she's off and just not into hockey like she used to be. She has an edge to her. Not her cheery self, and they don't know why, but McKenna does.

Max sees Maddie when he's warming up but never sees the smile he longs to see anymore. He keeps his distance and pauses his habit of tapping on the glass. He can tell she's still mad at him, although maybe not as much as before. She never acknowledges him or lingers after the games, as she did when they were together. He hears she's gotten into partying and is embracing the grunge scene. He wonders what's going on with her. But he never reaches out because he's afraid of being rejected, and he's afraid he'll hurt her again.

One weekend, the team has a tournament out of town. With Maddie's dad out of town for an Army drill, Maddie's mom agrees to let her go with the other girls with the expectation she'll stay in the girls' room and if she hears otherwise, there'll be no senior class trip for Maddie. Maddie agrees, especially since she had no intention of hooking up with Max or anyone else. Maddie is well versed in avoiding Max at this point and can just have fun with friends. The girls put some beer on ice in the tub when they go to the rink. After the games, they go back to the hotel and start partying. All the hockey parents are having their own fun and don't pay much attention to the kids; after all, they're seniors. The kids keep their hotel doors open and hop from room to room, sneaking beers with them. After a couple of beers, Maddie accidentally ends up in a hotel room with Max.

Tyler is in the room too. He still has his suspicions that something's going on between them, even though he couldn't ever get Max to admit it. This time he tries to get Maddie to slip up.

"Hey, Maddie!"

"Hey, Tyler," Maddie says in an annoyed tone as she realizes who else is in the room.

Max looks up at her from the corner of the bed he's sitting on. This time she meets his gaze. She holds it for a moment, not with butterflies in her stomach or a longing for him to kiss her, but with a fiery rage. Her normal welcoming smile melts into a clenched jaw. She stops breathing, afraid that if she opens her mouth, things she can never take back will come out. Her confusion about what happened has morphed into resentment that she's wasted her entire high school experience on him. The other girls in the room pick up on it but say nothing and concoct a reason to move to the next hotel room, sweeping Maddie up as they leave.

Once again, Max doesn't follow. He just watches her go.

"Dude, what was that?"

"I don't know. What?"

"What is with you two? You have some serious energy between you. Are you hitting that?" Tyler provokes Max.

"No," Max snaps.

"Do you want to? I know you were pretty into her. Why didn't you ever go after her?"

"You know why."

"What are you talking about?"

"My dad. He wouldn't let me date; it was hockey all the time."

"Did you want to?"

"Yeah, of course, I did. Of course, I wanted a girlfriend. But my dad was always hassling me about hockey. Now here I am, no hockey future, and no girlfriend," Max says, letting down his guard for the first time.

"Go get her."

"No, she doesn't want me. I fucked up when I took Nancy to prom."

"I knew it! I knew you liked her then. That's why I pushed Nancy on you, to see if you were into her, but you didn't even flinch. You just went with Nancy, so I figured you didn't like Maddie."

"I didn't want to, but I couldn't say anything. My dad would have killed me if he found out. No one knew; I couldn't risk it. I couldn't lose her."

"No one knew what?" Tyler says, realizing there's more to the story.

"Tyler, I've been in love with Maddie since the day I met her. We've been sneaking around all of high school, and I broke her when I went to prom. I haven't really talked to her since she found out. I can't imagine how big of an asshole she thinks I am," Max says as he slams his beer and reaches for another one.

Max begins to learn what Maddie already discovered: drinking makes the pain go away, and the thoughts become foggy memories. Max spends the rest of the night sulking and drinking.

♦ ♦ ♦

The next day on the trip home, Jessica asks, "Maddie, what's up with you? Things got really weird last night when you were in Max and Tyler's room."

Maddie is sitting in the front passenger seat, and McKenna is driving. McKenna gives her a side glance and sees Maddie's head drop.

Maddie is silent for a moment when another friend asks, "Yeah, Maddie, you haven't been the same all year. We're worried about you."

Maddie looks at McKenna and McKenna gives her a warm, reassuring smile and a head nod. Maddie starts to cry and shares the whole story. She tells them about their first kiss. She describes how they had a secret affair all through high school and how it ended when he asked another girl to prom a month later. She leaves out the part about homecoming, still unsure of what really happened.

McKenna, who knows the whole story, drives quietly as the other friends attack Max. They lecture Maddie about being too forgiving. They tell her he was clearly using her and didn't care about her. The words wash over her, and a new reality, one she was trying to convince herself wasn't true, sets in. Their words taint her memories that she cherished as a secret. What once brought her joy and anticipation now makes her feel stupid and used. Maddie cries the whole way home. She cries because she feels more rejected than ever because now her friends know, and it makes it feel real. She cries because she feels stupid that she trusted him and thought it was real. She cries because she mourns the loss of the last five years. She cries because she knows she has to move on and can't keep waiting for him to tell her she's wrong.

As her friends move onto a new subject, Maddie thinks to herself. She decides she's done waiting for him; she's done chasing him; done being a stupid, sad little girl. She decides it's her senior year, and she's done sulking; it's time to move on. She makes a promise to herself to stop wasting time and thoughts on Max. She's going to go back to being the happy, smiley person her friends miss.

At the next hockey game, Maddie flirts with a rival hockey team player she met over the years. Phillip is known to be a bit of a player, but she doesn't care. She likes the attention and the fact he calls her from the hockey locker room before practice, talks to her at games, and wants to be seen with her in public. He gives her little obvious gifts to woo her, and she knows it's all part of his game. She plays into it and asks for his hockey sweatshirt to wear, and he happily obliges. Phillip thinks he's getting somewhere with Maddie. Maddie, however, is making a point. Maddie proudly wears the sweatshirt to the rink and looks Max directly in the eyes when she goes out of her way to pass him intentionally.

"What's that shit?"

"My boyfriend's sweatshirt," she replies coldly as she keeps walking. He turns as she passes and watches her go once again, saying nothing. Seeing her in the sweatshirt and hearing those words cuts deep.

In that moment, Maddie feels triumphant, and a little bit of the anger fades. Only to reveal to her the hurt she still has and the feeling of rejection she hasn't gotten past.

A few weeks later, when Phillip makes it clear what he's after, Maddie breaks it off with him and returns the sweatshirt. It was nice to feel wanted, but she knows he isn't real boyfriend material, and she isn't about to give him what he wants. She learned her lesson with Max.

As the fall semester of her senior year comes to an end, the senior trip planning is just starting. Maddie goes to the senior trip meeting after school with her friends. There are about sixty kids in attendance, along with a number of parents and a travel agent explaining the trip logistics to Cancun.

Max is there with Tyler. Maddie and Max talked about this trip all through school. They planned a secret rendezvous on the white sandy beach. As Maddie remembers those plans, she glares at him with seething hurt. *How could I have been so dumb for so long?* He catches her staring, but from so far across the room, he can't tell if it's a glare or a stare. His buddy, Tyler, nudges him with his elbow and does a head nod towards Maddie to make sure she sees they're looking back. Tyler, always the instigator, Maddie thinks, and rolls her eyes, turning away.

"She totally still likes you," Tyler says.

"Doesn't look like it."

"You don't know girls. When they're that mad, it means they still have the hots for you." Tyler has pissed off enough girls in high school to know. He currently is dating another girl that Maddie has become friends with at the hockey games.

Maddie and Max both sign up for the trip. Max and Tyler are going to share a room with a couple of other hockey players, and Maddie is sharing a room with Lauren, Tyler's girlfriend, and a couple of other girls, Jessica and Stacey, who she has been partying with her senior year. McKenna is going to visit Tommy for the week, who is at his first year in college at the University of Minnesota—Duluth, and won't be in Cancun with them. Samantha is also skipping Cancun to go on spring break with her sisters in the Bahamas.

CHAPTER 15

Max and Maddie go on with their lives. The holidays come and go. Maddie's dad is done with drills for a while, and she gets back to being her happy self. Her friends are happy to have the old Maddie back. They don't know what has changed with her, but they like it.

At a Super Bowl party, Maddie meets a new boy, Connor. He's in the grade below her and is tall, with blonde hair, a warm smile, dimples and she thinks, he looks a lot like Leonardo Di-Caprio but with green eyes. Maddie's friends and his friends laugh at commercials, gossip about what's happening around school, and have a fun evening. Toward the end of the night, as people move around the party, Maddie finds herself sitting very close to Connor.

They have been chatting all night, and he makes her feel light and happy. The conversation is easy and fun with a little flirting mixed in. After the game ends, the other kids get up from the couch and get ready to leave. Maddie lingers, and Connor stays with her. When the room empties out, Connor leans in for a kiss. They kiss passionately until Jessica comes looking for Maddie.

"Maddie, where are you? It's time to go!" Jessica yells as

she walks down the stairs to the basement where they are making out on the couch. "Whoa!" she says as she walks in on them.

Connor and Maddie don't flinch. They keep kissing.

"Maddie, seriously, we have to go. School tomorrow. I'll drop Connor off if you want to keep at it on the way home."

They part for a second, looking at each other. Connor nods his head yes and scoops her up off the couch and carries her up the stairs to their coats. Jessica follows. Connor and Maddie pile into the backseat of Jessica's car and proceed to make out the whole way to Maddie's house.

Jessica drops off Maddie in her driveway. Maddie has to pull herself off of Connor.

"Call me!" she says as she shuts the door. Jessica is already backing out of the driveway as the door slams shut.

"I will!" Connor shouts out of the window.

Connor lives a few miles from Maddie and is at his place ten minutes later. By the time Maddie says hi to her parents and heads downstairs to her room, the phone is ringing.

"Hi!" Connor says on the other end.

"Hi!" Maddie says, thrilled he's already called her.

"When can I see you again?"

"Tomorrow after school?"

"That's too long."

"I don't know, when else then?"

"Where's your locker?"

Maddie tells him.

"I'll be there waiting for another kiss tomorrow morning."

"What?!"

"I want to kiss you every day for the rest of my life."

"No, you don't. You just met me."

"I'm serious. There's something about you, Maddie. You make me feel," Connor pauses, trying to find the word to describe it, "I don't know the right word, magnetized. Like, I can't be away from you for a moment."

Maddie and Connor talk on the phone for the next two hours and fall asleep on the phone sharing stories with each other. The next morning Maddie gets up early to do her hair and makeup and find just the right thing to wear for a morning kiss. She puts on a long-sleeved black bodysuit, a pair of jeans, and black boots. She paints her lips with a soft pink gloss and spritzes perfume across her head before she heads off to school.

As promised, Connor is waiting at her locker with a single pink carnation he picked up from the gas station on the way to school. He looks like a model out of a J. Crew catalog, with a navy waffled shirt with three buttons open at the neck, a plaid shirt tied around his waist, jeans, and a pair of Timberlands. Maddie can't help but feel warm inside, and a smile grows across her face as she thinks about how attractive he is.

Maddie and Connor are inseparable for the next few months. She's in love. So is he. True love. She never knew it could feel so nice to be part of a real couple. No sneaking around. No mixed messages. Just pure attraction and happiness.

The week leading up to the senior trip, Maddie and Connor talk about how they are going to miss each other. They haven't been apart a single day since they met. They can't fathom a whole week apart without phone calls.

"Are you going to miss me?"

"I already miss you. I don't want you to go."

"I know. I wish you were coming with me. I'm not going to have any fun without you."

"You better not."

"I won't."

"Promise not to make out with any drunk boys."

"I promise, these lips are only for you."

"What about him?"

"Him, who?"

"Max."

"What about Max?"

"He's going on the trip, isn't he?"

"Well, yeah but what's that matter?"

"Because you two were a thing for a long time."

"We were never a thing."

"But you lost your virginity to him."

"Yeah, I wish I hadn't. I wish I had kept it for you."

"Oh? Does that mean you're ready?"

"No, still not. We've only been together a few months."

"But I love you."

"I love you more."

"Prove it."

"You know I love you. I don't have to prove it."

"Yeah, but don't do anything with him while you are there."

"Why would you say that? Are you worried?"

"I'm not dumb. You're going to be in Mexico. You're going to be drunk. You two have a history."

"Yeah, but I haven't talked to him since," Maddie pauses,

trying to think of when, "honestly, since way before I met you. I can't remember. Besides, he's a jerk."

"Just remember that. And remember I love you."

"Of course, I will. I love you. I wish I could see you right now. I'd show you how much."

CHAPTER 16

At Fat Tuesday's, a corona banner hangs above the outside deck that is a makeshift dance floor and says, "Welcome Spring Breakers." "Rump Shaker" is playing on the speakers outside.

A crowd of late teens and early twenty-somethings in short shorts and bright-colored tank tops are dancing, while Mexican waitresses pour tequila down their throats.

Maddie brings a tray of Jell-O shots around to her group that she got from the bar. She walks up to a small group of girls standing around a very drunk Max sitting in a white plastic chair.

As she hands out shots, she asks, "What's up with Max?"

She hands a shot to Kelly. Kelly shouts over the music, "We can't get him to dance. He won't dance with anyone."

"I could get him to dance," Maddie says with boozy confidence.

"Trust me. No one can get him to do it. We've been trying for the last hour."

"Hold this," she says as she hands the tray to Kelly and takes a shot. "I can do it."

Maddie walks up to Max and stands in front of him. His head is slumped down like a drunk old man. He slowly looks up at her. They lock eyes. Looking into his blue eyes always makes her smile. She puts her hand out for him to take. He takes it and stands up. Without a word, she turns and leads him out to the dance floor. The group of girls stare in disbelief. She leads him to the middle of the dance floor. He wraps his big arms around her and they begin to sway like an old married couple still in love, dancing to a slow song. In the background, "Cotton Eyed Joe", a fast country song, plays. They are completely out of sync with the dance music and lost in their own world. He leans in to kiss her and she turns her head; he buries his face in her neck. He starts kissing it, and she melts. The girls watch in shock and have no idea what is unfolding in front of them. Max pulls his head back and looks her in the eyes. He leans in for another try at a kiss, and this time she doesn't turn her head. They kiss for the entire rest of the song. All their friends just stare in disbelief, mouths wide open.

As the song comes to an end, his buddies grab him and one of them shouts, "Time to go." He stumbles as they drag him off and reaches out for her hand. As she's about to turn away, Tyler picks her up and throws her over his shoulder and runs up to the group.

They leave in a mass and take over the sidewalk headed down the street toward their hotel. Tyler sets Maddie down next to Max. They drop toward the back of the group and hold hands, saying nothing. There is a sweetness about it like the first night they met. They walk silently to the hotel, happy to be next to each other once again.

They go up to Maddie's hotel room. It is full of people making more drinks. The two slip out onto the balcony to be alone.

Still holding hands, he turns and faces her, and then he leans in to kiss her again. She pulls away.

"I can't. I have a boyfriend," Maddie says as she comes to her senses. "I know where this is headed, and I don't think I'll be able to stop. Can we just talk?"

"I love you," Max blurts out. It is the first time he has ever said it to her.

"No, you don't. You're drunk," Maddie defensively says. She wants to believe him, but she's been so hurt by him she thinks it's just a line to get her to sleep with him. It makes her mad, and she snaps out of the drunken trance she fell into with him.

"I do. I've always loved you," Max bravely says. He can't believe the words are coming out of his mouth, but he knows it's true. He wants to tell her all of the reasons why, but he can't get the words to form.

Angry now, Maddie says, "You're just saying that so you can get laid."

Still unable to spit out his thoughts, he says, "No, I love you."

Maddie pauses. She looks at him, wanting to believe him. Instead, she says, "That's not fair. I've waited all of high school for you to be serious about me. And you tell me now? When I'm finally happy. When I have a boyfriend at home? I don't believe you. You just want to get laid. You're drunk."

Max looks down, shakes his head no. "I've always loved you. This was supposed to be our trip. And then you went and got a boyfriend right before..."

"You didn't want me. You had five years to date me. I was only good enough to sneak around with. Now I've met someone who really cares about me and isn't afraid to show it," Maddie says, hurt.

"I always loved you," Max says again. He so badly wants her to know it but can't believe he is saying it and knows how bad he hurt her by the way she is responding.

"Are you telling me you finally want to be my boyfriend?"

"No, not exactly. We could just see what happens," Max says, afraid of more rejection.

Maddie chuckles. "Yeah, that's what I thought. You don't love me. You just want to screw me."

The balcony door opens, and a crowd of drunk people come out. Two drunk boys pick up a really drunk girl and hang her off the edge of the balcony by her feet. The girl is screaming, and Maddie shifts attention there. She switches focus from what is going on with her and Max to calmly convince the boys to bring the girl back onto the balcony before they drop her. As she does, Max slips away feeling rejected.

Maddie ushers the drunk kids back inside so they don't do it again and looks around for Max but knows he is gone. She can't decide if she is sad or angry as she wanders into her bedroom and passes out.

♦ ♦ ♦

The next morning, Maddie wakes up, showers, and heads into the kitchen area. A group of her girlfriends are sitting around the kitchen table, gossiping about last night. Empty beer cans are tipped over next to cereal bowls.

"Did you hear that Max and Kelly hooked up?" Jessica says.

Maddie looks stunned. "What? No. He was here last night."

"No, it happened. I just came from her room, and he's there now," Lauren, Tyler's girlfriend, says.

"I don't believe you," Maddie says, feeling deeply betrayed.

"Come with me. I'll show you," Lauren offers.

Maddie and Lauren walk into the other hotel room. She sees Max and Kelly sitting next to each other in two chairs.

Kelly has a big grin on her face when she sees Maddie. "Good morning," she says, triumphantly.

Maddie looks like she just got punched in the gut. "Morning," she responds, clearly annoyed.

Maddie turns and looks at Max. Max says nothing, just looks at her with a blank look. She stares at him in an awkward silence and shakes her head in disbelief. As she walks away, she says, "Fuck you!"

Once again, Max does not go after her. He has no idea what he did this time.

That night all the girls go on a booze cruise while the boys hit the clubs. The girls dance and drink as they cruise to a private island. When they get there, the rum drinks are flowing like the endless thumping coming from the speakers.

Maddie is mad at herself for thinking for a second that Max could have meant what he said. She oscillates between having fun and feeling free, to being seething mad and dancing out the anger. She's determined to drink and dance her feelings away. She wants to get lost in the night and not think about how much of a fool she's been.

Maddie drinks so much that when the music stops and the party hosts start asking for volunteers for some competition on the grand stage, she makes a beeline for the stage. When she gets to the group of girls surrounding the stage, she gets picked out of the crowd and pulled up behind the stage. She has no idea what competition she is entering, half because she can't hear what the host is saying over the roar of the crowd, and half because she simply can't understand from the sheer amount of alcohol she's drunk. Regardless, she's confident whatever it is, she's going to win.

She's handed a white t-shirt to put on, and she does. Next thing she knows, she's on stage in a wet t-shirt contest, getting sprayed with a hose as she dances, trying not to slip in the puddle of water that is the stage. Maddie ends up in the finals, and her friends are shouting her name. The girl next to her clearly is not new to wet t-shirt contests and tears her shirt from the neck down until her chest is totally exposed to the crowd. Maddie bows to her and walks off the stage; she's drunk but not that desperate for attention. She puts her shirt back on and ties the wet t-shirt to her head like a crown. On the cruise back to the hotel, half the passengers are puking over the side of the boat. Everyone is super drunk and got their money's worth of free cheap Mexican rum, Maddie and her friends included. They stumble back to the hotel after the ship docks.

Max went to the clubs with the guys and drank about as much as Maddie did. He didn't say anything to his guy friends about what had happened the night before. When he and Tyler go back to the hotel, they meet a couple of random guys in the lobby. Tyler has a key to Maddie's and Lauren's room. Max, Tyler, and the randoms go to Maddie's hotel room, which is on the same floor as Max and Tyler's room, to wait for the girls to return. Tyler immediately passes out in Lauren's bed. The rest of the guys continue to drink. Max, in a drunken stupor, lets down his guard and starts talking about Maddie since he doesn't know any of them.

"I love Maddie," Max says to the random guys.

"Who is Maddie?"

"She's the girl that got away."

"Is she here?"

Max nods his head yes. "This is her room."

"Does she have a boyfriend?"

Max nods yes.

"Is he here?"

Max shakes his head no.

"Does she still like you?"

Max shrugs his shoulders like he doesn't know.

"I still like her, but I think she's mad at me and I don't know why. Why is she mad at me?"

"Why'd you break up?"

"We didn't break up."

"Then how did she get away?"

"She started dating another guy. A younger guy. He's tall and doesn't even play hockey."

"While dating you?"

"No, we never dated. I just loved her, and she would kiss me and make me feel good."

"Why didn't you date?"

"My dad got my mom pregnant in college and it ruined his hockey career, so now he forces me to play hockey, and he won't let me date girls because he's afraid I'll make the same mistake. But I love her."

"Dude, that's messed up. You can't help who or when you fall in love. You need to tell her."

"I did, last night. She didn't believe me and then told me to fuck off this morning."

"No one knows, so you can't tell anyone. My dad can't find out, or he will kill me."

"Dude, we don't know any of your friends, so your secret is safe with us."

"You can't tell my dad, or he will seriously kill me!"

"You two sound like a country song."

Maddie and Lauren walk in. Max looks up from the table and just stares at Maddie. She stares back.

"Whoa! What's going on here?" a random guy asks.

Max and Maddie are silent and just stare at each other. Maddie is too drunk to decide if she's angry or happy to see him, and she gets stuck in the thought.

"Is this her?"

Max drunkenly nods yes.

"Do you know he loves you?"

Maddie shakes her head no. Max can't take his eyes off her.

"You need to leave," Maddie says after a minute of staring at Max.

Max continues to stare at Maddie.

"You need to leave now!" Maddie shouts at Max. She decides she's angry.

Maddie walks over to Max and grabs his hand to drag him out.

"He hasn't stopped talking about you all night."

"He's an asshole. He doesn't give a crap about me."

Maddie pulls Max up from the chair and walks him out the door and leads him down the hall toward his room. He falls down in the hallway. She tries to help him up; he pulls her down onto him. She resists a little but gives in. They start kissing on the floor in the hall. The random guys look out the hotel room door and see them, and they smile.

♦ ♦ ♦

The next morning, Max's hotel room door bursts open. A bunch of loud, rowdy boys spill through the doorway, just getting back from drinking all night. Maddie and Max are passed out on the pullout bed in the living room.

"Oh, look who got some last night," one of the boys shouts as he points to the bed in the living room.

Max wakes up and jumps out of bed and joins the others in the kitchen as they razz him.

Maddie looks around for her shirt and finds the white one she wore in the contest first, and the night starts to flash back to her. She gets dressed under the covers after she finds the rest of her clothes by the side of the bed. She slips out without saying goodbye and does the walk of shame down the hallway.

Maddie walks into her own hotel room, completely hungover and looking like it.

"Where have you been? We've been worried about you," one of her roommates says.

"Down the hall," Maddie says as she looks at her feet with regret.

"No!" the girls all shout in unison.

Maddie shakes her head yes slowly, ashamed.

"I screwed up. I was so mad at him. I kicked him out of here, and next thing you know, I'm waking up in his room. I don't remember anything after he fell down," she says as her mind flashes back to the kiss. "I feel awful. I love my boyfriend. I've ruined it."

"It's Mexico. What happens in Mexico stays in Mexico," one of the girls says.

"Yeah, we won't tell," says another.

"I have to tell him. It'll get back to him. I have to. Oh God. What did I do? I don't even know what I did. What do I tell him?" Maddie asks, looking for an answer she knows she won't find.

Maddie mopes around for the rest of the trip, and Max avoids her.

When Maddie gets home from Mexico, she immediately calls her boyfriend.

"I'm home!" Maddie says cheerily when her boyfriend answers.

"I'm coming over. I've missed you so much."

"Umm. Before you do, I have to tell you something," Maddie says sheepishly.

"What?" he replies, already guessing what it might be.

"Umm... I accidentally kissed a boy."

"How do you accidentally kiss a boy? What boy was it?"

"You know what boy it was." She pauses. "I was being really good, and then one night I got back from the booze cruise, and he was in my hotel room. I kicked him out right away."

"So how did you accidentally kiss if you kicked him out?"

"We both were really drunk, and he fell over in the hallway as I was kicking him out. I tried to help him up, and he pulled me down, and then he kissed me."

"Anything else happen?"

"That's all I remember. I kicked him out. He fell, then he kissed me."

"Are you sure?"

"Honestly, that's all I remember. I don't remember anything else." She neglects to tell him about the first night. "We were so drunk. I felt awful and thought about you the whole rest of the trip. I didn't have any fun. I didn't see or talk to him the rest of the trip; I promise," Maddie says, trying to convince him, and herself, that it was that innocent.

"One of my sister's friends told me they saw you looking pretty sad before she left Cancun."

Maddie is surprised that is all he heard. "I was. I love you, and I never meant to hurt you. Can you forgive me? Please?" Maddie begs.

"I'm not happy. But if that is all it was... You have to stay away from him. He's no good."

"I know! Come over, and I'll make it up to you," Maddie says, suggestively.

"You're going to have to try really hard to make it up to me."

"I can think of a few ways."

"I'm on my way."

CHAPTER 17

Maddie is packing for college in her university of Minnesota-Duluth sweatshirt when the doorbell rings. She answers the door and sees Max standing on the other side in his University of Michigan hockey sweatshirt.

"What are you doing?" Max asks when she opens the door.

"Packing for college. What are you doing?" Maddie replies, not knowing why he would be there.

"I was just driving around, and then I found myself here," Max says softly.

"Oh. Why?" Maddie asks quietly back.

Max shrugs his shoulders and looks down at his feet.

Maddie stares at him, at a loss for words.

Max looks up and asks, "Want to go for a drive?"

Maddie shrugs her shoulders.

"I guess." She yells to her mom with no explanation, "I'm going out!" as she shuts the door behind her.

Maddie hops into Max's Bronco he got for graduation. They cruise around like they did so many other times over the years, eventually stopping at a secluded park.

"Are you excited to go to college?" Max asks.

"Yes and no. I'm excited for college but I don't want to leave home," Maddie shares.

"You mean, leave Connor."

"Yeah, him too. It's going to be hard. McKenna and Tommy made it work and I am sure we can too."

"How about you?"

"Not really. I should be going to Michigan to play hockey."

"I'm really sorry about that. I can't imagine how crushed you are."

"If only my dad would have let me accept on the spot. I'd at least still be going to school there while I work on getting back to where I was. I could have worked with their rehab team."

"Didn't they want to work with you still."

"Yeah, but I didn't accept and there's only so many spots. The Juniors team couldn't hold a spot for me forever."

"So where are you going?"

"I'm going to Bemidji part-time so I can stay eligible for the NCAA. My varsity coach knows some former Juniors coaches that live there that are going to train me and they have arranged with the Bemidji hockey coaches to let me practice with the team. If I can get my speed and strength back Michigan convinced the USHL to let me tryout when a spot opens up. They said they still want me if I can make a comeback."

"Wow, you've got a whole lot of people helping you. Your dad must be happy."

"My dad doesn't know. My varsity coach did all of this for me. My dad gave up on me when I didn't play varsity this year. He wouldn't even talk to the coach when he recommended I play rec instead. My dad thought I was throwing my whole hockey career away."

"Why did your coach want you to play rec?"

"We talked a lot about what to do before the decision was made. He knew with the condition I was in I wasn't going to get much playing time on varsity and that would be worse for me then playing rec hockey. He worked it out with the rec coach to give me as much time as my body would allow so I could keep my skills sharp."

"Do you want it that much that you'd risk getting hurt before you're healed?"

"I guess. I mean, it was always my dad's dream and he pushed me so hard but the fact is, I'm good. At least I was. I love hockey and I was so close to playing for Michigan. My dad gave up on me but my coach didn't. I don't want to let him down and honestly, I want to prove to my dad I am good enough."

"Oh, Max, I'm sure he thinks you're good enough. You'd be playing if you weren't in an accident."

"Trust me. My dad doesn't think I'm good enough. He never has."

"I think you're good enough. I believe in you."

Sammy Kershaw's "Double Wide Trailer" comes on the radio.

"Would you?" Max asks Maddie changing the subject.

"Would I what?" Maddie asks curiously.

"Come home and eat onion rings with me?"

Maddie is confused and tilts her head as she looks at him and says, "What are you talking about?"

"In the song, she runs away from him and he chases her and finds her with another man and he says, come home with me and eat some onion rings," Max explains and then asks, "So, would you?"

"Eat onion rings?" Maddie says, still confused.

"If I asked you to, would you leave him for me?" Max asks seriously.

"Yeah, if you asked," she says directly and without hesitation, surprising herself.

Maddie keeps looking into his eyes, a gaze they haven't held in a long while, and waits for him to ask. The song ends.

Max breaks the gaze and starts the Bronco. "We should probably go." He drives Maddie home in silence.

Maddie is dying inside, so confused about what just happened, and feeling guilty about being with Max when she loves her boyfriend. She especially feels guilty for saying that she would leave her boyfriend if Max asked. She knows she meant it, and then Max says nothing but brings her home. She shakes her head to herself, not knowing what to say or do on the silent drive home. *Why did he ask if I would, but then didn't ask me to be his girlfriend?*

When he pulls up to her house, she gets out of the truck and watches him drive away. She doesn't know if she'll ever see him again and wonders why he came over in the first place. As she watches him drive off, she thinks that is probably the last chance they ever had and now it is really over. She's headed off to college and so is he. They had a hard enough time seeing each other in high school, living a mile away from each other, now they will never see each other. She feels a profound loss as he slips out of sight.

Maddie goes inside to finish packing. She sees she has twenty missed calls on her caller ID. All from her boyfriend, which is unusual. She wonders if something happened and calls him back immediately.

"Where have you been for the last three hours?"

"On a drive. Why did you call so much? Is everything okay?"

"You tell me. Who were you on a drive with? Were you with him?"

Maddie pauses for a moment. This is not what she wants to happen right before she goes to college. "Yes," she calmly says.

"Did anything happen?"

"No, I swear. We just drove around and said goodbye for good. I don't think I'll ever see him again." As those words sink in, she feels the sadness deepening and pushes it aside as she worries about what this is going to do to her relationship.

Maddie and her boyfriend talk for hours. The drive revealed some worries her boyfriend had about her going off to college without him. They talk about how they are going to make it work and how they are going to be the couple that survives the long-distance curse. Maddie reassures him that McKenna and Tommy made it work and they can too. They plan out all of the weekends Maddie can come home and see him. She can tell trust has been lost and vows to be the best girlfriend ever when she leaves.

♦ ♦ ♦

Maddie and McKenna's dorm room phone rings.

"Hello?" Maddie answers.

"Who's this?" a strange voice asks on the other end of the line.

"This is Maddie. Who's this?"

"This is Dave, Max's roommate. Who are you?"

Maddie's heart stops. *Why is he calling? What happened to Max?* "I'm Maddie. Why?"

"Max never talks about you when he is sober, but when he gets drunk, really drunk, all he wants to do is talk to you."

"Sounds about right," Maddie says dryly, now that she knows he is okay.

"Who are you?"

"No one special. Just a girl he went to school with."

"Can we come and visit?"

"No!" Maddie says loudly.

McKenna looks up from studying, intrigued with the conversation now.

"He really wants to see you."

"He can't. I have a boyfriend. He knows that. You cannot come here."

McKenna grabs the phone. "Come!" she excitedly shouts into the phone.

Maddie in the background yells, "No, don't!"

"You have my permission to come. She talks about him too, all the time. How long until you get here?"

"It's about a two-hour drive. Will you be there?"

"You won't get here until 2:00 a.m., but yeah, I'll be here."

"If it gets him to shut up, it's worth it to drive in the middle of a cold winter night."

"They can't come. I would never be able to explain that. We are already on rocky ground."

"See you soon," McKenna says as she hangs up the phone.

Maddie shakes her head no. "He can't come. That would be the final straw with Connor."

Secretly, she can't wait to see him, and McKenna knows it. Maddie and McKenna wait for hours. The boys never show up. Worried, Maddie calls Max's dorm room. The roommate answers.

"Hello," the voice says groggily.

"You guys okay? We've been worried."

"Oh yeah, we didn't ever make it out of the parking lot. Sorry."

"Real quick, why tonight? Why did he want to visit tonight?"

"Hockey tryouts."

Maddie hangs up without saying goodbye or asking if he made the team. She looks at McKenna. "They never left the parking lot," Maddie says, annoyed. "Let's go to bed."

"Boo, Max, boo!"

CHAPTER 18

The toll of being apart and living separate lives has worn on Connor and Maddie. They've managed to navigate the first three months, talking on the phone nearly every night. But the phone bills are adding up, and the distance between them feels like it is growing wider.

"I can't wait to see you for Christmas break," Maddie says to Connor over the phone.

"I can't wait to see you. When do I get to see you?"

"I'm coming home as soon as finals are done. I'll be in your arms by Thursday night."

"It has been too long. I can't wait to kiss you all night."

Maddie grins, thinking about it. "It's a date then. I love you so much! We get a whole two weeks together. I won't have school, work, or any other obligations. You can have all of my time."

"Can I have all of you?"

"Maybe," Maddie teases. "Listen, I have to cram for finals. I'll call you tomorrow. Only a few more days. We can do this. I miss you so much."

"I miss you too. I love you—for eternity."

"I love you for eternity."

They hang up the phone.

"I love you for eternity," McKenna teases Maddie. "You two are too cute. It makes me sick."

"Stop. I do love him."

"I know you do. I'm happy for you. It'll be good for you two to see each other. I for one can't wait to go home and be done studying."

"Oh God, me too. I am so sick of these books," Maddie says, pushing the books off her lap.

♦ ♦ ♦

For New Year's, Maddie and Connor join McKenna, Tommy, and some other high school friends at the University of Minnesota for a house party. They park on the street a few blocks away and make their way to a rundown house on campus. Groups of people are walking into the party. They recognize some of the other people from different grades in high school.

As midnight gets closer, the party is crowded, with barely enough room to move.

McKenna grabs Maddie's arm and says, "Don't look now, but Max just showed up."

Maddie, looking around the house, says, "No, where? This is not good."

"I said don't look. He is straight behind you. I can see him now. I don't think he has spotted us yet," McKenna says, looking over Maddie's shoulder.

"Okay, let's grab the guys and get out of here."

"It's almost midnight. It'll be fine. We can go right after."

"I don't want Connor to see him."

"We will have to walk right by him to get out of the door. You are better off keeping him occupied. After midnight, the party will thin out, and we can make a break."

"Okay, good point. Where are the guys now?" Maddie says, scanning the room for Tommy and Connor.

"They are grabbing drinks from the kitchen. Let's go find them," McKenna says as she pulls Maddie toward the kitchen.

"Hey!" Maddie shouts at Connor as they get to the kitchen.

"Hey! Here's your beer," he says as he swoops in for a kiss. Maddie kisses him back trying to stall him.

"Let's stay in here."

"Why?"

"I'm thirsty. I might want another before the ball drops."

"You're drinking a lot tonight," Connor says, a little concerned.

"Yeah, well, it's New Year's, and I'm happy I get to be with you."

He kisses her again.

"Let's get out of here so we can be alone after the countdown."

"Sure!"

McKenna is keeping a watchful eye on the crowd when she sees Max walk into the kitchen with his buddies.

"Maddie!" McKenna shouts, trying to get her attention. Maddie is busy kissing Connor and doesn't hear her, but Max does and spots the couple. "Oops," McKenna says to herself, wishing she hadn't shouted Maddie's name.

When Maddie and Connor pull apart from their embrace, Connor sees Max. Maddie can feel Connor stiffen as his whole demeanor changes. She turns around and sees Max staring down Connor.

Connor and Max glare at each other as the crowd moves in and out past them. Maddie turns back around and puts her hands on Connor's chest to hold him back. She can feel Connor start to lean forward to move toward Max.

"Connor, no! Please don't!"

Connor pushes forward, and Maddie pushes hard back on him. McKenna grabs Tommy and moves closer to them, shaking her head no at Max. Max begins to move toward Connor.

Maddie can't stop Connor. They get about a foot apart and are locked in a stare down. Neither of them says a word to each other, but their body language does. The crowd around them takes notice and starts to encircle them, preparing for a fight.

Maddie tugs at Connor's arm, "Connor, don't. Let's go!"

Connor doesn't budge. Maddie reluctantly turns toward Max. Max doesn't break his concentration from Connor as Maddie looks at him. So many feelings are racing through her, and she doesn't know what to do next. She freezes, and McKenna steps between the two guys and says, "Hey Max!"

Max still doesn't flinch. Tommy slides next to McKenna trying to help break them up.

Maddie faces Connor again, waving her hand in front of his face and shouts, "Hey, look at me, not him."

Around them, people chant 10-9-8-7... and erupt in "Happy new year!" When this happens, the crowd swells in celebration, and Max and Connor get shifted, separating. Maddie drags Connor out of the party.

"What was that, Connor?" Maddie shouts at him outside.

"I'm going to kill him!" Connor shouts back.

"Why?"

"Because I hate him."

"Did something happen while I was away?"

"You tell me?"

"What's that supposed mean?"

"Why is he here? Did he come to find you?"

"What are you talking about? We're at a party. Look around. There are a ton of people from school here. I had no idea. If I had, I wouldn't have come," Maddie says, shocked at what he asked.

"When is the last time you've seen him?" Connor asks again, with even more accusation in his voice.

"Max? Before I left for school."

"What happened when you went on that drive?" Connor asks, revealing his lack of trust.

"Connor, I told you, nothing. Nothing happened. We said goodbye. That's it. I haven't seen him since then. I didn't know he was going to be here. I promise. Why are you so angry?"

"He's no good for you, Maddie. I love you. He doesn't."

"I know, Connor. That's why I'm with you, not him."

"If we ever break up, promise me you don't go back to him."

"I absolutely promise you. But let's not break up. Why are you even talking that way?"

"I love you, Maddie. He is no good for you."

"Connor, let's go home. You've had a lot to drink too. You're not making sense. There is nothing between Max and I. I came home for you. I love you. I want to be with you. Forever. For eternity, remember?"

McKenna is still in the house with Tommy. "Max, what was that?"

"What was what?"

"Between you and Connor. You two looked like you were going to kill each other."

"Ask him! I didn't do anything. I just walked into the kitchen, and he seemed like he wanted to fight me," Max says defensively. "You saw it, Tommy. Tell her."

"You kind of seemed like you wanted to fight him too," Tommy says.

"I'm never going to back down from a fight. Especially if I didn't do anything," Max says with an edge to his voice. "He better not be hurting Maddie."

"Connor?" McKenna laughs. "He's the sweetest guy. I don't think he could ever hurt Maddie if he wanted to. He adores her. It's sickening how much those two love each other."

"Yeah? You let me know if that ever changes."

"I will, Max. Until then, stand down. She's happy. Speaking of, where did they go? We have to find them. Happy New Year!" McKenna says, looking around. "Tommy, let's go."

"Happy New Year, Chief! Good to see you and congrats. I heard you made the team," Tommy says.

"Yeah, happy new year!" Max says, thinking he's had better.

♦ ♦ ♦

A few nights later, Maddie's phone rings.

"Hello?"

"Hi," Max is on the other end.

"Oh, hey."

"Hey," Max says. "You sound surprised."

"I am. I didn't expect to hear from you."

"What are you doing?" Max asks, ignoring her statement.

"Watching a movie set in the 1800's. You probably wouldn't like it."

"What's the plot?" Max asks, making small talk.

"Guy meets girl. They fall for each other but can't be together. Girl never stops loving the guy and tries to keep her distance. Guy marries a nice girl and is a good husband but never forgets his first love. They spend a lifetime longing for each other and having chance encounters that keep the fire alive."

"Sounds juicy."

"It's beautiful and heartbreaking. Kind of like Samantha's aunt."

"Huh?"

"Remember the first time we met. Samantha told us about her aunt who met her soulmate and lived her whole life without him but still loved him?" Maddie reminds him.

"Oh, yeah, sort of," Max says, vaguely remembering the conversation. "I do remember you in a swimsuit, though. Good memory."

"Stop, you can't think about that."

"Why not?"

"Because I have a boyfriend."

"Doesn't mean I can't think about you."

Maddie pauses for a moment before responding. "Do you?"

"Yeah. Do you think about me?"

"I shouldn't."

"But do you?"

"Yeah."

"What do you think about me?"

"Most recently, I was thinking why did you look like you wanted to fight Connor? And before that just about what you're doing, how school is going, you know, just stuff."

"School is fine. It's nice to be home for a bit and see you." Max doesn't tell her about making the team.

"That was nice? I thought the two of you were going to kill each other. What was that about?"

"You tell me," Max says defensively, putting up a wall. "I didn't do anything, and next thing you know, your boyfriend wants to fight me. Actually, it's why I called. I just want to make sure you're okay."

"What do you mean?"

"He's not hurting you, is he?" Max asks with genuine concern.

"Connor? No, he's an absolute sweetheart. I've never once seen him aggressive until New Year's. He was so angry."

"Why?"

"I think he thinks there is still something between us. Turns out he's still mad about that day we went for a drive before we left for school."

"How's he know about that? Did you tell him?"

"No, his best friend saw us. He was pissed—especially after what happened over spring break."

"What does he think happened over spring break?"

"I told him we kissed and that I didn't remember anything else."

"That's all he knows?"

"That's all I remember, besides waking up in your bed. I certainly didn't know how to explain that, so I left it out."

"Probably smart. Yeah, I guess I could see how he might not like me. Do you promise, though, he's not hurting you?"

"That's sweet. I promise. He would never, and I would never stand for it."

"So, is there?"

"Is there what?"

"Is there something between us?"

"Between us? I didn't know there was ever an us. You never wanted to be my boyfriend."

"Sure, I did."

"Like when? Every time I brought it up, we got in a fight."

"I always wanted to be your boyfriend. I just couldn't be because of hockey."

"That's BS. Plenty of guys have girlfriends and played hockey."

"Yeah, but it was different for them."

"Different how?"

"It's hard to explain. I just couldn't; it wasn't an option—then. So, is there?"

"Something between us?"

"Yeah."

"Don't make me answer that."

"Why not?"

"Because I'm happy. Please don't do this to me."

"Do what?"

"Get me thinking about you again. You're like a drug. You're an addiction. It takes me a long time to get you out of my system."

"So, there's still something?" Max asks again with a little hope in his voice.

"Max, there will always be something between us, but you're no good for me. I get hurt every time, and I'm happy now. I don't want to ruin it."

"We're kind of like your movie."

"How so?"

"We can't be together, but we want to be."

Maddie takes a deep breath as she thinks about it. Max can hear her contemplating it.

"If you had to choose, who would you choose?"

"Max, that's not fair! You made your choice over and over again, and it was never me."

"I didn't have a choice. You do."

"Max, I haven't talked to you for months, and before that months, and now you're telling me I have to make a choice. You're incredible," Maddie says, deflecting the question.

"I am pretty incredible," Max says, trying to defuse the tension. "Watch your movie. Let me know how it ends."

Maddie sits in silence, not wanting to hang up but knowing the conversation is going nowhere good.

"Okay. It was nice to hear from you."

"Yeah, have a happy new year. I'm glad you're happy."

"I hope you're happy too. Happy new year, Max," Maddie says, not wanting to hang up.

Max hangs up. Maddie is stunned and keeps thinking about what Max asked her. She wonders if he's just feeling nostalgic being home or if he is serious. She finishes watching her movie. At the end of the movie, the two characters have the opportunity to finally be together. The woman waits for him and the man stands outside her window looking up at her and doesn't go to her, choosing instead to let her live her life and not hurt her again. Maddie bursts into tears. *Why doesn't Max ever choose me?*

Max thinks about their conversation too. He knows Maddie still has a thing for him, even though she won't fully admit it. He wants to be with her, but he is scared he'll break her as he does every time. She's happy now with Connor. As long as she's happy, that will have to be good enough for him. He loves her, but he doesn't know how to love her out loud.

CHAPTER 19

Maddie comes home for spring break. Things haven't been the best with Connor. They have been fighting a lot about her going out so much and them never being able to see each other. She's hoping spending time together this week will help get them to summer break. Connor picks Maddie up in his new car and drives her to the dam at the lake.

"What made you decide to come here?"

"This is where we come before hockey games; no one is ever here this time of year."

Connor started playing rec hockey thinking it would make Maddie like him more and to pass time while she was off at college.

"Why would you come here before games?"

"To get high."

"To get high?"

"Yeah, it's no big deal."

"It's actually a really big deal. You and I made a pact not to do drugs."

"Whatever, you're an alcoholic. Pot is at least natural."

"I'm what?"

"You drink all the time. What's a little pot?"

"I'm in college. That's what you do. You're getting high before a game. What's the point?

"Okay, okay. I don't do it that much. I'll stop."

"Promise?"

"I promise. Will you stop drinking as much as you do?"

"If it means that much to you, I will."

"Okay, it's a deal then. I don't want to fight while you are home. There's something I'd rather do," he says as he pulls her closer.

♦ ♦ ♦

The next day, Maddie looks at her clock. It's 2:00 p.m. Connor was supposed to be at her house an hour ago. She tries calling his house to see if he's there. His sister tells her he's at Andy's, his best friend. Maddie calls over to Andy's house.

"Hey Andy! How are you?" Maddie says cheerily.

"Hey Maddie! Are you coming over?"

"Is Connor there?"

"Yeah, one second," Andy says as he yells for Connor, "It's Maddie!"

"Hey."

"Hi, are you still coming over?"

"Yeah, I just had to stop at Andy's. I'll be there soon."

"You were supposed to be here an hour ago. What are you guys doing?"

"Nothing."

"Nothing? What did you need to stop over for then?"

"I just did. I'll be there soon."

"You don't have to come over if you'd rather hang out with Andy."

"I'll be over in a half-hour."

"Connor, are you getting high?" Maddie asks, not wanting to know the answer.

Silence on the other end of the phone.

"You are, aren't you?" Maddie pushes. Her heart sinks.

"Yeah," he reluctantly says.

"You promised."

"It's not a big deal," Connor says, as if he is talking to his mom.

"It is to me. I'm home to see you, and you'd rather smoke pot with your buddy you see every day than be with me. Do you know how that makes me feel?"

"Do you know how it makes me feel when you go out drinking all the time?"

"I told you I'd stop. Do you want to see me or not?"

"I do want to see you; I'll come over when I'm done," Connor says, not wanting to leave.

"I don't want to be your second choice. I don't want to play second fiddle to Mary Jane. You have to decide," Maddie says, giving him an ultimatum. She thinks back to her conversation with Max about having to choose.

"I told you, I'll be there soon," Connor says stubbornly.

"Okay, so you decided. I get to decide too, and I'm not going to watch you get sucked into this world. I've lost too many friends to drugs, and I can't lose you too. If you stay, we're done."

Silence again on the other end of the phone.

Maddie can't believe the words that come out of her mouth next, "We're done. I love you, but we're done. I can't."

"I love you too, Maddie, but I'm young, and I just want to have fun. I'm sorry."

Maddie hangs up the phone and bursts out crying. Her heart is broken. She loves Connor with all her heart. Drugs are her deal breaker. She doesn't know what to do with all the feelings that are flooding to the surface inside of her. She turns the radio up as loud as it goes to try to drown out her thoughts and silence the hurt. "Total Eclipse of the Heart" is playing.

"Dude, everything okay?" Andy asks, looking at Connor's surprised face, holding the phone.

"Maddie just broke up with me?" Connor says as he hangs up the phone.

"Why? You two are so in love."

"Because I wanted to smoke some pot with you before I went to see her."

"When did she get so uptight? She's acting like your mom."

"I don't know. It's not like she doesn't party."

"Does that mean you have the rest of the day to hang?"

"Guess so?"

"Are you sure you don't want to go see her and work things out?"

"I don't know; we've been fighting a lot lately. Maybe we need a break. I'll call her tomorrow. Let's get high. I don't want to think about this now."

"Want to try acid? I got some from my brother. You'll forget her for sure if you take a trip with me."

"Sure, why not? I've got all day now."

♦ ♦ ♦

The next day, Maddie's grandma arrives at her house. Maddie is still crushed over her breakup. She's feeling hurt that her boyfriend hasn't called. When she sees her grandma show up unexpectedly, she thinks, *Grandma will make me feel better,* and smiles for a second.

Her grandma gets out of the car and has a suitcase with her. *That's odd,* Maddie thinks. She runs to open the door and greet her grandma.

"Grandma!" Maddie says cheerily.

"Hi, sweetie," her grandma says and gives her a long hug like only grandmas do. She holds it longer than usual.

Maddie senses something is wrong.

"Is your mom home?"

"No, she's out grocery shopping right now. Come in."

They go inside, and Maddie asks, "Are you staying with us?"

"For a little while."

"Where's Grandpa?"

"He's in the hospital."

"What? Is he okay?"

"He's not. His kidneys are failing. He needs a transplant."

"He can have one of mine."

"Sweetie, he's lived a good life, and you have your whole life ahead of you," her grandma says as she turns to look out the front window. "Looks like your mom is home."

Maddie's mom comes in from the garage.

"Hi, Mom, what are you doing here? Everything okay?"

"No, your dad is in the hospital. His kidneys are failing. I need to stay with you while they take care of him."

"Of course, anything you need. Can we see Dad?"

"He doesn't want any of you seeing him like this."

"Well, he's my dad, and of course, I'm going to visit him," Maddie's mom says. She looks at the clock, "What time are visiting hours over?"

"7:00 p.m.," Maddie's grandma says. "I just came from there and need a little rest before I go back."

"Yes, let's get you settled in. Maddie gets the groceries from the car while I help Grandma."

"Mom, is Grandpa going to be okay?" Maddie asks.

"I don't know, honey. I'm going to take Grandma back to the hospital and find out."

"Can I go with you? I want to see Grandpa."

"Not today. I need you to stay with your brother while I figure out what is going on. Maybe tomorrow. Can you do that for me?"

"Yeah, I can do that. Tell Grandpa I love him."

Maddie stays home with her brother. They watch movies that night, waiting for her mom and grandma to return. Maddie is sad about her breakup but so busy worrying about her grandpa she doesn't notice her boyfriend hasn't called. She knows they broke up but figured they'd at least try to talk things out. Her mom calls to say they are staying late at the hospital and not to wait up. After putting her brother to bed,

Maddie falls asleep thinking about the two of them and missing her dad who is overseas again fighting another war.

♦ ♦ ♦

The next day, her mom and grandma head back to the hospital. Her brother is off to a friend's house for the day.

"Can I go with you today?" Maddie asks since she doesn't need to watch her brother.

"Grandpa really doesn't want anyone there," Maddie's mom says.

"How come you get to go?"

"Because I won't take no for an answer."

"So why do I have to?"

"Because he is already mad enough at me. Let's give it another day to see if they can get him stable and then we'll get you and your brother to see him. Deal?"

"Okay," Maddie says, not wanting to agree.

Maddie's mom and grandma leave for the hospital. Her brother puts his backpack on, hops on his bike, and is off to the neighbor's house for the day. Maddie is all alone with nothing to do.

The sadness starts to creep in. She wants to call her boyfriend and work things out. She wants to cry to him about her grandpa. She decides not to call him and goes to her room. She crawls back into bed and cries. She cries for her grandpa, not knowing really what is happening with him, and she cries because she wants to be back together with her boyfriend, but she knows they have grown apart, and she cries because she misses her dad. She cries so much she falls asleep in the middle of the morning. She's emotionally exhausted.

When she wakes that afternoon, she decides she's going to call Connor and ask to pick up some of her stuff. She thinks it's a good excuse to see him, and maybe they can work things out. They talk briefly, and he says he'll pull it together so she can pick it up. Maddie does her best to cover her swollen eyes with makeup and look as cute as possible for him. She drives over to his house and sees a box of her stuff on the step outside. Her stomach drops. He doesn't want to see her. She gets out of the car slowly and looks up at his front window. He's standing in the window staring out at her. She smiles. He doesn't move. She walks up to the door where the box is. She leans down to the step to pick it up, lingering for a second, hoping the door will open, and he will appear. It doesn't. She picks up the box and turns to go back to her car. She puts it in the back seat. Maddie looks up at the window again before she gets into her car. He's still standing there, watching her. Her heart breaks into a thousand pieces again. She quickly gets into the car and starts it as fast as she can. She's racing her tears out of the driveway. She doesn't want him to see her crying. Maddie sobs the whole way home. She knows it is really over. She thinks to herself, *How did he not even come outside? No last goodbye?*

Connor watches Maddie walk up to the stairs and grab her box of stuff. He knows he should run outside and scoop her up like he has always done, but his body won't move. He feels nothing. He watches her turn and go back to her car. He still doesn't move an inch. When she looks up at him the last time, he can tell she's about to cry, and he still feels absolutely nothing. He knows he should feel something for this girl, but he feels dead inside. She drives away. He turns around and calls out to his mom.

"Mom!"

"What is it?" she says, walking into the front living room.

"Something is wrong with me. I think I need to go to the hospital."

"What are you talking about? You look fine."

"Something is wrong in my head. Maddie was just here, and I couldn't move to open the door to say hi to her. You know how much I love her, and I feel nothing."

"Oh, honey, you're just sad because you two broke up. That's normal."

"Is it normal to think you're either an angel sent to save the world or the devil sent to destroy it?"

She looks at him in horror. "What are you talking about? That's not funny."

"I know, Mom, but that's what's going on inside of my head for the last few days. I honestly don't know which I am, and I feel nothing inside."

"Oh, God, I'll get my keys," she says as she runs to the kitchen. "Let's go." Her heart is beating a thousand times a minute. She knows what is happening to her son but prays the whole way to the hospital it isn't true.

♦ ♦ ♦

The next morning the phone rings at 7:00 a.m. Maddie answers it.

"Hello?" she says, still sleepy.

"Hi," Connor says.

"Hi, what time is it?"

"7:00 a.m."

"Why are you calling so early? Is everything okay?"

"Yeah. I don't know why I'm calling."

"Okay, can I call you when I wake up?"

"Yeah, okay."

"You okay?"

"Yeah. Call me later."

"Okay," Maddie says and hangs up the phone, falling back asleep.

She calls when she wakes up, but his mom says he isn't there. Maddie runs up to the video store to return the videos she and her brother watched.

"Connor was wild the other night at Andy's house," one of the store employees says to her, "why weren't you there?"

"We broke up."

"That explains it. He was so messed up. He kept telling everyone he was either an angel sent to save the world or the devil sent to destroy it. He was pulling at his hair, saying, 'Get these demons out of my head.' It was funny."

"What? What was he on?"

"I think he was dropping acid."

"What? Seriously? We broke up because he was smoking pot, and now he's doing acid?" *What a jerk*, she thinks, hurt that he chose more drugs over working things out with her.

Another girl chimes in, "I heard he went to the hospital, and they locked him up."

"I just talked to him this morning. He just called me." Maddie says, trying to tell them they are wrong.

"From where?"

"Home, I assume."

"I heard from his sister's best friend's sister that he's still in the hospital."

Maddie grabs the store phone and calls his house. His sister answers this time.

"Is Connor there?"

"No."

"Where is he?"

She is silent.

"Is it true? Is he in the hospital?"

"Yes. It's so scary."

"Oh, no. Which one? I'm so sorry. I'm sure it'll be okay."

"North Memorial."

"Can I visit?"

"Yes, but he's not himself. I don't recognize him. Prepare yourself."

"Why? Did something happen to his face?"

"No, his personality. He's not the same person right now."

♦ ♦ ♦

Maddie arrives at the hospital, and after a little paperwork, they let her in to see Connor.

"Thanks for coming and talking with me. That was really nice of you," Connor says after twenty minutes of conversation about the weather.

"Of course, why wouldn't I come?" Maddie asks, thinking that was an odd thing to say after all they had shared.

"Because I don't even know you. Who are you?" Connor says, not joking.

Maddie stares at him for a while and watches his once bright green eyes search for a memory of her. But there are none.

"You don't know who I am? Do you recognize me at all?"

"No, should I?"

"Well, you called me this morning."

"Yeah, you're the only number I can remember. Who are you?"

Maddie smiles sweetly at him and says, "I've been your girlfriend for the last two years. We broke up recently, but we loved each other very much before then."

She watches his eyes again. He's searching for a memory to prove what she said is true. Again, no memory comes. He truly doesn't have any recollection of her. It's like she never existed.

Maddie hugs him and says she'll visit again. She turns to try to leave before she bursts out in tears. She walks over to the door; Connor follows like a zombie. She tries to open the door, but it is locked. She keeps trying to turn the handle and pull the door open, but it won't budge. She is desperate to leave; she can't hold the tears back any longer. They are streaming down her face. Connor stares at her with no compassion because the drugs won't allow him to feel anything.

She reads the sign on the door. It says to push the intercom to get let out. She asks for them to unlock the door so she can go. Her words are choppy as she fights back the tears. As she waits for the nurse to come, Connor speaks.

"Don't go back to him."

In that moment, a nurse opens the door to let her out. The nurse can see the hurt and says, "Don't worry, honey, when the meds balance out, he'll be better."

Maddie smiles politely and pushes past her. Maddie turns back to Connor. As the door closes, Connor says, "He's no good for you."

Maddie turns and runs, holding back her emotion. Once out of the building, she begins sobbing. She makes her way to the parking lot and gets lost looking for her car. She is devastated and confused. Connor was her first real love and he had no idea who she is. It was like she never existed—except, what was that last thing he said to her—don't go back to him? Was he talking about Max? She knows there is no hope they are ever getting back together, and she knows it deep in her bones. Maddie cries in her car until she can get control of herself to drive.

When she gets home, her mom, grandma, and brother are standing silently in the kitchen. They all look sad, and it is eerily quiet. Maddie's heart sinks. She has a feeling why they are silent.

"Maddie, your grandpa died today," her grandma says flatly.

Her mom hugs her but says nothing, still in shock. Maddie looks at her younger brother, who doesn't know how to react either. Her grandma picks up the phone and returns to calling people to tell them what happened. Maddie is devastated at the news but doesn't know how to react. It is the first person she has lost, and she is out of tears. Her mom and grandma are in shock, not expressing any emotion. Maddie is too young to understand this. She is confused why no one is crying.

Later that night, her dad calls from overseas and is also non-emotional. Maddie answers the phone when he calls. He says he is sorry about grandpa and asks to talk to her mom. She doesn't want to give the phone to her mom. She wants to tell her dad about Connor, how bad she hurts, how sad she is about Grandpa—but she does what she is told. "I love you Dad," she says and hands the phone to her mom.

Maddie goes to her room to cry. The tears don't stop. She's lost her boyfriend. Not just a break up but lost. He's a shell of the person she once knew and loved. He doesn't remember her or know her. Her grandpa is gone and she didn't get to say goodbye. Her best friend is out of the country on spring break—really most of her close friends are. She's lost and has no one to turn to, not even her dad.

That night Max starts calling.

CHAPTER 20

Maddie is snug in her bed, sleeping soundly after crying herself to sleep. Her phone rings, waking her up. It rings again. She reaches out from under the covers and answers it.

"Hello," she says sleepily.

"What are you doing?" Max asks.

"Sleeping. What time is it?"

"It's 2:00 a.m."

"What do you want?"

"Can you come out?"

"No, I'm sleeping. Are you in town?"

"Yes. I'm home for break. I've been out with the boys tonight and want to see you."

"Call me tomorrow—during the day, when you're not drunk," she says as she hangs up.

The next night the phone rings late again.

"Hello."

"What are you doing?"

"Sleeping, just like last night."

"I want to see you."

"Why?"

"I miss you."

"That must be why you called me during the day like I asked."

"I couldn't."

"Whatever."

"Come out."

"I can't. It's the middle of the night."

"And your boyfriend would be mad."

Maddie pauses, her heart breaks thinking about Connor.

"We broke up."

"When?"

"Couple of days ago."

"You okay?"

"Not really. I'm heartbroken."

"What happened?"

"We grew apart. Long distance got the best of us, I guess," Maddie says sadly, not telling him the real reason they broke up.

"I'm sorry. Come out. Come see me."

"Not tonight. Goodnight," Maddie says, hanging up the phone. As she falls back asleep, she lets the thought of the two of them cross her mind.

The next night, same time, the phone rings again. Maddie once again reaches out from under the covers to answer the phone.

"Hello."

"What are you doing?"

"Waiting for you to call."

"Really?"

"No. I'm sleeping. Were you out with the guys again?"

"Yeah, but I want to see you."

"No, you don't. If you did, you'd call me at a decent hour."

"Come out. For old time's sake."

"No. You know the one thing Connor asked me to do when we broke up? It was not to go back to you. You're bad for me."

"I'm headed back to college tomorrow. Come out. I want to see you before I go."

"Why? So, you can no-show like you did last year?"

"You told us not to come."

"Your roommate said you were on the way. We waited up for you, and you never showed up."

"The radio in the car broke."

"And you couldn't call to let us know?"

"I fell asleep while trying to fix it. Come see me. Please."

Long, silent pause.

"No. You're going back to college. It's the middle of the night. It's not a good idea."

"Please. For old times. Meet me at the tracks between our houses. Like we used to."

Long, silent pause.

"You know you want to," he pushes, sensing the hesitation.

"Fine. But just as friends. Not like old times. I'll be there in fifteen. I need to get dressed."

"No, you don't."

"Fifteen minutes if you're lucky." Maddie hangs up without saying goodbye.

Maddie mutters to herself, "What am I doing? This is stupid. This is a bad idea." Maddie goes anyway to escape her house of sadness, hoping Max could make her feel better.

The full moon lights the sky. Maddie runs down her neighborhood street as she has done a thousand times before. She cuts through the woods and appears on the other side where the old abandoned railroad tracks are. Max is waiting. Maddie pauses for a second and catches her breath. All the feelings she ever had for him come rushing back—excitement, hate, lust. She pushes them aside and thinks to herself, *Who knows, maybe it'll be different this time.* She shrugs her shoulders, shaking the thought off, and walks up to him.

"You came."

"Said I would."

"I didn't know if you'd show. Are you still mad at me?"

"That was a long time ago. I'm over it."

"At least you didn't have to explain to Connor why I showed up at your college."

"Yeah, I'm lucky. That would not have gone over well. Doesn't matter now, anyway," Maddie says sadly, thinking about Connor.

"But you're not together now?"

"No, I told you, long distance took its toll. We grew apart over the school year. I came home for spring break to try to make it work. Ironic that here I am again with you on spring break, when I should be with him."

"Lucky me," Max says with his mischievous grin.

Maddie looks at him inquisitively.

"I get to see you," he explains, reading her face.

"Yeah, in the middle of the night like we're kids sneaking out. I'm too old for this. You could have called me during the day."

"I couldn't."

"Sure, you couldn't call me but you had time to call the boys. Whatever. I'm here," Maddie replies, not wanting to fight. She doesn't have the energy. She's too sad.

"Remember what we used to do here and at the church when we'd meet?"

"Yes, but that's not happening."

"Not even for old times' sake?"

"Nope, not even."

Max moves towards Maddie.

Maddie's heart races. He moves closer. She doesn't move away. He leans in and kisses her. She doesn't resist. She feels the loneliness of her breakup and the sadness of her grandpa dying slip away. She hopes that now maybe the timing is right for her and Max. She lets down her guard, and Max gets his way.

Max buttons up his shirt. Maddie brushes the dirt off the back of her pants. He starts to act strange, walking from side to side of the tracks almost as if he is drunk.

Maddie looks at him. "Are you okay?"

"I'm drunk."

"Shut up. No, you're not," Maddie laughs, thinking he is being silly, forgetting her sadness for a moment.

"Yes, I am."

Max pretends to stumble and then starts walking towards his house. Maddie follows him, not understanding why he is acting that way.

"You're not drunk. I've been with you for the last hour, and trust me, you weren't acting drunk."

Max keeps walking away, not looking back at her.

Maddie yells, "Stop! What's going on?"

Max stops. Turns slowly around. Looks down at the ground. "I'm sorry."

"About what?"

"I have a girlfriend."

Maddie stands there for a moment letting the words land on her ears and sink into her heart. "I have a girlfriend," he had said. *Did she hear him right? A girlfriend? Why has he been calling all week? Why did he want to see me? Why did I come out after saying no over and over? Why did I let him kiss me? Why did I just sleep with him—on the old railroad tracks? Why didn't I listen to Connor? Oh, Connor.* Her thoughts flood her mind, building until tears explode from her eyes.

As the hurt bursts out, Maddie screams, "What? Fuck you! Seriously, fuck you! Don't ever fucking talk to me again. Ever!"

"Maddie," Max says, reaching his arm out towards her.

Maddie turns and runs towards home. Tears stream down her face, her back to him. He's hurt her before but never like this. *How could he? He knew I was hurting from my breakup. He didn't care. He took all of the broken pieces and smashed them into tinier bits.* Maddie feels like a fool again. Connor, who truly loved her, warned her not to go back to him, and she didn't listen. As she darts into the woods, she realizes he's not even trying to stop her. *He's a selfish asshole. Why doesn't he ever chase after me?*

What Max didn't know, was how much pain Maddie already was going through. How this moment decimated the last of her normally happy soul. She was crushed, and that moment altered the course of her life.

Max watches her go and doesn't follow her. His head drops in shame as he turns and walks towards home. He did have a girlfriend and he should have told her. He never meant to sleep with her that night. He just wanted to see her, but once he did, he couldn't help himself.

Max wasn't lying when he said he couldn't call during the day. He had been with the boys all day. All week, in fact. They'd been helping him pack up his mom's belongings. His parents were getting divorced.

His dad was having an affair. It turned out it had been going on for years, and no one knew. That was why Max's dad started being so happy and lenient. Now he knew it wasn't because he had finally made his dad proud, but because he didn't care anymore. Once Max went off to college and his hockey career was cut short, Max's dad left his mom. His mom asked Max to come home over spring break and help her move. They were selling his family home.

Max enlisted his buddies to pack up their trucks and help him move his mom. They had spent every day packing and moving boxes and furniture. At night, he'd take them out for drinks to thank them and to escape his feelings. Like every time he drank too much, Maddie would creep back into his mind and he'd want to talk to her. He missed her. She always made him feel good, and he needed that right now. But once again, he hurt her while trying to make himself feel good. Max vowed never to hurt her again, if only he knew how.

Part 2
Circumstance Conspires To Part

CHAPTER 21

"How was spring break?" McKenna asks.

"It was awful. My grandpa died, I broke up with Connor, and then he lost his mind—literally—and doesn't remember me. I hooked up with Max to make myself feel better, and then, right after, Max told me he had a girlfriend. How was yours?" Maddie says, dropping bomb after bomb on McKenna.

McKenna's jaw drops. "Not nearly as eventful as yours. Oh no, how are you?"

"I'm broken. Absolutely broken." Maddie starts to tear up.

"I can't even imagine. Where do we start? I'll get the queso," McKenna says, going to the mini fridge in their dorm room.

"I've cried for the past week. I don't have anything left. I'm just going to throw myself into my studies to get school wrapped up, and then I'm going to run away."

"Yes, summer will be here soon, and things will get better."

"Not just summer. I'm dropping out of school and am running far, far away. I don't know what I am doing. I need a break from reality."

"You can't drop out."

"I know, I shouldn't but I'm going to. I'm not happy here.

I'm not happy anywhere. I don't know what I want anymore. I'm lost."

"You're going to want to graduate; you'll figure it out. You're just really sad right now. It'll get better."

"Yeah, but you know what you want. You've got a major, a great boyfriend that you'll probably marry, a future. What do I have? Nothing. I need to figure out what I want. I don't even know what I want to do. I've been so wrapped up in Connor I never gave it much thought. Now that's over..." Maddie trails off as tears well in her eyes.

"Okay, maybe just get through the end of the year and figure it out from there. If UMD isn't for you, maybe you transfer to another school? I'll miss you, but it could be the fresh start you need. You've got plenty of time to figure it out."

"Yeah, maybe, but right now all I want to do is run away. Maybe I'll go travel the world with Samantha."

"Um, I think your parents would kill you if you did that. You know what your dad always says."

"Be the best Maddie you can be," they say in unison.

"I know, I'm just sad and lost and broken. I don't know what the best Maddie is anymore."

"Just take it a day at a time. You'll get back to you and knowing what you want. You've been through a lot!"

♦ ♦ ♦

Maddie moves home for the summer, and McKenna stays in Duluth to work at her first internship and live with Tommy. Maddie decides to visit Samantha in Chicago for the first weekend of summer.

Samantha moved to Chicago after graduation to become a flight attendant for United. Maddie is excited to see Samantha and hear about her latest adventures and juicy stories.

Maddie's dad is off to Germany for another mission and sees Maddie off before heading to his gate to catch his flight. Maddie boards the plane and finds her seat in the back of the plane. When the flight takes off, she feels a little nauseous. She thinks to herself *That's strange; I don't normally feel sick when flying.* At first, she thinks it is probably just being in the back of the plane. Then she realizes she's been feeling this way for the last couple of days in the morning. She reasons it must be the exhaustion from finals catching up with her. *What else could it be?*

"Please don't let me be pregnant," she says to herself quietly. "It's not possible, is it?" She thinks back to the last time she had sex and does the math. *Two months ago,* she thinks and then says out loud, "Shit." The passenger sitting next to her looks at her. Maddie looks back and says, "I forgot something." The other passenger nods their head knowingly and goes back to reading.

Then another thought pops into Maddie's head. *If I am pregnant, whose is it?* She relives the afternoon at the dam with Connor and then the night on the tracks with Max. *No, no, no, no. This cannot be. This is not good.*

Maddie spends the rest of the short plane ride convincing herself that it is just stress catching up with her and that she's dehydrated and tired. When she lands, Samantha is waiting for her.

"Sam!" Maddie yells when she gets off the plane. "I've missed you."

"Hey! You ready for a wild weekend?"

"Of course, I'd expect nothing less from you," Maddie is determined to have fun and not think about the last few months.

Samantha and Maddie hop on the train and head into the city. They drop Maddie's bags off at Samantha's place, freshen up, and head out to lunch at an outside patio overlooking Lake Michigan. Over lunch, they catch up. Samantha tells her about her first year flying, and Maddie tells her about college and breaking up with Connor and her grandpa dying. She leaves out the part about Max. Samantha lays out the plan for the weekend. Clubbing tonight, Cubbies' game tomorrow to get some sunshine, and then bar hopping afterward. They do a little shopping on the Magnificent Mile after lunch and then head back to Samantha's to rest up and get ready for dancing.

As they get ready, "Girls Just Want to Have Fun" blaring, they take a couple of shots of vodka Red Bulls to start off the night. Samantha is dressed in a skin-tight black leather mini skirt with a silky red tank top that screams look at me. She wears very high chunky heels and a choker around her neck to finish the look. Maddie is wearing a slim, short black dress also with heels, but not as tall as Samantha's. She sprinkles a little glitter across her eyelids and dusts her bare arms too. She falls right back into her sidekick role, and they are ready for a night out on the town.

Samantha introduces Maddie to the club scene in Chicago. They hit a couple of different clubs checking out the vibe until they find one they like. Samantha is on a mission to find a new man tonight. At the third club, they find a packed house, good music, and great-looking guys. They proceed to have a fun night, drinking, dancing, and feeling the freedom that only twenty-somethings do. A few hours into the night, Maddie feels a sharp pain in her stomach; it takes her breath away. She goes outside for some air. The pain passes. She sits on the curb for a few minutes, staring at the night sky. It reminds her of the night she met Max on the tracks. Crystal clear sky, full moon, stars shining bright. *Please don't let me be pregnant,* she thinks to herself again. She stands up, ready to go back into the club for another shot to erase the memories. When she turns towards the door, the sharp pain returns, making her double over. It feels like a sword has been stabbed deep into her belly and is being twisted around. She lets out a loud groan and drops to her knees. The pain doesn't subside this time, and she can't catch her breath it hurts so bad.

A guy they had been dancing with earlier walks outside for a cigarette and sees her and rushes over.

"Are you okay?"

"No," Maddie groans… "Get Samantha."

"Tell me what's wrong."

"My stomach, it hurts, so bad, it hurts," she manages to say as another sharper wave of pain comes over her, feeling the invisible sword twist around again.

"Could you be pregnant?"

"I can't be," Maddie cries out.

"But could you be?"

"I don't know, maybe."

"We need to get you to the hospital."

Maddie, on her hands and knees, starts to sob. "Get Samantha!"

The guy runs inside and gets Samantha. When he comes back out, he has Samantha and flags a cab for them. They all hop in the cab and race to the hospital. Maddie is crying partly from the pain but mostly from fear that she is pregnant.

When they arrive at the hospital, the guy gets out with them.

Samantha says, "I can take it from here."

The guy says, "My name is Griffith. I'm a med student here. I'll get someone to see her quickly."

He disappears behind the double doors leading back into the emergency area. Samantha watches him go and thinks, *Now, there is a man of action*. She takes note and makes a point to remember his name.

"Are you pregnant, Maddie?"

"I don't think so, but it's possible."

"Connor's, I assume, or is there a mystery man I should know about?"

"I don't know."

"Oh! I was teasing. Is there a mystery man?"

"Not a mystery man," Maddie says, wincing.

Samantha looks at her for a moment, thinking about who she could possibly mean. Then she gets it, "No!"

Maddie nods her head up and down as another wave of pain strikes.

"Max?!"

Maddie nods again, bent over towards the floor.

The med student appears again with a wheelchair and guides Maddie into it. "I'll take her back; she'll be in good hands. Then I'll come and find you, Samantha." He wheels her away. Samantha watches her go in disbelief.

The nurse gets a health history from Maddie and has her pee in a cup. Later, the doctor comes in and tells Maddie her pregnancy test came back positive, and he is concerned there may be something wrong with her pregnancy and wants to do an ultrasound. Maddie thinks about how much she's been drinking and tells the doctor. The doctor tells her she needs to stop drinking immediately for the health of her baby but assures her that the pain she is feeling isn't because of that. The nurse wheels in a sonographic machine. "I'm going to put this device inside you to see what is going on." Tears stream from Maddie's face. She doesn't try to stop them. She assumes the nurse and doctor will think it is from the pain, but it's not. It is from the overwhelming news that not only is she pregnant, but there is something wrong with the pregnancy too. *How did this happen to her?*

As the doctor performs the ultrasound, his face is emotionless. He consults with a nurse in the room, pointing at the screen. When he is done, he says to Maddie, "You're going to need surgery. You have a heterotopic pregnancy."

"What's that?"

"Essentially, you are pregnant with two different babies. One is inside your uterus, and the other outside. It is very rare and even more rare to happen naturally."

"Is it possible to be from two different people?" Maddie asks, wondering if she could have got pregnant by both Connor and Max, even though she and Connor were safe.

"No, it's twins. One fertilized egg implanted in your fallopian tube, which is called an ectopic pregnancy. It means the pregnancy isn't viable since it is outside of the uterus. It has ruptured your fallopian tube and is bleeding internally, which is why you are in so much pain. The other egg is a viable pregnancy that you may lose during surgery or likely miscarry during your pregnancy."

"Twins?"

"Yes, twins. Do twins run in your family?"

"The father's," Maddie says, thinking about Max.

"Actually, twins are determined by the mother's side."

"As far as I know, we don't have any twins in our family."

"Very unusual then for you to be in this situation. We're going to get you prepped for surgery immediately and do everything we can to save your viable pregnancy and your fallopian tube. Is there anyone you want to call before we get started? The father perhaps or your parents?"

Maddie is completely overwhelmed with the news. The doctor asks her again. "Maddie, is there anyone you want to call before we get started?"

Maddie thinks to herself, *No, I really don't want anyone to know about this*. She says to the doctor, "Can you bring my friend Samantha back here?"

"Yes, I'll go get her," the nurse says.

"Okay, I'm going to get ready for surgery. I'll see you shortly. You're going to do great."

Maddie nods her head in agreement. Tears still streaming from her face.

Samantha enters her room. "How are you? What is going on?"

"Oh, Sam! I can't even," Maddie sobs.

"Are you okay? Maddie, what did they say?"

"I'm pregnant, and they have to do surgery," Maddie cries. "You have to help me through this. No one can know. No one, not even my parents."

"Of course, what do you need? Why are they doing surgery?"

"He said it is an ectopic pregnancy and not viable. My fallopian tube has ruptured, and they need to remove the pregnancy and try to save my other tube."

"Holy shit, Maddie!"

"I know."

"Are you sure you don't want to call your mom?"

"Absolutely not! She and my dad can't know. They would be so disappointed in me. I mean it, no one can know. Swear on your life."

"I do. I swear. I got you. Do you want me to call Connor or…"

"No, especially not him," Maddie cuts Samantha off before she can say Max's name. "Never speak a word of it to anyone."

Samantha agrees and, in that moment, knows it must be Max's.

The nurses prep Maddie, and she sobs the whole way through the prep. She didn't tell Samantha about the other pregnancy, assuming she was going to lose it anyway.

Samantha holds her hand until the nurses take her away. Then she goes back to the waiting room where Griffith, the med student, is waiting for her. They wait together until Samantha can visit Maddie in recovery. Samantha gives the med student her number before she leaves to be with Maddie. He gives his to her and tells her to call him when she needs a ride home.

Surgery goes well. They keep Maddie overnight to monitor her. The next day, Griffith visits Maddie to check on her. While he's there, he asks about Samantha. Maddie thinks to herself, *Even in the hospital, recovering from surgery, I'm Sam's wingman.* It makes her smile and is a bright spot in her day. Samantha arrives a short while later, looking absolutely stunning. No one would ever guess she had been out clubbing and then in the ER until the wee hours of the morning by the way she looks. Griffith is still there and takes notice of how well she looks.

"Good morning," Samantha says cheerily, greeting Maddie, pretending not to see Griffith.

"Hi," Maddie groans.

"How are you doing today?" Samantha asks.

"I've been better," Maddie says, feeling wiped out.

"She's doing really well," Griffith chimes in.

"Oh, I didn't see you there," Samantha says, acting a tad surprised. "Nice of you to check on Maddie."

"Of course, I wanted to make sure she was doing okay," he says. "Last night was a close call."

"How do you mean?" Maddie asks.

"Do you mind if I share in front of Samantha?" Griffith asks.

"Of course, she knows all my secrets," Maddie says.

"If you'd gone home to try to sleep this off, you could have died from internal bleeding. Your fallopian tube ruptured, and if it wasn't treated immediately, you could have died from loss of blood or infection."

Maddie and Sam look at each other in shock. "Oh, my goodness. I had no idea it was that bad."

"The doctor will be in later to tell you more, but yeah, you got lucky."

"It doesn't feel like it," Maddie says.

"Oh, honey," Samantha says, uncharacteristically of her.

Maddie looks at her weird for a moment until she realizes Sam is putting on a show for Griffith.

"Thank you for your quick action."

"No problem, this happens to be the area I'm studying, so you really got lucky. I figured by looking at you that was what was happening,"

Maddie smiles a little. "I guess I am lucky we danced with you."

"Actually, I'm the lucky one, dancing with two pretty girls like you," he says and smiles directly at Samantha.

At that moment, the doctor comes in. "Good morning, Maddie. How are you doing today?"

"Tired."

"I can imagine, last night was pretty traumatic on your body. We almost lost you. I'm going to do a quick exam and see how you are healing," the doctor says.

"We'll let you have some privacy," Samantha says as she extends her hand for Griffith to follow her. She gives Maddie a wink as she leaves the room.

Maddie shakes her head and thinks, *Only Sam can pick up a doc in an ER while her friend is lying helpless in a bed.*

The doctor does his exam and then pulls up a chair next to Maddie.

"You are healing really well. I'm going to send you home today, but I need you to take it easy for the next week or two. Can you do that?"

"I'm supposed to fly home to Minnesota tomorrow."

"Is someone going to fly with you?"

"No."

"Can you have someone go with you?"

"No, but I could see if I could change my ticket, I guess. When you say take it easy, what do you mean?"

"After a couple of days, you can go back to normal activity, but nothing too strenuous. I want your body to have time to heal. It's also the best chance of keeping your baby."

"What baby?"

"Maddie, do you remember I told you last night you were pregnant with twins?"

"Yes, but you said I'd lose them during surgery."

"No, I said you could. I wanted you to be prepared if you did. We had to remove your fallopian tube and ovary, but we were able to save your viable pregnancy," he says, very clinical. "You will have a harder chance of getting pregnant in the future with only one fallopian tube and ovary."

"I'm still pregnant?"

"Yes, we were able to save the baby, but you have to be very careful so you don't have a miscarriage."

"I'm pregnant?"

"Yes, you are still pregnant with one baby. You're about eight weeks along. I can't tell if you're happy or sad about that news."

"Shocked. That's a lot to process. I didn't know I was pregnant yesterday. Then I find out it's twins, and I think I lost both, and now I'm learning I have one baby and it's going to be hard to get pregnant in the future. What do I do with that?"

"That's up to you, Maddie," the doctor says. "I can tell you what your options are if you're not sure you're ready to be a mother."

"Mother? I'm just a kid. I just finished my first year of college. This was a weekend to let all that stress go."

"Do you want me to get your friend?"

"No! I don't want anyone to know I'm pregnant until I figure out what I want to do."

"You have options. You can keep the baby, and if you decide to do that, you need to find a doctor as soon as you get home and have them monitor you closely. You can put the baby up for adoption, and there are a variety of programs to support you through your pregnancy if you choose that option. You can also terminate the pregnancy, but you'll need to make the decision quickly. There is also a strong possibility you still lose the baby. Your body has experienced a lot of trauma. Maddie, it'll be hard for you to get pregnant in the future but we have things like IVF that can help with that too. Take time to think this through. Every decision has implications on your future."

Maddie nods her head in thought as tears stream down her face.

"I'll give you some time to adjust to this news. I'll check back on you before you are released and bring you some information on what happened to you, your care instructions, and your options."

Maddie nods her head again, signaling that she understands. The doctor shows himself out of the room. Maddie sobs uncontrollably when he leaves. Samantha comes back in the room and sees her.

"Oh no, now what, Maddie?"

"The doctor…" Maddie gasps for breath, searching for the words. "The doctor said it's going to be hard for me to have kids in the future. He removed one of my fallopian tubes and an ovary. And I'm…" She sobs some more. While sobbing, she decides not to tell Samantha the other news until she makes a decision.

Samantha lets her guard down for a moment and crawls into the bed with Maddie and holds her. Maddie continues to cry.

"Can I stay with you this week while I recover?"

"Sure, anything you need."

"I'm sorry we're going to miss the game."

"It's okay. We can sit on my balcony and get some sun. I just wanted to go to the game to scope for guys anyway. You did good and landed me a big fish last night. Always a good sidekick."

Maddie laughs. "Only you, Sam! Only you. Do you already have a date scheduled?"

"Yep. Call me old-fashioned, but I'm going to marry this one. Don't tell him though."

"Oh, Sam! You say that about all the cute ones."

They both laugh and cry.

"Ouch, laughing hurts."

"You okay? Want anything?"

"The pain is beginning to get worse. Yeah, if they have something."

"Hit the call button. I'm sure they can give you something for the pain."

"Okay, good idea," Maddie calls for a nurse.

A nurse comes in a few minutes later.

"Everything okay?" the nurse asks.

"I'm really starting to hurt," Maddie says.

"We can give you something for that. You're going to hurt for a while as your body recovers. You've been through a lot. This may make you sleepy, but you need your rest anyway."

"Thanks," Maddie says as the nurse administers morphine into her IV.

"I'm going to head home, but I'll be back to get you later."

"Will you call McKenna and tell her what's happened? Maybe she can come visit and help take care of me this week."

"Did you really think I wasn't going to call McKenna when you went into surgery?"

"I told you not to tell anyone."

"Maddie, I've known you a long time, and I knew you'd want her here. Plus, what if something happened to you?"

"What did she say?" Maddie asks as she yawns.

"She's on her way. Should be here soon. I only told her about surgery. Not the baby."

"Okay, that's wonderful. I feel so tired. I think something is wrong. I think I am going to…"

Before she can finish her sentence, she is out.

Maddie spends the week recovering at Sam's. She contemplates what to do about her pregnancy and really struggles with her options. She knows she's not ready to be a mom. She knows her parents would be disappointed in her, and she can't bear to tell them. She also knows she always saw herself having Max's babies, just not like this. How would she even tell him? What would she want from him? She never wants to talk to him again after how badly he hurt her. Maddie heads home with McKenna at the end of the week, undecided.

When she gets home, she flips through the mail her mom left on the counter. There's a thick envelope from Michigan addressed to her. She opens it. It's an acceptance letter to the School of Journalism at the University of Michigan. Maddie thinks a moment about how and why she would be getting this letter. She calls McKenna.

"Know anything about the School of Journalism at Michigan?" Maddie asks when McKenna answers.

"I might. What do you know about it?"

"Apparently, they heard how amazing I am because they want me to go to school there."

"Ahhhh! You got accepted. I knew you would!"

"I didn't even know I applied?"

"You were so sad at the end of school that I applied for you. I wanted you to have options if you didn't want to come back to school with me. You are too smart to drop out, Maddie. You have a gift for storytelling. Go explore that for a bit. Get out of town, get a fresh start."

"Ha! I tried to do that last weekend, and as you know, that turned out to be a disaster."

"Oh, Maddie, I am so sorry. This really hasn't been your year. Go to Michigan. Get a fresh start. You need it."

CHAPTER 22

Instead of studying for her finals so she can graduate, she flips her books shut. On a whim, she dials 411 and asks the operator for Max's number. She didn't think she'd get it, but the operator came back with the number and asks Maddie if she wants to be connected. Without thinking, Maddie says yes. Panic comes over her as the phone rings. She hears the phone click, and Max answers.

"Hello."

"Hi."

Max recognizes the voice instantly and lets out an excited "hi." He never thought he'd hear her voice again after their last night together.

"How are you?" Maddie asks nervously.

"Fine, how are you?" Max responds instinctively.

"Fine," Maddie says, unsure what to say next.

"Umm, can I call you back later?"

"Yeah, sorry, did I catch you at a bad time?"

"Yeah, kind of. I'm uh, studying for finals."

"Oh yeah, me too. Just trying to blow off some steam. Sorry, call me when it's good for you," Maddie says, a little disappointed but trying not to show it.

"Yeah, I will. Thanks for calling."

"Max, who was that?" Ashley, his girlfriend, asks.

"An old friend from school calling to say hi."

"Did you tell them you just popped the question?" Ashley asks, handing him a glass of champagne.

"What?" Max asks, lost in thought.

"Did you tell them we just got engaged?"

"Um, no, I said I was studying."

"Why did you say that? You're done with finals, aren't you?"

"I don't know, I guess I just wanted this moment to be for us. Plus, we should probably tell our family before I start sharing with a friend I haven't talked to in years, right?" Max says, snapping back into the moment.

The phone clicks, and Maddie hears a dial tone. Hmm, he didn't ask for my number, she thinks. *Oh well, he's got my home number. He can leave a message there*. Maddie reopens her books and goes back to studying, now with her mind occupied by thoughts of Max. She studies late into the night, and the phone never rings. Max never calls, but she sees him in her dreams that night.

Late that night, Max lies next to Ashley wide awake, thinking about Maddie. He hadn't thought he'd ever talk to her again after what happened at the old railroad tracks. Now, the night he proposes, she calls out of the blue. *What did she want? Why tonight? Did she know? How could she know—I just popped the question? No one knows.*

♦ ♦ ♦

In Maddie's dream, Max and Maddie are back at the railroad tracks. It's a brisk spring night with a full moon lighting their faces.

"Hi, Max," Maddie says, walking up to him.

"Hi, Maddie," Max says, taking a step back.

"What's wrong, Max?"

"I have a girlfriend, Maddie."

"Why aren't I your girlfriend, Max?"

"I want you to be. I love you, Maddie."

"Then ask me to stay with you."

"I can't, Maddie."

"Why not, Max? You love me, don't you?"

"I do Maddie, but I don't deserve you. I'm not good enough. I've never been good enough."

"How come you're not good enough, Max?" Maddie asks sadly, feeling like it's her fault.

"Ask my dad. I've never been good enough, and he doesn't let me forget it."

"You're a dad, Max."

"What do you mean, Maddie?"

Maddie's alarm clock wakes her. She can't shake the sadness of the dream. She looks at the clock. It's 7:00 a.m. She checks her messages; none at her apartment, none at her home line. She knows Max won't be calling. She can feel it—her dream told her so. She feels sad and stupid for reaching out. It's been three years since she last talked to him. She pushes the feelings down deep, as she is so used to doing with him. *Why did I rip that wound open?* She thinks, *I don't have time for this, I* have to get to class, or I won't graduate.

♦ ♦ ♦

After graduation, Maddie moves home as she interviews for jobs. She's chatting on her cordless phone in her parent's basement.

"Come out to Fletcher's tonight. It's the last big night of the summer. Everyone is going to be there," Samantha says.

"Yep, that's exactly why I don't want to go."

"Why, because of Max?"

"Yeah. I do not want to see him, ever!"

"He won't be there. I haven't seen him all summer. I don't even think he came home from college. Tell you what. I promise I'll call you if he's there, and then you don't have to come out."

"Promise?"

"Promise. It's my last night in town before Griffith and I head off for his residency. You have to be there. I never get to see you since you ran away to Michigan."

"We could go somewhere else."

"We're meeting all of our friends there. You have to come! You're the reason we're together."

"Fine. I'll see you in a couple of hours," Maddie concedes. "But that's our secret!"

Maddie gets a ride with some other friends from high school to Fletcher's on the Lake. Fletcher's is a bar on the lake that has been around for ages. During the day, it's a family favorite for locals to eat. At night, it turns into a party scene, with people coming off the lake in swimsuits and arriving by car, all dolled up, looking for a good time. It's an eclectic mix that always makes for great people-watching—a favorite hotspot for young people and old rich guys looking for new girlfriends.

The place is packed, as it is most summer nights. Her friends head to the bar, and Maddie walks through the crowd looking for Samantha. She swears it's like a class reunion as she sorts through the crowd. She spots Tyler. She quickly turns to avoid him, but he spots her before she can disappear into the crowd. He yells her name, walks toward her, picks her up, spins her around, and sets her down.

"Maddie! There's someone here who was hoping to see you," Tyler says as he steps aside, revealing Max.

Her heart stops. She looks around and sees her friend Samantha. Maddie shakes her head in disbelief at her. Samantha smiles and shrugs, putting her hands out as if to say "oops." Maddie mouths "I hate you." Samantha laughs. Maddie should have known better. She turns and looks at Max again.

"Nope," Maddie says as she pushes past him, thinking of how he never called her back during finals. She mutters, "I need a drink."

Maddie walks straight to the bar and tells the bartender, "Give me the strongest drink you've got."

The bartender hands her a Long Island. Tyler follows her.

"He really wants to talk to you."

Maddie ignores him, thinking, *Yeah, well, he could have called me.*

"Give him a break," Tyler insists.

Before she can respond, Tyler grabs Max as he walks by and pushes them together.

"Hi," Max says.

"Hi," Maddie replies coldly.

"How are you?"

"Fine, how are you?"

"Fine."

"How's your dog?"

"He died last year."

"Oh, I'm so sorry. I loved Bear."

"He never barked at you. He barked at everyone else, but never you."

"He was the only one at your house who liked me. Well, technically, the only one that knew I existed. Speaking of, how are your parents?"

"They got divorced."

"Oh, I'm sorry to hear that too."

"I'm not. It gives me hope."

Maddie looks confused. "Hope?"

"My dad ran off with his high school sweetheart."

"That sounds like an episode straight from *Jenny Jones*. Why would that give you hope?"

"Because I hope to run off with my high school sweetheart someday."

Maddie, feeling like she just got punched in the gut, asks, "Who is your high school sweetheart?"

"You know."

"Nancy?" Maddie asks, remembering his prom date.

"No."

"Kelly?" Maddie guesses again, thinking of spring break.

"No."

"Who?"

"You."

"Me? We never even went out on a date. We just snuck around," Maddie says, shocked.

"It was you. It was always you," Max affirms.

Maddie stares at Max in silence, trying to register what he just said.

"Listen, I'm really glad you're here. I owe you an apology."

"Yeah? For what?"

"Yeah, in fact, I owe you a lot of apologies for what happened in high school."

"And freshman year of college," Maddie reminds him.

"Especially then. I'm really sorry about," he pauses, "that night." His eyes drop to the floor as he remembers it.

"Me too. You have no idea how bad that hurt. My heart was already broken..."

"I can explain," Max interrupts before she can tell him more.

A classmate looking for a drink stumbles between them. He tries to strike up a conversation while he waits for his drink order. Neither of them encourages the conversation. He buys them another round, and they wait for him to leave as they drink and stand there awkwardly. Max starts to apologize for all the things he can think of and Maddie points out a few that he forgot. They talk for two hours, never stopping to notice anyone around them.

"Can you ever forgive me?" Max asks.

Maddie pauses. "You know I always do. But you still owe me a call."

Max smiles.

"Max, you have a spell cast over me. I shouldn't forgive you, but I always do. Honestly, I wouldn't change a thing. It's shaped who I am." She can feel her anger melting away and old feelings creeping in.

"I'm glad I got to see you tonight. I didn't think I'd ever see you again when I heard you moved to Michigan." He pauses. She looks up, and they lock eyes. "You know I wasn't lying back in Mexico. I did love you. I do love you," Max says honestly.

"You've got a messed-up way of showing it," Maddie responds, not breaking his gaze. She can't believe what he is saying. "Why didn't you call me back during finals if you love me?"

"I know. I need to explain why..." Max trails off.

"I had something I really wanted, no needed, to tell you."

A tall, slim, redhead walks up to them. "Max, who are you talking to?" she asks. She looks at Maddie and says, "Who are you?"

Maddie knows by now those words are never followed by anything good.

"Who am I? I am Maddie," she answers the woman, bracing herself for what's next.

"I'm Max's fiancé, Ashley," the woman says.

Maddie looks at Max, clearly crushed once again. "Hmm?" she says in disbelief, biting her lower lip so she won't cry.

Ashley notices and says condescendingly, "And you are?"

Feeling betrayed again and stupid for letting her guard down, Maddie says, "I'm just Maddie. Good ole naïve Maddie."

"Max has never mentioned you. I don't know who you are or why he's spending so much time talking to you," Ashley says, marking her territory.

"You're his girlfriend from college, right?" Maddie asks, making a guess.

"Yeah. How do you know that? I have no idea who you are. He literally has never mentioned you, not once," Ashley says, implying that Maddie was nobody to Max. "Max, how much longer are you going to be? Come see your friends."

Maddie interrupts her, "Max told me about you the last time I saw him. I never would have guessed you were a redhead. He told me that's not his type. I guess things change." Maddie turns to Max and asks with a hurt look on her face, "I think we're done here?"

Not waiting for an answer, she slowly nods her head yes at him while showing how disappointed she is in him, her heart broken once again.

"Yeah, we're done, really done," Maddie says, with a mix of sadness and anger in her voice. Looking at Ashley, Maddie pauses, then says, "I'll never forget the night when Max told me about you. You should ask him about it sometime. But no worries, I won't take any more of his time. He's all yours."

Maddie walks away. She can hear Ashley demanding answers from Max, "Who is she? Who IS she, Max?"

Max once again stands there and watches her walk away, wishing he could grab her arm and make her stay. He knows he can't. He knows he hurt her again, and if he chases her, he'll hurt Ashley too. He thinks to himself, *How am I going to explain Maddie?*

"Max, seriously, who is she? How does she know about me?" Ashley demands again, her fiery Irish-side showing.

"She's Maddie," Max says, longing for her to turn around while he watches her walk away. When she doesn't, Max turns to Ashley and says, "We went to school together," hoping that'll be enough, while thinking to himself, *she's the one that got away*. He walks back to his group of friends, Ashley following, still upset with him.

It wasn't enough for Ashley. "You went to school with all these other people and you haven't been talking to them. Why did you spend the whole night talking to her?"

"Because we were supposed to eat onion rings together," Max says and turns to the group, trying to ignore her.

"You ordered onion rings?" Ashley asks, still confused.

Before interrupting Maddie and Max, Ashley asked the group of friends who Maddie was. Every single one of them answered, "That's just Maddie," as if it was no big deal they were talking. Ashley's intuition told her it was a big deal. Why would Max be talking to a girl she's never heard about the whole night? She asked a couple of the girls in the group if Max and Maddie ever dated. They all shook their heads no and said they couldn't remember Max dating anyone in high school.

Tyler, always the instigator, says, "Yeah, but remember spring break?"

One of the girls recalls, "Oh yeah, like how Max wouldn't dance with anyone until Maddie walked up and they started making out on the dance floor?"

Ashley pushes for more details, "And then *what*?"

The girl says, "And that was it. Maddie had a boyfriend, and she moped around the rest of the trip, feeling guilty."

That's when Ashley decided to break up their conversation. She knew there must be something more.

CHAPTER 23

A few weeks later, as Max is mindlessly dropping wedding invitations into the mail as his soon-to-be wife instructed, a name jumps off an envelope. It's Maddie's name.

"How did this get addressed? Where would her name and address come from?"

He can't figure it out and begins to wonder if it is a sign. He always thought he'd marry Maddie. He thinks, *Would she come if I invited her? What would I do if she showed up?"*

He dumps the rest of the cream envelopes into the mailbox and then stares at Maddie's invitation a while longer. He imagines her walking into the church. Then he imagines their church. He lets his mind follow his heart as he imagines reaching for her hand and walking her out of their church to the tree they always sat under. The pastor who once caught them is waiting to absolve them from their premarital sins and unite them in wedded bliss. The sun shines on Maddie's face, making her glow with happiness. He feels his heart swell inside of him as he pictures her saying "I do" while staring into her eyes.

"Hey buddy! You gonna mail that or what?" one of his coworkers says as he walks by towards the police station.

Max looks down at the envelope, breaking from his trance. "Ah, no, I think it might be the wrong address." He turns to walk with him into the station and slides the envelope into his coat pocket, forgetting about it.

That night, Ashley finds the envelope in his pocket. She pulls it out and throws it away. She purposely addressed the envelope in a different color ink and put it on top of the pile so it would pop out from the others. She wanted to know if he would mail it and if Maddie would come. She's happy that Max found it and didn't mail it. Maybe she was just overreacting to him catching up with an old schoolmate at Fletcher's.

Later that week, Tyler hears—but doesn't tell Max—that Maddie took a job out of state. For once, Tyler doesn't interfere; he can tell if he does, Max might not go through with the wedding. Max and Ashley get married as planned, and Maddie moves back to Michigan.

CHAPTER 24

Maddie has thought about Max off and on over the last five years, with an occasional dream reminding her of her deep feelings for him. She has tried over the years to push him out of her thoughts, especially after hearing he actually married his college girlfriend. As their ten-year class reunion gets closer, the dreams become more frequent. Maddie can't remember the last time she dreamt about Max this much. *It must have been since high school, or maybe the start of college,* she thinks. No, it was finals week of her last year of college, she remembers. The dreams are coming more frequently, and they switch between Max being really sweet to her and feeling peaceful and Max ignoring her and her feeling hurt. She's heard he's working the night shift now and wonders if, when he's patrolling the quiet streets, he's thinking about her. She wonders if he has ever busted kids making out at their church.

Max, in fact, is thinking about Maddie as the reunion draws near. He shares with Tyler how conflicted he is about seeing her. He wants to see her but knows how much she must hate him and how he hurts her every time they talk. He debates whether he should go to the reunion. Maddie is picking up on his indecision in her dreams.

Maddie flies home for the reunion and stays with McKenna and Tommy for the weekend. The night of the reunion, Maddie is really nervous about running into Max, not knowing if he is going to be there, but she hopes he will. It's been five years since she last saw him.

Many of her other friends who got married right out of college are getting divorced, and she wonders if Max will get divorced too. Samantha married Griffith after he completed his residency in New York and then divorced him a few short years into her marriage when she grew bored of him never being around. She found a wealthy Manhattan businessman in her spare time to keep her occupied. Samantha doesn't come home for the reunion because she's busy traveling through Europe for the summer with her new husband. McKenna and Tommy are still going strong—true high school sweethearts.

The reunion is at Bayside, a popular event center on Lake Minnetonka. It neighbors an even more popular restaurant, Maynard's, which is always busy in the summer due to its scenic views and great people spotting.

Tommy, McKenna and Maddie go to the bar at Maynard's and have a couple of drinks to warm up before the reunion.

"He keeps sneaking into my dreams at night," Maddie says to McKenna.

"Who, not Max?"

"Yes, can you believe after all of these years, I'm dreaming about him again? Just when I think he's finally faded from my memory, there he is, clear as day. And the dreams are so haunting. They feel real, and we either have deeply intense conversations, or he completely ignores me. I sometimes wonder if he's thinking about me, and that's why I'm dreaming again."

"He probably is. What else does he have to do in the middle of the night? Should we go and see if he's there?"

"Ahh, I guess. Let's go," Maddie says as she musters up the nerve to see him.

They pay their tab and walk over to the reunion at Bayside. At the reunion, there is a large crowd; they do a lap to see who's there. They recognize everyone but don't see Max. They settle into the reunion and have fun laughing and reliving old memories with their classmates.

Later in the evening, as they work their way through the crowd, Maddie bumps into Tyler. Tonight, Tyler picks Maddie up and spins her around, but when he sets her down, there is no Max.

Maddie looks at Tyler and then looks around and back at Tyler.

"He didn't come. He had to work," Tyler says, knowing who she was looking for.

"Oh, how's he doing?" Maddie asks, pretending not to be too interested in the answer.

"He's okay, but night shifts are really hard on him. He doesn't get to see his friends or family much."

"He couldn't get tonight off?"

"No, it was his shift. He has no seniority."

"That's too bad. How are you?" she says, changing the subject.

They chat for a while, and she gets to know Tyler's wife, Sheila. Tyler gets the bright idea that they should call Max and pulls out his cell phone.

"Hey, I've got someone here who wants to say hi," Tyler says into the phone. He hands the phone to Maddie.

"Hey, you should be here tonight. Lots of people want to see you," she says, meaning herself. As she finishes her sentence, the phone beeps, and she realizes Tyler had her talk to his answering machine.

"Tyler, you are such a jerk!" she says as she hits his arm. "How did you marry this guy?" she says to Sheila.

Sheila gestures that she doesn't know.

"You are such a dick!"

"He misses you, Maddie."

"Yeah, well, what do you want me to do about it? He could have come here tonight to see me."

"He had to work."

"We've known about the reunion for months. I'm sure he could have asked for it off if he really wanted to be here. I managed to make it back from Michigan. He had to, what, drive down the road? Can't say that's much effort he'd have to put in to see me if he really wanted to. But then again, when did he ever put the effort in to see me?"

"He thinks about you all the time," Tyler says, trying to justify Max's lack of action.

That makes Maddie remember her dreams. She looks at Tyler and says, "then tell him I still dream, and I've been dreaming a lot lately."

"Oh, juicy."

"Keep it in your pants, Tyler. Not like that. Just tell him I still dream. He'll know what that means."

Tommy comes up to Maddie. "McKenna is drunk. Do you want to go?"

"Yeah, I'm drunk too, and ready to leave," Maddie says, making a disappointed face at Tyler.

They stumble out of the reunion and grab a cab back to Tommy and McKenna's house.

CHAPTER 25

Maddie feels like death the next morning at breakfast.

"How much did we have to drink?" Maddie asks McKenna as she prepares eggs for them.

"Too much, as usual," McKenna says, pouring them both orange juice from the fridge. "Are you going to be okay to fly tonight?"

"Yeah, after a good breakfast and a cold shower I should perk up. How are you doing?"

"I'll be okay. But I don't need to do that again for a long time. I am so glad you came home, though. I've missed you."

"I've missed you too. It was really fun."

"Are you ever going to move home again? Hasn't it been long enough?"

"Maybe. I was really nervous about seeing Max last night, but he didn't even show. Maybe it's time for me to move on once and for all. It seems he has."

"Not according to Tyler."

"Screw Tyler. I'm sure he was just saying that to get a rise out of me. If Max wanted to see me, he would have been there. He didn't show, and actions speak louder than words."

"Are you ever going to tell me why you moved so abruptly?"

"You're the one who applied to Michigan for me."

"Yeah, but you could have stayed the summer and visited before you started school in the fall."

"I needed to get out of here. It was all too much with Connor and Max. I needed to escape. I was broken—literally broken, like someone cut me open and took a piece of me," Maddie says, metaphorically, but she really means it literally, thinking about her emergency surgery as she unconsciously moves her hand to her belly.

"I get it. I just miss you. Are you ready to come home?"

"I'm getting there. I'll know when it's time. I trust the universe will give me a sign."

Later that night, Maddie's flight to Detroit gets delayed. She waits out the delay in the Delta Sky Club, ordering a glass of vodka on the rocks to take the edge off her hangover. The man next to her inquires whether it's been a long weekend or if she's gearing up for a long week. They end up chatting, and she learns he is on the same flight, grew up a few towns over from her, and is on his way to Detroit for work. His name is Jordan; he's a patent attorney and travels frequently between Minneapolis and Detroit for work. They share another drink before it's time to head to their gate. Before they board, Jordan asks for her number and says he'd love to grab dinner while he's in town. Maddie agrees.

Chapter 26

"I got my sign," Maddie says to McKenna the next time she talks to her.

"What sign?" McKenna asks, forgetting about their conversation.

"The sign, if it is time to move home."

"What? What was the sign?"

"I met someone at the airport. We've been seeing quite a bit of each other."

"Which airport? Is he from here?"

"Yes, on my way home from the reunion. My flight got delayed, and I met him in the Sky Club. He flies to Detroit about twice a month, and we've been seeing each other the last few months."

"Tell me more."

"His name is Jordan. He's an attorney for Ford. Never been married. Workaholic like me. Doesn't want kids. He checks all my boxes."

"Is he cute?"

"Of course! C'mon, I still have good taste."

"So, are you moving home?"

"We've talked about it. We're getting pretty serious. Plus, I miss my family. And you."

"Well, that's good because you're about to be an aunt."

"What? Are you pregnant?"

"Yes! I haven't told anyone else. Well, except Tommy, and my mom, and my grandma."

"Oh my god. Congratulations!!!! I am so excited for you. You're having a baby!!! That settles it. If Jordan isn't a sign, then your being pregnant is. I'll start looking for a job."

"Just quit and come home. You need to be here with me as I grow this baby."

"I'm so happy for you."

CHAPTER 27

Maddie tells Jordan she is ready to move back to Minnesota and that McKenna is pregnant. The next time she sees Jordan, he proposes, and Maddie accepts. It is a very simple and unceremonious proposal. Maddie likes the lack of drama and how calm and easy it is with Jordan. He's an introvert, driven by routine, and it is safe for her. No surprises. No letdowns.

Maddie moves home a few months later and starts reconnecting with old friends, including Lizzy, who she knew from her neighborhood. Lizzy is a couple of years younger and a few grades behind Maddie and McKenna. She's an avid runner and invites Maddie to run with her on weekends. Maddie takes up her offer to help get in shape for her wedding. Lizzy is friends with McKenna too, as their husbands work together. They throw McKenna a baby shower. After the shower, McKenna, Lizzy, and Maddie are cleaning up.

"Thank you for a beautiful shower," McKenna says to both of them.

"It was our pleasure," Maddie says. Lizzy nods her head in agreement.

"You're next, Maddie," Lizzy says.

"Oh no, I'm not having kids. I'll be a good aunt."

"Why aren't you having kids?"

"Yeah, you and Jordan should have kids, and we can raise our kids together."

"You know why."

"Just because it'll be hard to have kids doesn't mean you can't have them."

"It's settled. Jordan doesn't want kids, and I don't really either."

"You don't *really* either? Really?"

"There was only one person I ever saw myself having kids with, and that time has passed."

"Who was that?" Lizzy asks.

"You probably wouldn't know him, a guy in our grade, Max."

"Sure, I know him, too well. I saw Max last week."

"Oh, how is he?"

"He is good. Still a cop. He's helped me a few times with my ex, who, by the way, is now in jail."

"Small world. What did your ex do?" Maddie asks, trying to change the subject now that she knows Lizzy talks to Max.

"Domestic assault. Thank God we're not together. My brothers would have killed him if he ever laid a hand on me. Anyway, I told him I was throwing McKenna a shower this weekend with you. He asked when you were coming home for it, and I let him know you moved home to get married. He seemed surprised. Doesn't he know?"

"I doubt it. I haven't talked to him in a decade."

"Oh, I thought you guys were close, weren't you?" Lizzy asks, looking between McKenna and Maddie. "You and McKenna talk about him like you were."

"Once upon a time, we were."

"What happened?"

"Nothing. Nothing ever happened. We were really close, and I always thought we had a connection, but he never wanted to date me. Then, when I wasn't or he wasn't available, he'd tell me how much he loved me and wanted to be with me, and then nothing. The last time I saw him was literally a decade ago. He was so sweet, told me he hoped to marry me someday and then that same night I met his fiancé. Unbelievable. Honestly, now that he knows I'm getting married, I wouldn't be surprised if he shows up at the wedding to tell me again how he wants to be with me."

"You don't think for real he would do that, do you?"

Maddie laughs. "No, not really, but at the same time, it wouldn't surprise me."

"Me either," McKenna agrees.

"You know he and his wife have been having a hard time getting pregnant?" Lizzy shares. "You've got that in common."

"I always wondered why they didn't have kids," McKenna says, knowing Maddie had wondered the same thing.

"Why is it hard for you to have kids?" Lizzy asks Maddie.

"My fallopian tube ruptured, and they couldn't save it and had to take an ovary too," Maddie shares.

"I'm sorry; that must have been hard. My sister had that happen too with her last pregnancy. Luckily, they were done having kids, but it still hurt to lose the baby."

McKenna looks at Maddie and sees a tear form at the corner of her eye. She looks at Lizzy and says, "Maddie wasn't pregnant; it was in college."

"Oh, sorry, I just assumed. I thought that was how fallopian tubes ruptured—with an ectopic pregnancy?"

"I had something else wrong with my ovary, too," Maddie chimes in, letting Lizzy off the hook. She avoids eye contact with McKenna. She can tell McKenna is looking at her.

"Either way, still hard," Lizzy says.

"We should probably get the trash out of here. That cake smells good, and I'm about to dig in and find some scraps," Maddie says jokingly as she grabs the trash and takes it outside. When she gets outside, she lets out a few tears she was holding back. She wipes her eyes and heads back in.

McKenna looks at her when she returns. "Is there something you're not telling me?"

"I don't think so," Maddie says. "Why?"

"That was a weird conversation. Were you pregnant when you had surgery?"

"What? No. It was my ovary. I told you that."

"My motherly intuition is telling me otherwise."

"No, it must be your hormones. Here comes Lizzy; let's drop it. I don't want to hear about Max trying to get his wife pregnant anymore," Maddie says, distracting McKenna.

♦ ♦ ♦

Maddie is in a beautiful old church. It is a bright day, and the sunlight is beaming through the stained-glass windows.

She looks around at the place she is going to get married with happiness in her heart.

She sees Max. Max has an aura of sadness around him today, not like his usual jovial self.

Maddie walks up to him by the back pew and asks, "What's wrong?"

"I got divorced."

"What? When?"

"A few weeks ago. I haven't told anyone."

"Are you doing okay?"

"Yeah, I'm back at my parents' house."

There is a stillness in the room. A peace settles around them. Max moves toward her and takes her hand. They walk outside together. Maddie looks back at the church she is getting married in, and it turns into the church by her house where she used to meet Max. They walk outside over to their hill.

"I never got over you."

"I never got over you."

They gaze at each other for a moment and are drawn toward each other. They try to resist but eventually give in and start kissing like they did back in school. At first, it is a slow, sweet kiss that turns more passionate. Max runs his hands over Maddie's body, trying to capture every inch of her. He kisses her neck, and she tilts her head back to take a deep breath of air.

She wakes up as she breathes in, gasping for air.

Sitting straight up, she blinks her eyes a couple of times to make sure she really is awake. Then she puts her head back on the pillow, shuts her eyes, and tries to enter her dream where she left it. But it is gone, and it's time for her to start her day.

The feeling of the dream haunts her, and she wonders if Max is thinking about getting divorced.

As the wedding draws closer, the dreams intensify. Max has not stopped thinking about her since Lizzy told him she was getting married.

CHAPTER 28

Maddie is dressed in a long-sleeved, fitted, cream-colored lace wedding dress. She looks very delicate. Her hair is smooth, swooped up into a low bun at the nape of her neck. Her makeup is flawlessly done, and her nails are painted a soft pink. Today is her wedding day.

Maddie meticulously planned out the day, and the bridesmaids are running ahead of schedule. McKenna and Maddie take advantage of the time to relax.

"Are you ready?" McKenna asks.

"Yes," Maddie says with a huge grin on her face.

"You know, I always thought you'd end up with Max."

"I know, deep down inside I think I did too. But honestly, I'm glad I didn't. Jordan is so good to me. He's the one I'm meant to live happily ever after with, not Max."

"What would you do if Max showed up like in the movies and yelled 'Stop'?"

Maddie laughs, "That would be just like him. He'd wait until I'm super happy and then decide he wants to give it a go."

"Do you still love him?"

Maddie pauses and looks at McKenna, "No, I never loved him."

"Not ever? Not after everything you've been through and the connection you had, have?"

"No, he never let me. Every time we'd get really close, he'd push me away. The only time he ever really opened up to me was when he was drunk and his guard was down. Every other time he'd pull me in, make me feel like we had something but kept me just at a distance, and if I managed to get too close, he'd push me away and break my heart."

"I don't believe you. I've seen how you look at him. I've seen how he's hurt you and you always forgive him. There's no way you don't love him."

"You mean loved him," Maddie corrects her. "But no, I can say I never did."

"Look me in the eyes and tell me you don't love him," McKenna dares Maddie.

"I never loved him," Maddie says confidently, looking at McKenna.

"But I said, tell me you don't love him," McKenna challenges.

Maddie stares at McKenna. She thinks about what McKenna is saying before answering. She says, "I'm marrying Jordan today. I love Jordan. He's good to me."

McKenna says, "Okay, I'll drop it, but only because it's your wedding day."

They both laugh.

♦ ♦ ♦

Max and Tyler are sitting at a bar down the road from where Maddie is getting married in the same sleepy lake town where they first held hands.

"What's going on, Chief? Why are you so down today?" Tyler asks.

"She's getting married today over at the inn," Max says, not specifying who.

"And?"

"She should be marrying me," Max mutters into his drink.

"But you're already married, and you two haven't talked in years."

"A decade actually, but it should be me," Max says as he finishes his drink. He signals the bartender for a round of shots.

The bartender brings over the shots and asks, "Celebrating anything special?"

"Yeah, a wedding," Max says as he picks up a shot glass.

"To Maddie," Tyler says as he clinks glasses with Max.

When they are done with their shots, Tyler asks, "Want to walk over there and see if she wants to grab a drink with us?"

Max looks at Tyler for a second and contemplates it. "She's probably too busy," Max says, jokingly.

"We could walk over and see if we can get a glimpse of her from the street."

"No, she's better off without me around today," Max says, wondering if she saw him if she'd still get married. He thinks she probably would, but also knows he may not have if she had shown up at his wedding. He thinks back to the day he asked her if she'd eat onion rings, and she said yes. Maybe he should have mailed that wedding invitation. Maybe they'd be together today.

"I should probably go to church," Max says as the last shot settles on his brain.

"Church? It's Saturday afternoon."

"Oh yeah," Max laughs it off as he thinks about the church he and Maddie used to frequent. He'll go later for old time's sake, he decides.

They order another round of drinks.

♦ ♦ ♦

A short while later, Maddie's nerves are beginning to get the best of her. The conversation about Max jostled something loose, and she can't stop thinking about him.

"I'm doing the right thing, aren't I, McKenna?"

"What?" McKenna asks, not understanding what Maddie is asking.

"Marrying Jordan?"

"Of course, you love him."

"The same way you think I loved Max?"

"No, what you and Max have is like a cosmic connection. I've never seen it before, and I doubt I'll ever see it again. It's like he's got a spell over you."

"What if he does?"

"What are you talking about?"

"I don't think I can do it."

"Do what?"

"Get married."

"You're getting married in a couple of hours. The guests are going to start showing up soon. You're just having cold feet," McKenna says, trying to reassure her. "It's my fault. I shouldn't have said anything about Max."

"I think you're right. I think he does have a spell over me. I can't stop the dreams. They are so intense. They feel so real. I literally miss him when I wake up. I can't shake him. I waited for so long for him. He's moved on. He's married. It's my turn to get married, but I can't stop thinking about him. I can feel him. It's like he's nearby. I keep waiting to see him. That's crazy, right? Tell me he won't show up here today."

"No, that would be absolutely crazy. He won't show up," McKenna reassures her. "Maddie, this is totally normal. You're about to get married. Today is full of emotion. It's just your nerves. Have you had anything to eat today?"

"No, I was too nervous to eat this morning."

"Let's sneak out of here for a bit and grab a quick bite and maybe a drink to calm your nerves. All we're going to do is wait around. You're all set, the other bridesmaids are set, nothing left to do thanks to your top-notch planning. Plus, it's tradition to kidnap the bride before her wedding. I'll go get Samantha and the rest of the girls."

"Okay, yeah, you're right. I'm just nervous, my blood sugar is low. Let's get some food and a little something for my nerves, maybe."

McKenna rounds up the other bridesmaids, and they walk down the street to Haskell's. The fresh air feels good on Maddie's face. She takes a few deep breaths and begins to calm down. The other girls are walking ahead with Samantha leading the way.

"Want to know something ironic, McKenna?"

"Yeah, what is it?"

"This is the same sidewalk I first held hands with Max."

"When was that?" McKenna asks, already knowing the answer.

"First day I met him. We walked up and down this sidewalk from here to the beach and back to the corner looking for Samantha," Maddie laughs for a second. "She actually hooked up with Tyler that night, and the rest is history."

"Well, today we're walking to the bar, which I'm sure you didn't do that night," McKenna points out.

"Ha, no, just the phone booth across the street."

They arrive, and Samantha leads the bridesmaids in ahead of Maddie and McKenna. Max and Tyler look up from the bar as girls fill the tiny bar. Tyler gets a huge grin on his face. Max freezes.

"It can't be," Max says as he sees Samantha directing the bridesmaids into the door.

"Oh, Chief, I think you may get your wish after all," Tyler says, trying to look past the blur of bridesmaid dresses to the girls coming in behind them.

Max abruptly stands up, turns, and sprints towards the back door.

"Chief!" Tyler shouts after him.

Max doesn't turn around. He can't see Maddie in a wedding dress. His heart is in his throat, and he feels like he's about to lose the shots they've been putting back.

Tyler slaps a hundred-dollar bill on the bar and goes after him.

Samantha looks towards the bar and sees Max going out the back as Tyler is putting money on the bar.

McKenna and Maddie hear Tyler shout "Chief," too. They stop dead in their tracks before they walk into the bar.

"Noooo," McKenna says low and slowly, in disbelief.

"I can't go in there," Maddie says as she stops at the entrance.

"I'll look; stay here," McKenna slips through the door and makes a quick lap. She doesn't see Max or Tyler. She asks Samantha if she saw them, and Samantha says it's all clear, not mentioning what she just witnessed. McKenna goes back to Maddie. "We both must be hearing things; he's not here."

Maddie's heart is racing. She takes a few deep breaths before she says, "Okay, I'm going to need a very strong shot right now."

They walk up to the bar and grab the seats Max and Tyler just left. They see the hundred-dollar bill sitting there. The bartender comes over and asks them what they'll have.

"Shots, something strong," Maddie instructs.

The bartender nods and grabs the bill from the bar and wipes it down.

McKenna says while gesturing towards the hundred, "Looks like someone was hitting it hard before we got here."

"I'm guessing you know them," the bartender says.

"Why do you say that?" McKenna asks.

The bartender looks at Maddie and says, "Is your name Maddie?"

Maddie's heart stops; she hesitantly says, "Yes, why?"

"There were two guys in here earlier toasting to your wedding. One of them seemed pretty bummed about it. He made a beeline for the back door when you guys came in."

"Do you know who it was?" McKenna asks.

"No, but by the looks of it, I'm guessing she broke his heart. They were talking about crashing your wedding, but he said he'd better go to church."

McKenna and Maddie stare at each other in disbelief.

"Bring us the bottle," McKenna says without breaking eye contact with Maddie and to Maddie she says, "You sensed he was near. What is it with you two?"

Maddie shakes her head in disbelief. "I'm cursed!"

"What are you going to do? Are you going to get married today?"

Maddie sits in silence until someone plays "I Hate Myself For Loving You" on the jukebox. The bartender brings over shots and puts a bottle of whiskey behind them. She turns towards the shot glasses, presses her lips together in deep thought, takes a big deep inhale, and, as she lets it out, she says, "Nope," and reaches for the first shot glass, tips it back, slams it down, and reaches for the second shot glass, and slams it down. She remembers the last time she drank whiskey when she vowed never to drink it again.

Maddie looks at McKenna, "Why did he run away?"

"For the same reason you couldn't walk in the door when you heard Tyler yell his name," McKenna says.

"Why is that?" Maddie asks, looking for McKenna to tell her the truth.

"Because you love him, and he loves you, and that love is so powerful it makes it impossible for you two to be in the same room together. I swear the longer you two are apart, the larger that love grows, and the larger the power is to keep you apart. It's like your magnets facing the wrong direction—you're inseparable when you're facing the right way, and it is impossible to be together when you're facing the wrong way. I think you may be destined to love him the rest of your life."

"Sometimes the heart has to endure love silently, singularly," Maddie mutters.

"No, it was 'sometimes the heart has to endure love alone,'" Samantha says as she walks up and grabs a shot from the bar.

"What?" McKenna asks.

"The day I met Max, Samantha told us about her aunt who never got over her first love—it's what she used to say. I thought it was so beautiful."

"It was pathetic," Samantha says. "It was, and it still is."

"I think you're right, and I was wrong," Maddie says, agreeing with her.

"Why is that?" Samantha asks.

"Cuz, here I am, about to call off my wedding for a boy who wasn't brave enough to stay. It's not beautiful. It's pathetic."

"It's not pathetic. It is the most beautiful gesture of love I've ever seen and also the most heartbreaking," McKenna says.

"No, it's just pathetic," Samantha says. "Are you really going to call off your wedding? He just ran out the back door!"

"How am I going to do this? I'm going to break Jordan's heart. What am I going to tell my parents?" Maddie asks them both, looking for a good answer.

"They'll understand, Maddie. They love you," McKenna says, encouraging her.

"Seriously, Maddie, you've been waiting around for Max your whole life. He's not good enough for you. It's time to move on. Snap out of it!" Samantha demands.

"You're right. What am I thinking? I'm crazy. No, I'm going to pull myself together, and I'm going to get married. Screw Max. He ran out of here. If that's not a sign, then I don't know what is. He doesn't want me. He's had plenty of opportunities. If he had stayed and talked to me even, that would have been a sign that we were meant to be together. But no, he ran. Jordan doesn't run; he asked me to marry him, and that's what I'm going to do. Let's get married!" she says as she takes one more shot, slams it on the bar, and hops off the stool.

"Okay, let's do this!" Samantha says.

"It could have been a sign…" McKenna says.

The rest of the bridesmaids surround them, they do one more shot, and head back to the wedding venue. The booze starts to hit Maddie, mixed with the emotion she feels about Max and Jordan she can feel the butterflies churning in her stomach. As they reach the steps of the building, Maddie pauses. The other bridesmaids go inside.

"McKenna, I don't feel good," Maddie says, holding the railing on the steps.

"You'll be okay; take a few deep breaths," McKenna assures her.

"I think something bad is about to happen."

"You're just a little jittery from the booze," McKenna says. "Let's get you some water and bread."

"No, I can feel it; something bad is about to happen," Maddie turns and throws up on the side of the stairs.

When she stands up, McKenna asks, "Feel better now?"

"I don't feel nauseous anymore, but something is wrong. I just know it. I feel it in my body."

As she finishes her sentence, Jordan comes running out of the door looking for her.

"You can't see the bride before the wedding," McKenna shouts at him, jumping in front of Maddie, trying to hide her. Maddie wipes her face off from being sick. "It's bad luck."

"Too late," Jordan says, moving towards Maddie. "It's your dad, Maddie, something is wrong. He collapsed a minute ago. The ambulance is on its way."

"What are you talking about? Did he fall?" Maddie asks as she starts up the steps to go inside.

"No, he didn't fall. He was telling a story to us, and then he started to sweat and got breathless. Next thing he is grabbing his chest, and he collapsed to the floor."

"Take me to him."

Maddie, Jordan, and McKenna race to the room he is in. Her mom is by his side. He is lying on the floor with a jacket under his head. Her brother is by his side, keeping him calm and monitoring his breathing. He is still conscious but barely.

"Daddy!" Maddie yells as she enters the room. She runs to him and drops to the floor. "Daddy, what's wrong?"

Her dad bends his arm up and pats her the best he can and whispers "sweetheart."

She leans in and hugs him, tears welling up in her eyes. "You'll be okay. You have to be."

He smiles at her, and she smiles back. He nods his head in agreement and gives her a thumbs-up.

The paramedics arrive, and Jordan pulls Maddie back from her dad. They check his pulse, blood pressure, and oxygen levels. They tell him that he is going to be okay but he needs to go to the hospital to figure out what is going on with him. His blood pressure is very low, and his body isn't getting enough oxygen. He agrees to go, and they slip an oxygen mask over him and lift him onto the gurney they brought with them. They wheel him out to the ambulance with his family in tow. Maddie and her brother give him a big hug before they load him into the ambulance. Her brother helps their mom into the ambulance to ride with their dad and says he'll follow behind. The ambulance leaves.

Her brother turns to her, "What are you going to do? You've got a wedding coming up here."

Maddie turns to Jordan and looks at him without saying a word.

"I'll take care of it. Go be with your family," Jordan says. "I'll be there as soon as I can."

Maddie gives him a huge hug, "I am so sorry… I love you," Maddie pulls back and looks at Jordan, then McKenna.

"Go, I'll help him. Take care of your dad," McKenna instructs.

Maddie turns to her brother and says, "Let's go," and they head for his car.

"Maddie, wait," McKenna shouts and runs up to her. "Your purse."

McKenna hands Maddie her purse and hugs her. "It's going to be okay. Your dad is going to be okay."

"I told you something bad was going to happen. I guess the universe really doesn't want me to get married today."

"If this isn't a sign, I don't know what is. Now, go!"

♦ ♦ ♦

Max and Tyler are walking around after leaving Haskell's and see the ambulance arriving at the inn where Maddie is getting married. Tyler and Max stand down the road and watch as they load an older man into the ambulance. They see Maddie and her brother leave shortly after. Max knows then it is her dad that they took to the hospital.

Tyler looks at Max as the ambulance drives away. "Looks like you still have a shot, Chief."

"You're such a dick, Tyler. They just took her dad away and that's what you're thinking?"

"Aren't you?"

Max shakes his head no, but his heart says yes.

Later that night, after hours of tests, the doctors finally confirm that Maddie's dad has an infection that has spread throughout his body and is affecting his organs. He likely picked it up overseas. They say it is treatable, but they are going to have to use aggressive treatments to get it under control.

Jordan and Maddie decide they are going to hold off on rescheduling the wedding until her dad has recovered and can walk her down the aisle like she had planned. Maddie thinks that will be good motivation for her dad to fight hard. Maddie's dad and mom agree, that's a good goal to work towards.

CHAPTER 29

"Hi Mom!" Maddie answers the phone. "I'm just walking the dog. What's up?"

"Hi Honey. I'm at the hospital with your dad. He just went into cardiac arrest, and they are working on him now. Can you talk to me until they get him back?" Maddie's mom says matter-of-factly.

"What? What happened?" Maddie asks, alarmed.

"Your dad had a bad reaction to the medication, so we brought him to the ER. The nurse gave him a shot of morphine to take the pain away while we waited for the doctor, and his heart stopped immediately. They were ready, though, and had a crash cart right there. It should only be a few minutes to get him back," Maddie's mom details, as if this is a routine procedure.

"Are you in the room with him?"

"No, they kicked me out. They are working on him now. He was fine a minute ago. He was just telling stories to the nurses. It should just take a minute. They had a crash cart," Maddie's mom says, trying to reassure her it's not a big deal.

Maddie realizes her mom is in shock and talks to her for a while to keep her calm and distracted. After a while, Maddie asks, "Mom, how long have they been working on him?"

"I think it has been about twenty or thirty minutes now."

Just then, an ER doctor enters the room where Maddie's mom is waiting and says, "You need to decide if you want us to keep working on him. It's been thirty minutes."

"Do you want them to keep working on your dad?"

"Will he have brain damage?" Maddie asks.

"Will he have brain damage?" Maddie's mom repeats to the ER doctor.

"We can't say for sure, but that long without oxygen to the brain, he most likely will. It will most likely affect his speech if we get him back."

"What do you want to do, honey?" Maddie's mom asks, as though she were asking what she wants for dinner.

"Mom, Dad and I were just talking last week, and he said he'd rather be dead than not be able to communicate." Maddie pauses and then says without hesitation, "We have to let him go."

"Let him go," Maddie's mom repeats to the ER doctor.

As Maddie listens to her mom tell the doctor their decision, someone in the background shouts, "We've got a pulse."

"Let me call you back," Maddie's mom says.

Maddie's brain is trying to process what has happened. She is still standing outside in the middle of her walk. Her dog is looking at her, wanting to go home. Maddie keeps thinking she just made the hardest decision to let her dad go, and, in that moment, he comes back to them. *What just happened?* she thinks to herself. *Is he alive?* Maddie waits for her mom to call back and walks the dog home.

Maddie's phone rings. It's her mom again. "Your dad hasn't woken up. His heart won't beat on its own. They want to give him a pacemaker. What should we do?"

"What did they say about brain damage?"

"He will probably have it and won't be the same person he was, but we won't know for sure. It'll be a long road for him to recover, and his organs are still failing with his infection."

"Mom, I don't want to let him go, and that was the hardest decision I ever made. Now we have to make it again?"

"Yes, honey," her mom says like it's a chore she has to do and better do it soon.

"He may or may not survive surgery. He'll have a pacemaker and recovery, and he'll likely have brain damage. Dad would be in a living hell. I don't think he would forgive us. He's a warrior, not a patient. I don't want to, but we have to let him go. It's what he would want," Maddie says, holding back tears from her mom.

"I know. I don't want to let him go either. I'll call your brother and let him know," Maddie's mom says and hangs up the phone.

The phone clicks off. Maddie stands in silence, trying to process what just happened. The wind picks up around her, swirling her hair around her face. She pulls it back behind her ears and soaks in the moment. The sun is shining. The sky is blue. The neighbors are going about their business all around. It started off as a beautiful day full of promise. Now it's the day her dad died. The day she had to make the decision to let him go. And it is his birthday. The last gift she'll ever give her dad is letting him go when all she wanted to do was fight and hold on for as long as she could. She knew it wasn't what he would want, and she honored that in the hardest way possible. "We have to let him go," the words ring in her ears as reality crashes in. Maddie always had to let her dad go; he was always needed somewhere else.

CHAPTER 30

That night, the pain is gone. Maddie is at peace. She is holding hands with Max at the church—their church. Max tells her everything will be okay, and she believes him. Being with him is comforting and simple. It's where she is supposed to be. She sits with him in silence and doesn't want to leave.

Her phone rings. As she looks at it, she wakes up.

Maddie sits up in bed, mascara smeared down her face, stains on her pillowcase. She looks at her phone by the bed until it stops ringing. Then she drops her head back down onto the pillow. She rolls over, staring up at the ceiling, feeling really confused. Jordan walks into the bedroom.

"Who was that?" Jordan asks.

"I don't know," Maddie says groggily.

"How are you doing?"

"I don't know. Did my dad die, or did I dream it?"

"Yes, he died yesterday. I'm sorry; I wish it were just a dream. I loved him too."

"Oh, okay… I thought I dreamt it. It really felt like a bad dream."

CHAPTER 31

"How are you holding up?" McKenna asks.

"I'm devastated. I just didn't see this coming. I loved my dad so much. No one is ever going to love me as much as he did," Maddie sobs to McKenna.

"I know. It'll get better with time."

"I'm just so broken right now. I never knew someone could hurt this much."

"Are you taking anything to help numb the pain?"

"No. But the dreams have started again, and they seem to help."

"Dreams? No, not about Max?"

Maddie nods her head yes while looking down at her feet.

"That's got to be traumatizing."

"Not quite. They are so peaceful. We just hold hands, or he is just present. It's the only place I escape this pain. I just don't understand why him? He's treated me like crap my whole life. Why in my darkest hour is my mind choosing him to help me cope?"

"You guys are clearly connected. I bet he heard the news and is thinking about you. You two should be together. I've never figured out why you're not."

"Frankly, he never picked me. He told me he loved me, but he never once did a thing to follow up on it. No dates, no phone calls, nothing. All he ever had to do was ask—or at least not run away. I was right there, waiting for him. Next thing you know, decades have passed, and I'm crying myself to sleep, and he's waiting on the other side to catch me."

"We've got another reunion coming up in a few months. Might be good for you to share about your dreams. Make peace with your past. As much as I hate to say it, you need to let him go and move on with your life. Your dad would want you to be happy now."

"I know! I've tried. You were there; I almost got married. I don't know why he's haunting my dreams now. Although I'm sure my brain just picked him because it was a time of innocence in my life, and losing my dad kind of represents not being a kid anymore. It's so strange, but the dreams feel so real. It's a nice little bubble to live in to avoid the pain."

♦ ♦ ♦

Leading up to the reunion, the dreams begin to change. The peaceful dreams seem to fade away, and they are replaced by more frequent dreams that alternate between being really passionate or being rejected. They haunt Maddie, and she can't shake the feelings all day. Some days it's a warm glow wrapped around her, and other days it's a feeling of rejection as deep as it was in high school. As she thinks about the dreams, she realizes they perfectly describe how she felt in school when she was running around with him. It was high highs when they were in sync and low lows when they were not.

The dreams are a direct reflection of what Max is thinking. Some nights, his mind slips into memories of the two of them when they would meet up at the church. Other nights, when she creeps into his mind, he does his best to push her out of his thoughts. He's married and he knows he shouldn't be thinking about her. It frustrates him. He wants to see her, but the last time he saw her, he regrets what happened. He knows how deeply he hurt her. He imagines she is still fragile after losing her dad so recently, too. He wants to be able to tell her how sorry he is. Sorry for the loss of her dad. Sorry for what happened that night. Sorry that he hurt her so bad. But he knows he still has deep feelings for her and is afraid they will pick right back up where they left off. He hates his dad for what he did to his mom, and at the same time, he is jealous that his dad gets to be with his high school sweetheart. His feelings on the situation are complex, and he struggles to sort them out.

Max can't decide if he wants to go to the reunion. It is also the only way he thinks he'll ever get a chance to talk to Maddie again. He's conflicted and struggles with the decision. He loves his wife, but he misses Maddie.

"Are you going to the reunion or what, Chief?" Tyler asks.

"Not sure. I'm scheduled to work right now," Max says.

"Dude, you worked the last reunion. Are you going to avoid her the rest of your life?"

"Yep, that's the plan."

"She really wanted to see you at the last one. Did I ever tell you she let it slip you guys hooked up the last time you saw her in college? Is that true?"

"Maybe," Max shrugs.

"Why didn't you tell me?"

"Well, that's because right afterward, she screamed in my face and told me never to talk to her again."

"Umm, what? Were you that bad in the sack?"

"No, worse."

"How can it get worse than that?"

"I told her I had a girlfriend right after we were done."

"What? When was this? You've only had one other girlfriend, and you married her."

"That's the one."

"What? When? How?"

"It was the spring break we moved my mom out of the house. I was so messed up learning about what my dad had been doing. You guys were so great helping me move her, and then we'd go out and drink at night. I couldn't sleep in that house. I just wanted to escape. She was always my escape when I lived there. I called her every night that week. She blew me off every night, but just hearing her voice on the phone was enough. The last night, somehow, I convinced her to meet me, and she did."

"And?"

"And I took one look at her, and it was like the very first day I met her. I was head over heels again. I was at peace for a moment, and the feeling consumed me. She looked up at me, and one thing led to another. It happened so fast; I just got lost in the moment, in her. I was transported back to the days when everything was so much easier. Then I realized what I had done. I hated my dad for cheating on my mom, and that is exactly what I just did to Ashley. I felt like such a hypocrite. I panicked. I started acting drunk to get away, and Maddie called me on it. I had to tell her the truth. I told her I had a girlfriend, and she ran away before I could tell her the rest of the situation. You should have seen the look on her face. No one has ever been more disappointed in me than her at that moment. Not even my dad, when he learned I couldn't play hockey for Michigan. I didn't deserve her, so I let her go. I've never talked to her again like she told me, until we ran into her at Fletcher's. I never told anyone about that night until now. I've had to live with what I did, but I deserved it. I never thought I'd see her again."

"Man, you've loved her all of your life. That was your moment. Why didn't you go after her? Why didn't you stop her from getting married when she walked into Haskell's?"

"Because I don't deserve her."

"You have to tell her. You have to talk to her."

"I can't. I'm married."

"Dude, her dad just died. Don't you want to say something to her? See how she's doing?"

"I do, but what do I say? 'Hey, I know you hate me, but I just want you to know I'm thinking about you'?"

"Sure, why not? Hey, that reminds me. She told me at the last reunion to tell you she still dreams. What does that mean?"

"Wait, what did she say?"

"Something about dreaming, and that you'd know what it means. We were both pretty drunk, so maybe I don't have that right. Sorry, just remembering that now."

"She still dreams?" Max says as he wonders if that means what he thinks it means.

"What's that mean?"

"She used to dream about me in school. She said it was like we'd have whole conversations in her dreams, and the creepy thing was she normally was spot on with what I was thinking about before I would even tell her."

"What is she, like a mind reader or something?"

"Or something. She said I could always find her in her dreams. I wonder if she knows what I'm thinking now?"

"Wouldn't she have known after that night?"

"Maybe, but I don't think it ever worked when she was mad at me. She must have blocked me out or something. I mean, I screwed up so many times in high school. If she really was a mind reader, we wouldn't be where we are today, right?"

Chapter 32

The day of the reunion is hot and humid. A couple of hours before the reunion, storms roll in, and it starts raining. Maddie and McKenna meet their friends at a bar to wait it out. To get to the reunion, they'll need to take a boat, since it is being held at a classmate's cabin on Big Island.

"Do you think it will stop raining?" one of the girls asks.

"Yes, it doesn't rain on Lake Minnetonka," Maddie answers.

"Sure, it does," another girl says.

"Trust me, it doesn't. There's like a little bubble around the lake. It's going to clear up and be perfect."

"Let's get some drinks while we wait the rain out," McKenna suggests.

The girls and their friends share stories over a round of drinks and get in the reunion mode. Their husbands, and Jordan, enjoy a beer and talk sports, not knowing any of the people in the stories the girls are sharing. Thankfully, they are friends and plan to hang out together as they fully expect their wives to forget about them once they get to the island.

"You were right, Maddie," one of the girls says. "Looks like it stopped just in time, and the heat burned off the rain."

"I told you. It never rains on the lake, at least not when something important is happening."

"Are you ready for tonight?"

"I think so. Are you?"

"Yeah, it's going to be fun. Let's go."

Maddie and McKenna get to the island before Max and his friends. They settle in and make the rounds. When Max and friends pull up, Maddie spots him instantly.

"He's here," Maddie says to McKenna.

"Are you going to talk to him?" McKenna asks.

"I think so. Why not? We're adults, right?"

"Do you want to go say hi now?"

Maddie takes a deep breath and says, "Screw it. Let's rip the band-aid off so it isn't awkward all night."

Maddie and McKenna walk up to the group of classmates and their spouses getting off the boat. Max spots them instantly and pretends like he doesn't see them.

He was leery about seeing her tonight, but he never imagined that after all this time she'd look better than she did the last time he saw her. She grew into a beautiful, confident woman. He notices that she is dressed in a light pink sundress that, in the light breeze, has just enough lift to make Max wonder what is underneath. That's exactly what he is doing as she walks up to him. If they were alone, he thinks, he'd back her up against the wall without even saying "hello" and press himself firmly against her as he kisses her, like he used to when they were teens.

His buddy Tyler jabs him with his elbow and says, "There she is. Are you going to talk to her tonight?"

The question snaps him from his thought as Maddie and McKenna start to walk towards him and emotions flood him.

"Ladies, let's get some drinks," Tyler leads his wife Sheila and Max's wife Ashley towards the bar, leaving Max on his own as Maddie and McKenna approach him.

"Hi," Maddie and McKenna say in unison.

"What do you know?" Max says, not ready to talk to Maddie yet.

"I'm still waiting for you to return that call…" Maddie says with half a laugh.

Still coming out of his quick daydream, he defensively snaps back, "I can't believe you're still waiting for that…"

Maddie, thinking that would have been a funny icebreaker after a decade, instantly puts up a wall too and snaps, "I'm not. I think I got the hint by now."

McKenna jumps in and says, "Hey, how are you it has been ages?"

Max mutters, "Man, I don't even have a beer yet."

"I'll grab you one," McKenna offers and heads to the bar, leaving the two standing there alone.

In an awkward silence, they stare past each other, trying not to make eye contact.

Maddie asks, not knowing what else to say, "How is your dad?"

"I don't talk to him anymore," Max says defensively.

"Oh, I'm sorry," Maddie says, surprised.

"I'm not. He's an asshole," Max jerks back.

"Okay…" Maddie begins to say.

A number of other classmates walk up and join the conversation. Max is grateful and focuses on their questions, completely shutting Maddie out. Minutes later, McKenna returns with Tyler, Sheila, and Ashley. Ashley hands him a beer. McKenna looks at the extra beer in her hand and gives it to Maddie.

Maddie was really looking forward to sharing how her dreams about him helped her survive her dad's sudden death. Instead, she experienced real-life feelings she hadn't felt for decades wash over her like a tidal wave. The feeling of rejection, like it was just yesterday, she stood there listening, smiling, and he wouldn't even glance at her. She drifts away from the conversation and walks away.

She tries to push aside the hurt as McKenna comes up to her and says, "Let him get a couple of beers in him and relax. We probably spooked him. It's been a long time. Hey, at least he didn't run away this time."

Maddie laughs, "Sure, you're probably right, or he's just trapped on an island and has nowhere to run."

"Let's go dance," McKenna suggests.

"Okay," Maddie welcomes the opportunity to do something to forget what just happened.

Maddie dances her heart out like she used to do to let the emotions go. Max watches from afar and knows he hurt her again. He can tell by the fire in her moves. When "Poison" comes on he listens to the lyrics and watches her and McKenna sing along with Alice Cooper.

Max thinks to himself, *Maddie is poison. Poison to my marriage. I have to stay away.* He decides not to talk to her for the rest of the night.

Later that evening, Maddie finds herself walking towards the bar, but to get there she has to pass a group of people Max is talking to. She thinks she'll try again and, as she walks up to the group, he abruptly splits, so she keeps walking to the bar as she says hello in passing to the group. Coming back from the bar, she tries again with the same result. At this point, it is crystal clear to her that Max wants absolutely nothing to do with her. Ashley notices too.

Tyler appears just like clockwork. "Maddie!" he yells as he picks her up and spins her around. "Max wants to talk to you."

"No, he doesn't!" Maddie says aggressively.

"Yes, he does we talked about it before we came here. He didn't want to come at all but he came to see you," Tyler says, a little stunned at her aggressiveness.

"No, trust me, he does not want to talk to me," Maddie says, very seriously.

"Yes, he does. He told me," Tyler insists.

"Come with me. Watch this," Maddie says as she drags him towards a group Max is talking to. Max sees them and quickly diverts to another group of people across the room.

Tyler looks at her and says, "He must not have seen us. He wants to talk to you."

"No, he doesn't. Watch." She leaves him standing there and walks up to the group. Once again, as she is approaching, Max slips away. Maddie turns and walks back to Tyler instead of joining the group.

"What the hell is he doing?"

"You tell me."

"I swear, he wants to talk to you. We talked about it. Stay here, I'll find out what's going on."

Maddie grabs Tyler by the arm and says, "Tyler, do you swear? Promise you're not messing with me. If you are, I will pour this beer over your head in front of everyone and not for one second feel bad about it."

Tyler stops in his tracks and stares at her, trying to figure out if she's drunk or serious. Maddie reads the look on his face and says, "I'm serious. I cannot take it if you are toying with me."

"I am serious. He said he's afraid that if he saw you tonight the two of you would run off and get married."

Maddie laughs, "Get married? We're stuck on an island. Who's going to marry us, the ship's captain?"

Tyler doesn't laugh and repeats, "He really is afraid the two of you are going to run off and get married. Stay here. Don't move an inch."

Maddie does what she is told. Standing alone, she wonders if that is why he ran away the day of her wedding. What would he have done if he saw her in her wedding dress? Rush her down the aisle before Jordan could beat him to it.

Tyler walks up to Max, no problem, and hauls him off to the bathroom. They are in there for enough time for Maddie to drink her beer. When she's done, she wonders why she is standing alone, waiting for a guy that clearly wants nothing to do with her. She's about to walk away when Max walks out in front of Tyler.

Max purposively does a sharp right turn, never even glancing ahead to see her. Tyler follows and stands in the doorway and looks at her and puts his hands up in the air, gesturing his confusion. He follows Max. Maddie stands there for a minute longer, nodding her head to no one, thinking, *I told you so.* She tips back her beer, realizes it is empty and heads to the bar. *Time to drown the feelings*, she thinks to herself.

Maddie walks up to the bar and says to the group standing there, "Let's do some shots."

Everyone, feeling good, lets out a collective "woo" as the bartender pours out a round of shots.

They clink the shot glasses in cheers and tip them back. Maddie slams her glass on the bar and orders a stiff drink. She pushes the pain deep down and slaps on a drunken smile. She mingles, she laughs, and she forgets about him. McKenna finds her again and pulls her back to the dance floor. They dance for what seems like an hour, and for that moment in time, she forgets about him.

"I have to go to the bathroom," Maddie shouts at McKenna over the music.

"Okay!" McKenna shouts back and keeps dancing.

Maddie takes the long way to the bathroom and catches sight of Max. She's still hoping he'll talk to her, but he doesn't.

As the night is coming to an end, the crowd thins out and makes their way across the lake to Maynard's for the afterparty. When they get there, Maddie tells McKenna to order her a drink and heads inside to use the bathroom and freshen up. On the way in, she passes Max. He is talking to one other person, and there is no one else around. She stares him down as she walks past him to the bathroom, and he doesn't even flinch as she passes him. He never breaks from his conversation, and she's like a ghost floating by, invisible. Like she never existed. It reminds her of when she visited Connor in the hospital. She can feel the bubble she's living in crack a little.

She touches herself up in the bathroom and walks out, expecting to see him there still. He's gone, another crack in the bubble. Maddie goes back out and sees Jordan waiting for her with McKenna and Tommy.

Two circles of classmates form next to each other. Max and Maddie stand back to back, ignoring each other, but not breaking distance until the bar closes. Security ushers the summer mob out, pushing Maddie and Max shoulder to shoulder in the crowd. They still don't speak, another crack in her bubble. The silence, the indifference, makes Maddie feel like she never mattered to Max.

Jordan grabs her hand and leads her through the crowd to the parking lot. Maddie looks back at Max, hoping to at least catch his eye for some sort of connection before the night is over. She's waited patiently to talk to him for ten years since their last conversation. He's looking in her direction, but he's not looking at her. He's eyeing Jordan up and down, refusing to acknowledge her existence.

All of the feelings she drowned in alcohol that night start floating up, pushing on the cracks in the bubble she built. She feels the bubble about to burst. Jordan, tired, drives Maddie home. As she attempts to keep her feelings at bay, Jordan suddenly pulls off the highway and turns into the first parking lot he sees. It happens to be the hotel she spent her senior homecoming at with Max. He parks in almost the exact spot Max and Maddie had their final high school encounter.

"What are you doing?" Maddie asks Jordan as he starts to get out of the car.

"I have to pee," Jordan says.

He runs inside to the hotel, and Maddie is thankful because as the door shuts behind him, she can't contain her feelings anymore. The bubble bursts, and her feelings spill out in an explosion of tears. She turns the music up to cover the wail she lets out. She's utterly broken and feels like the bubble she's been living in has been shattered. She accepts that she didn't matter to Max. She realizes she never did. He couldn't even look at her or mutter a word of acknowledgment. He literally went out of his way to avoid her. The nonsense Tyler put in her head about wanting to run off and get married—like he actually cared for her—why did she think for a second that could be true? She fell for it again. Her world crashes down, and she has nothing left to keep the feelings in check. The loss of her innocence. The loss of her bubble. The loss of her dad. She hates herself for taking solace in a memory that wasn't real, and she sobs until Jordan returns. Maddie wipes the tears with the back of her hands and slides on a pair of sunglasses. She rolls the windows down to let the wind dry her face, "Nothing Else Matters" plays on the radio. Maddie sings loudly, while she pushes the pain aside, like she did when she was young. Jordan knows Maddie is drunk and doesn't think twice about it.

◆ ◆ ◆

Max, Tyler, and the rest of their crew head to Tyler's house for the after, afterparty. They light a fire in the backyard and wind down, telling stories from the night. After an hour, people start to depart. Max's wife wants to go too, but Max is being stubborn. She goes inside with Sheila to wait for him. Tyler and Max finish drinking a beer and let the fire die down.

"What was that tonight?" Tyler asks when everyone is gone.

"What are you talking about?"

"You! You were so ready to talk to Maddie, and then you acted like she had the plague."

"No, I didn't."

"Yeah, you did. It was super obvious. She even pointed it out to me."

"I wasn't avoiding her. I talked to her when I first got there."

"I wouldn't call that avoiding, more like running from her. She couldn't get within five feet of you without you running away."

"Whatever."

"Seriously, what got into you tonight?"

"I didn't want to talk to her. I changed my mind, that's all."

"Bullshit! You wouldn't have gone if you didn't want to talk to her."

"Honestly?"

"Yeah!"

"I mean, did you see her tonight? Of course, I wanted to talk to her. That's not all I wanted to do. I couldn't trust myself to be around her."

"What do you mean?" Tyler says, laughing a bit, a little nervous about Max's intensity.

"I mean, it has been a decade since I last saw her. She grew into this incredibly beautiful woman. It caught me off guard. At the same time, when I looked at her, all I could see was the high school version of Maddie."

"Is that good or bad?"

"I don't know. My brain was registering how good she looks now, but it was like my soul, my heart, I don't know, my body, something more than my brain could see her, us, like a day hadn't passed." Max takes a sip of beer and thinks for a second. "It's hard to explain. It was like she was a magnet pulling me into her but not just her, into the past. I couldn't be by her. It was too much. I was going to get lost in her if I got too close."

"Why didn't you just leave then instead of running from her all night?"

"I couldn't do that either. I wanted to be by her, I just couldn't talk to her. I can't explain it."

"I told her you were afraid you were going to marry her."

"I would have done more than that if I'd had the chance."

"Nice!"

"Seriously, when she looked at me, it's like she was looking right into my soul, and it made me feel so alive. I didn't even know I could feel like that anymore. I don't think I've felt like that since," Max pauses, "college," Max pauses again, "no, the last time I was with her," thinking about the night on the tracks.

Behind them, they hear a twig crack as someone walks on it. They turn to look and see it's Ashley running away from them.

"Shit! How much do you think she heard?"

"I don't know, man. You better go after her."

"Crap, this is exactly what I didn't want to happen."

"Good luck!"

"Ashley!"

Ashley runs to the car and fumbles with her keys. Max catches up with her.

"Ashley," Max says as he touches her shoulder to turn her around.

"Fuck you, Max!" Ashley yells at him. "Fuck you!"

"What's wrong?" Max says, trying to calm her down.

"You know exactly what's wrong!"

"No, I don't. What's going on?" Max asks, trying to figure out how much he's going to have to explain.

"You were talking about *her*, weren't you?" Ashley accuses him.

"Her, who?"

"Maddie, that girl from Fletchers!"

"Why do you think that?"

"Don't play games with me, Max. I saw you tonight. There was something weird going on with you two."

"I didn't even talk to her. I said hello when we first got there and then I didn't talk to her the rest of the night."

"Yeah, that's what I mean. Every time she'd get near you, you'd walk away. You were going out of your way to avoid her—like you're hiding something," Ashley says, accusing him a third time.

"I'm not hiding anything. There is nothing to hide. I just didn't want to talk to her. That's all," Max defends himself.

"You know, I could have believed that if I hadn't just heard you telling Tyler how she made you feel when she looks at you. I thought for a second you were talking about me, saying something sweet about your wife, right up until the minute you corrected yourself and said you hadn't felt that way since the last time you were with her. You meant Maddie, didn't you?"

Max is silent as he thinks about how to answer that question. He takes a deep breath. He's about to tell her the truth and instead he says, "Listen, it's a reunion. Everyone I saw tonight stirred up old feelings and old memories, not just her. It doesn't mean anything. It's just a walk down memory lane. I love you. I married you. You are all that matters to me."

"Do you still have feelings for her?"

"Of course not."

"Then why do you get so weird whenever you are around her?"

"I've been around her, what, twice since I met you?"

"Yeah, the first time, it's like you two were in your own little world and you didn't know anyone else existed. You were in a funk for like two weeks after that. Tonight, you were acting like she had cooties and she was trying to give them to you. There is something weird between you two."

"There's nothing between us. You don't have to worry."

"I'm sure your mom thought that too," Ashley says carelessly.

Max tenses up and clenches his jaw. He can feel the anger brewing inside of him. She hit a nerve.

"What's that supposed to mean?" he says, clenching his fists, trying to keep his anger at bay.

"I mean, your dad ran off with his high school girlfriend. Promise you won't do that to me," Ashley says, being direct about what she fears.

"My dad is a selfish asshole. I'm not my dad. I would never, ever, do that to you. I can't believe you'd even think that," Max says, feeling guilty. "Besides, she was never my girlfriend. You're my one and only girlfriend."

"I'm sorry, I know, that was a low blow. It's just the stress of not being able to get pregnant and then hearing you talk about her tonight. It makes me feel like, like I'm not enough for you."

Max takes a deep breath and exhales. "Why do you say that?" Max says, feeling the anger leave his body.

"Because we can't have kids. I know how much you want kids and I can't give that to you. Maybe she can," Ashley says, testing him.

"Don't be silly, Ashley. I'm married to you. We will have kids someday. It'll happen for us. Do you want to go home and try tonight?" Max says, grabbing her hand.

"No, you're drunk and smell like a bonfire," Ashley says, pulling her hand back.

"Okay, well, do you want to go home?"

"Yes. I'm sorry, I'm tired. All these hormones are making me crazy."

"You're not crazy. Well, maybe a little. You did marry me." Max hugs his wife, thinking he just dodged a bullet and feeling bad about how he made her feel.

"So, who is she?" Ashley asks, after getting into the car, not letting her suspicions drop.

"Who, Maddie?" Max asks, realizing he did not dodge a bullet and he's trapped now until they get home.

"Yeah. What's her backstory? How do you know each other?"

"We went to school together," Max says, not answering the question.

"Obviously, she was at your reunion," Ashley says, a little annoyed. She knows Max is avoiding the question. "Who is she to you?"

"She's just a girl I once knew."

"Did you date her in high school?"

"No, I wasn't allowed to date girls. I've told you that. It was hockey all the time."

"Did you like her?"

"I told you. My dad wouldn't let me date any girls."

"That's not what I asked. I asked if you liked her? He can't stop you from having a crush on a girl," Ashley says, not letting him escape the question.

Max knows he can't reason his way out of this one. He concedes, "Yeah, I did."

"When did it start?" Ashley asks, digging deeper.

"The day I met her," Max says, being honest.

"When was that?"

"End of eighth grade, I think."

"How did you meet?"

"After school at a friend's house."

"Did she like you back?"

"I don't know."

"Why not?"

"I didn't talk to her after that."

"Are you telling me you met her once in eighth grade and never talked to her after that, and she still has that kind of a hold over you?"

Max chuckles. "She doesn't have a hold over me," he says, seeing the trap even though he's letting his guard down. "I talked to her again, just not right away."

"Oh, how long after?" Ashley asks, wanting to get to the truth.

"I don't know, a few weeks, months maybe. I don't remember," Max shares, not giving much detail, trying to downplay it.

"Okay, so you had a crush on her when you first met her, and then you didn't talk much?" Ashley tries to clarify, not believing him.

"Yeah, then we ended up riding the same bus in ninth grade," Max shares a little more.

"Did you still have a crush on her then?"

Max nods his head up and down but doesn't say anything more. Ashley can tell he's shutting down again.

"So, just a little school crush that you grew out of," she says, half asking, half stating a fact she hopes is true.

"Sure."

"Did you ever kiss her?"

"Yeah."

"Did you ever sleep with her?"

"Yeah."

"But you didn't date her?"

"Nope, like I said, my dad forbid girls."

"So, how did you sleep with her? On the bus?"

Max lets out a laugh. "No, we didn't sleep together in ninth grade."

"Oh, my mistake. When then?" Ashley says, getting annoyed she has to ask so many questions.

Max has to think about it for a second. "I guess it would have been our junior year."

"When did you stop sleeping together?" Ashley asks, a little afraid to know.

"When Connor showed up."

"Who's Connor?" Ashley asks.

"Maddie's big love."

"When did she meet him?" Ashley asks, trying to put the pieces together.

"I think somewhere towards the end of our senior year," Max says. "I'm not quite sure, we weren't talking then."

"So, you must have stopped sleeping together before him then?"

"I guess."

"What happened?"

"I went to prom with someone else," Max says, still regretting it.

"What? Let me get this right. You weren't dating, but you were sleeping together, and then you took someone else to prom? What's the story with the prom girl?"

"I didn't want to go to prom. It wasn't my fault, it was Tyler's. He tricked me into taking his girlfriend's friend. He didn't know about Maddie. No one did. I just figured my dad would have said no way, but that was about the time he started cheating on my mom, so he stopped caring about what I did." Max says, really defensively. "What was I supposed to do?"

"Whoa, Max, how come you've never told me about this before?"

"What's to tell?"

"Were you and Maddie sneaking around all of high school?"

"Yeah, so?"

"Hey, I'm not accusing you of anything. Settle down. I'm just trying to understand. I think it's terrible how your dad treated you, your whole family," Ashley says, trying to defuse Max.

"So, you went to prom with another girl, and that's where it ended?"

"Basically. I really hurt her, and we stopped talking, and then she started dating Connor our senior year."

"But prom is at the end of the year."

"Junior prom," Max corrects her.

"Isn't that when you started sleeping together?" Ashley says, putting the timeline together in her head.

"Yeah, like a month or two before prom."

"Did you guys lose your virginity together?"

"Yeah, why?"

"Max, tell me you're not that big of a jerk."

"What?" Max asks, defensively.

"You lost your virginity to each other, and a month later, you went to prom with another girl? Do you know how that must have made her feel? No wonder she didn't want to talk to you again. I get that, but I don't get why you two still have weirdness. I would never talk to you again if you had done that to me. Did you ever apologize?"

"I tried."

"What do you mean you tried. You either did or didn't."

"It's complicated."

"It's really not."

"She was really angry. Then my dad shipped me off to hockey camp for the summer. That was the summer I got hurt, and Michigan dropped me."

"What's that have to do with apologizing?"

"I was busy. I was trying to salvage everything I worked for that summer."

"Wow, are you that selfish?"

"I'm not selfish."

"Yeah, you are! You didn't have time to pick up the phone and say, 'I'm sorry'?"

"I broke her heart, and then I lost my chance at college hockey. Why would she want to ever talk to me again? I had nothing to offer. I was worthless. Ask my dad."

"Max, did you really think that? Do you think that?"

"It doesn't matter. I eventually apologized for all of it."

"All of it?"

"Let's just say we had a few not-so-great run-ins over our senior year. I get why she finally gave up on me and started dating Connor. Connor made her happy. I just always let her down."

"What happened senior year?" Ashley says as she pulls into their driveway.

"Nothing, I don't want to talk about it," Max says, shutting down.

"Did she forgive you?"

"She said she did, but it didn't matter by then."

"When did you finally apologize?"

Max unbuckles his seat belt and gets out of the car. "That night at Fletcher's," and shuts the door and walks inside.

Ashley sits in the car, taking in all the info. She thinks back to that night at Fletcher's. That explains why they were in their own little world. They had quite the memory lane to go down. She wonders why Max was still feeling bad all those years later about junior prom and whatever else happened senior year. So much so he had to apologize for it? *What happened senior year,* she wonders? Then she remembers somebody said something about them kissing and Maddie having a boyfriend during spring break. Ashley can't let it go. She gets out of the car and follows Max inside.

Max is in the master bathroom brushing his teeth.

"Max, what happened over spring break?"

Max looks at Ashley in surprise. *How does she know about spring break?* he wonders. *Is she guessing, or does she know?* He points at the toothbrush in his mouth to buy some time. When he is done, he responds.

"What are you talking about?"

"Your senior year. One of your friends told me that you two kissed, and then Maddie moped around the rest of spring break. Did something more happen?"

"No, I don't even remember that," Max says, lying and feeling relieved she didn't mean their freshman year of college. "I'm done talking about this. I'm going to bed."

"Do you still have feelings for her?" Ashley asks, not dropping it.

"What? No! Don't be ridiculous. I didn't even want to talk to her tonight," Max says, going back to his earlier excuse. "Seriously, let it go. It's time for bed." Max crawls into bed and closes his eyes, effectively shutting the conversation down.

Ashley gets ready for bed and crawls in next to him. She doesn't ask any more questions but she does think about it until she falls asleep. She decides she has to get Tyler or his wife to talk about what really happened.

Part 3
The Universe Waits Patiently

CHAPTER 33

"I'm dreaming about him again," Maddie says to her therapist.

"Max or your dad?" the therapist asks.

"Max. I think he's about to get divorced."

"Why is that?"

"That's what he is telling me."

"In real life or in your dreams?"

"My dreams. I haven't talked to him since our reunion, since I started seeing you."

"How does that make you feel?"

"Which part? Not talking to him or the dreams about him getting divorced?"

"You tell me; what do you want to talk about."

"Well, I'm here so I can let him go, so I guess not talking to him is the right step. However, the dreams are haunting, and it isn't helping me let go. Do you think talking about the dreams would help get him out of my mind?"

"Do you?"

"Well, not talking about him, trying not to think about him, pushing him out of my mind when he pops up isn't helping, so maybe talking about the dreams will."

"Tell me about your dreams."

"I wrote a few of them down so I could capture the essence of them. Can I share them with you?"

"Please do."

"I keep having this recurring dream of the last day of school. There is happiness and excitement all around, and all I can feel is sadness and loneliness. It's over, and I know I'll never have that feeling again. The excitement has ended. Like when the lights go on at the end of the concert. You know the band isn't coming back on stage and the feelings you had that evening are fleeting. Soon the high will flatten out, and the mundane and boredom will set back in."

"How often do you have that dream?"

"I have that dream, or a version of it, at least once a month. Sometimes more."

"It sounds like your life is missing something. That's not about Max; that is about you."

"Yeah, how about this one? School setting again. Max walks into the room and walks right by me. We make eye contact. There was no feeling behind his eyes. It was like I was a stranger looking back at him. Someone he felt indifference towards, an insignificant soul floating past him, not one his body had once been entangled with. My eyes drop to the floor. I couldn't bear the feeling of not knowing him, not having a connection with him. How could someone go from sharing their innermost thoughts and feelings to nothing, nonexistent?"

"That's a pretty powerful dream. How does that make you feel?"

"I miss him. I absolutely miss him. It feels like I have a big empty hole in my heart. The loss swells inside of me with so much intensity, it feels like my heart could explode. I hope it is sending a beacon to summon him home to me."

The therapist sits for a moment and jots a note on her pad of paper. "Who do you miss, Maddie? Max or your dad?"

Maddie starts crying. "I don't know."

"Your dreams are telling me that you feel invisible, that you are sad, and that you are lonely. That sounds a lot like grief to me. You're still grieving the sudden loss of your dad. Your brain is just processing it with Max. It's trying to protect you."

"How do I make it stop?"

"You don't, Maddie. You don't get to control grief. You have to live through it, feel it. You have to resolve your past with Max so you can process your feelings about your dad."

"Yes, sure, anything. Make him stop haunting me."

"You still have unresolved issues with Max after all these years. Why do you think that is?"

"I don't know; if I did, I would resolve them."

"I'm curious, Maddie. Do you want Max to get divorced?"

"What? No. Why would I want that?"

"You tell me. You said he's telling you he's getting divorced, but the dreams you share are about how you feel, not him."

"Oh, I have a whole stack of dreams here," Maddie says, waving her notebook. "Let me read a divorce dream to you."

"Okay," the therapist says. She puts her notepad in her lap to listen again.

"Oh, here is a good one," Maddie says, flipping through her notes. She begins.

I'm in my parents' home in the basement in my room. It is dimly lit when the phone rings. I answer it.

"Hello,"

"Hi," Max says on the other end.

I'm a little confused for a moment. I look around my bedroom. My friend McKenna is there. McKenna looks at me and says, "Is that him?" I nod my head yes.

"How are you?" Max asks.

"I'm okay. It's been years since I've talked to you. Why are you calling?" I ask, wondering if this is a dream—in my dream.

"I just needed to talk to you."

"I know this is going to sound weird, but did you ever talk about getting divorced with your wife?"

Max hesitates for a minute then answers, "Yes, our marriage is on the rocks, but we're not getting divorced."

"But over the years, have you come close?"

"Yes, we almost did. Why? Did you dream about it? No one knows that."

"Yes, a couple of times. Each time you came to me in a dream and told me."

"Yeah, then what happened?"

"You know what happened. You were there."

McKenna taps me on the shoulder and says, "This is really spooky, like off-the-charts ghost stuff."

I tell Max to "hold on for a second," to McKenna I say, "What is?"

"You and Max. You met in 1645. A witch cast a spell over the two of you. It's why you're connected."

"What are you talking about?"

"The witches, they cast a spell over the two of you, and it's why you're drawn to each other but never have the right timing."

"Witches?" I say. "Max, did you hear that? We've known each other since 1645."

There is silence on the other end of the phone line.

"Max," I say. "Are you there?"

I look at the phone. There is no dial tone and no one on the other end. I look around my room again. McKenna is gone. I am alone. Then I realize I am dreaming and I wake up.

"I literally woke up and for a fleeting second, I wondered if we did meet in 1645? I mean, a witch's spell would explain everything." Maddie laughs when she says it.

"I think it is wishful thinking. It would be easy to say you have a spell cast over you. But I see the same loneliness theme in this dream as the others. Let me ask you again, do you want Max to get a divorce?"

"No, it's not wishful thinking. It's him. We were like this in school too. I would dream what he was thinking. How about this one? I dreamt this one a few days later."

I'm walking through a dark, creepy parking lot. It's a cold winter night and I am lost and a little scared. As I walk by a conversion van, the door slides open and Max appears from inside.

"What are you doing here?" he asks.

"I don't know; I'm lost. What are you doing here?" I ask, relieved to see him.

"I live here," he says.

"Here?" I ask and look around at the parking lot.

"Here," he says as he points to the van.

"You live in a van?" I ask.

"For now. I just got divorced," he says.

"Why are you in a van?" I ask.

"Do you want to see it? You look cold," Max says.

"Sure," I say apprehensively.

I follow Max into the van. It is much bigger inside than I expected. Before I can say anything, Max is on top of me, kissing me. I push him away.

"What are you doing?" I ask.

"Kissing you," he says.

"I know that, but why?" I demand.

"Because you're here; you belong with me," Max says.

"You're married, Max. You had your chance with me. You didn't pick me," I say.

"Yes, I did. You just didn't know it. You always run away from me before I can tell you." Max says.

"You never follow me," I say.

"You don't want me to. You never look back," he says.

In the dream, I feel like it is my fault that things never worked out the way they should have. I look at him for a second and then realize it's not my fault for the way he treated me. It's my fault for always giving him another chance. Then I feel a ream of emotions flood through me. First, I feel hurt, then sad, then angry. When the anger starts growing in me, I turn to Max and shout, "I can't. I can't do this again." I open the van door. I hop out and start running. I look around trying to figure out where I am, and then I realize I'm in the church parking lot—our church parking lot. I look back at Max. He's standing in the doorway of the van. I wait for him to follow me, but he just stands there, like always. I turn to face forward, and I trip over a rock. I put my hands out to catch myself, and as I fall, I jerk myself awake just before I hit my head on the ground.

"I woke up from this dream and felt hurt and angry all day," Maddie says, looking up from her notes.

"That's called grief, Maddie. I hate to break it to you, but Max is a metaphor for your grief. He's not talking to you through your dreams. There is no magic spell binding the two of you together. You are grieving your dad. Grief has a funny way of showing itself, and unfortunately for you, it is manifesting itself as Max."

"But you said if I resolved my feelings about Max, I could make them stop?" Maddie argues.

"No, I said you needed to resolve your issues with Max so you could get to processing your feelings about your dad," the therapist corrects her.

"Okay, how do I do that? I've spent a lifetime trying to get over him."

"You have to find the root of what you are holding onto with him. What aren't you letting go of? What needs resolution? Think about that for next time. We're out of time today," her therapist says, closing her notebook and standing up.

"If I knew that, I wouldn't be here," Maddie jokes. Deep down she knows what she has to address.

"Whatever it is, it'll eventually catch up with you. Better you figure it before it consumes your whole life," her therapist says as a cautionary warning.

It already has, Maddie thinks as she leaves.

That night Maddie has another dream. This one scares her.

She is in a car, out of control, on the roof of a parking garage. It is night, pitch black out. She remains calm as it crashes through the barrier and falls off the top of the parking garage, eight stories down. The car doesn't crash but lands on a set of train tracks. The tires pop, and the rims grip the rails and start moving forward. Maddie tries braking, and the brakes don't work. She pushes them hard into the floor. Nothing. The car begins to gain momentum.

Max comes on the car phone speaker. "Hello! Maddie, are you there?"

"I am!" Maddie shouts.

"Maddie, are you okay?" Max shouts back.

"No, the car is barreling down a track with a train that's headed towards me!" Maddie says, still shouting and wishing he could jump through the speaker and save her.

Maddie waits for Max to say something. The train is getting closer, and she knows time is running out. She wants to tell him how she never got over him, but she can't do it. She holds back, waiting for him to say something. Death is certain, she thinks, but his silence is worse.

As the train is about to crash into her car, she opens the door and falls out of it. When she looks up, she's in a parking lot. She can see Max. He is drunk with his friends. She runs back to him.

"I wanted to tell you something, but I was about to die, and I couldn't," Maddie says, gasping for breath.

"Stop. You can't say it," he instructs.

"I have to. I never got over you and…" Maddie is cut off.

"Stop. Are you serious?" Max interrupts.

"Yes, but I have to tell you something…" Maddie starts to say.

Maddie wakes up before she can tell him the one thing she has been trying to tell him for years.

CHAPTER 34

Max has been thinking about Maddie a lot lately. Seeing her at the reunion unleashed a lot of old memories and feelings. Telling Ashley about Maddie hasn't helped either. He can tell she's still thinking about it too, and he goes out of his way to avoid her and the topic. That doesn't help them as they are going through their last round of IVF. They agreed if this round doesn't work, they are going to stop trying. The hormones are taking a toll on Ashley, and the cost is taking a toll on their financial situation. He longs for a less stressful time. His mind leads him to Maddie as a brief escape from reality. He imagines what it would be like if he and Ashley did get divorced and he was free to strike things up with Maddie again. Max thinks a life with her would be so much easier, simpler, freeing. But he can't figure out why. It's never been that way before; something always messes things up between them. Yet, he is still drawn to her. He misses her, and he can't stop thinking about her.

"Are we going to be okay," Ashley asks Max over dinner one night.

"Of course, why wouldn't we be?"

"What if it doesn't work again?"

"You can't think that way. This will be our time. It'll work, and it'll be worth everything we've gone through."

"But what if it doesn't. Then what?"

"We'll figure that out if we have to. We don't need to figure that out now."

"Will you still love me?"

"Yes. Will you still love me?"

"Yes," Ashley says and hesitates. "When did it get so hard between us?"

"I don't know. We just have a lot going on. Marriage is hard."

"Do you think it is hard like this for everyone?"

"I do. I see a lot worse every day when I go to work. We've got a great marriage compared to the people I help."

"I just thought we'd be in a different place by now. I thought we'd have a house full of kids thinking about what college they should go to, and here we are still trying to get pregnant."

"Yeah, but we've had fun trying."

"Do you ever think about what life would be like if we'd married someone else?" Ashley asks, meaning if he married Maddie.

The question catches Max by surprise.

"No, do you?" Max asks concerned.

"Sometimes," Ashley admits.

"Do you want to be married to someone else?"

"No, I just wonder if us not getting pregnant means we should have been with someone else. Why is it so hard for us, and other people get pregnant just by looking at someone?" Ashley asks near tears.

"That, I've wondered about. I've met plenty of people that have multiple kids with multiple people. It's like the universe is throwing it in my face," Max says, thinking about some of the terrible parents he has met on the job.

"Exactly! Why is it so easy for them and not for us? Are we just not compatible?"

"We've been together for fourteen years. I'd say we're pretty compatible."

"But don't you want more?"

"Yeah, of course, I do. We wouldn't be spending all this money and putting you through this if I, we, didn't want more. These are the cards we were dealt, and we just have to accept what we got."

"Do you think if you and Maddie had ended up together, you'd have kids?"

"What? Why are you asking that? Don't go there. You'll drive yourself crazy," Max says, trying to shut the conversation down. He does not want to explore that topic.

"You didn't answer my question," Ashley says, not letting it go.

"Ashley, don't do this. It's been a long day already," Max begs her.

"You do think about it, don't you," Ashley says, ignoring his plea.

"Enough. No, I don't!"

"I can't make you feel the way she makes you feel," Ashley says, starting to cry.

"She doesn't make me feel any way. She's not in my life. You are. I love you. I am here with you. I am trying to have a baby with you. Please let it go."

"I can't stop thinking about you two," Ashley says, tears streaming down her face.

"Why? She is my past. You are my present," Max says, getting up from the table and walking over to her.

"I just have this feeling it's not over between the two of you. I can't explain it. Call it women's intuition."

"It's the hormones talking, Ashley. It's been years since the reunion. I have no contact with her," Max says, hugging Ashley tight.

"I just don't get why we can't get pregnant. There is nothing wrong with either of us," Ashley cries into his chest.

"It's because I don't deserve a family," Max says, still holding her so she can't see his face.

"What?" Ashley asks, pushing back from the hug to look at him.

"That's the reason. I had a crappy dad. I have no idea how to be a good dad. If I had a kid, I'd probably screw it up. That's why we can't get pregnant. It's me. I'm sorry. I let you down. I let everyone down. No matter how hard I try, it's never good enough. I'm never good enough," Max says, backing up from her. "I can't do this tonight. I need to go for a drive."

"Max," Ashley calls out after him. "Max, don't go."

Max grabs his keys and walks out the door, gets into his car, and drives away.

Ashley sits at the table picking at her food, still crying.

Max had a hard day. He interviewed a young woman in the hospital. Her boyfriend had put her there after a dispute. The woman had told the man she was pregnant, and he accused her of cheating on him and beat her up. He beat her so badly she had a black eye, split lip, a couple of broken ribs, and she ended up miscarrying her baby. The case really got to Max today, and the stress of the last round of IVF was wearing on him. He really wanted to have a kid, but what he said to Ashley was true. He was afraid he'd be a bad dad. He was afraid he'd let her down. He was afraid he just wasn't good enough and that his dad was right. Max drove that night to the old church parking lot. He thought about what Ashley asked him. He thought about what life would be like if he and Maddie had ended up together. Would they have kids? Would they play hockey? Would he push his kids as hard as his dad pushed him or would he let them play for the love of the game. Let them have a normal childhood, go to parties, date, just be free.

He also wonders if he and Ashley are going to make it. He's not happy. She's not happy. They haven't been happy in a long time. He wonders if that is just what marriage is like—rough patches that you have to push through? Max wonders if Ashley thinks about if she was with someone else, if she'd have kids by now. He thinks about how great of a wife she has been, putting up with his family issues. Putting up with his job. Putting up with him. He's thankful for her. She's been a steady constant in his life. He tells himself things will get better one way or the other after they are done with this last round of IVF.

Max starts the car to head home. The radio comes on, and "Until Your Love Comes Back Around" is playing on the oldies station. He thinks this one was written for him as he sings along with the lyrics.

CHAPTER 35

A song catches Maddie's ear. It's familiar in the background. Her mind is consumed in a book, letting the song play in the background without really listening to it. While her mind is occupied, her heart isn't. Suddenly, she feels sadness creep up inside her. It stops her, and she looks up from her book. Sitting quietly, she hears the words from the song "Until Your Love Comes Back Around" floating through the air.

The words pierce her heart, and her feelings spill out. Just like the day her dad died, the ache and sorrow overflow for the man who left her life too soon. The sorrow catches her by surprise, and her eyes burst with tears. Streams of tears gush down her face. She can't stop them, rapidly trying to wipe them from her face. She can hear Jordan approaching the room. She tries desperately to get herself under control.

Her soul is screaming at her—you're missing a part of you. Her mind is screaming, "You belong with him, and you can't keep running. One of these days you have to face the truth one way or the other. You can't have both."

Jordan walks into the room and sees her crying in her reading chair. "What's wrong? Did something sad happen in your book?"

Maddie sobs when he asks her that. Trying to catch her breath to speak, she pushes out a sorrowful "no."

"What's wrong then? Why are you crying?"

"I miss him."

Jordan assumes she means her dad and picks her up out of her chair, holding her tight. He wants to take the pain away. "I miss him too, Maddie."

That makes her cry harder. She knows he thinks she is talking about her dad. Jordan holds her until she calms down.

"You okay?"

"Yeah, thanks. I sometimes get these waves of feelings that catch me off guard," Maddie says, drying her tears.

"Is therapy helping any?"

"I'm trying, but I don't know. She just keeps telling me it's grief, and I have to feel it."

"She's right. It shows up differently for everyone."

"Will it ever go away?"

"I think you'll always miss him, but eventually, it shouldn't feel as intense as it does now."

"I hope so. I don't know how long I can last feeling like this. I just want to get all the feelings out of me," Maddie says, thinking about Max.

"Have you tried writing?"

"Sometimes, I write down the dreams that haunt me."

"That's a good start. But like right now, that was a big wave of emotion. You should sit with those feelings for a bit instead of trying to run from them. Write it down. Get it out of your head and heart and onto paper."

"For a guy who is so practical, when did you get so smart?"

"As you know, I'm not a very emotional person. But when I've got something on my mind I can't work out—a patent, a case, a problem—I just free flow write. It helps. I trust my subconscious will figure it out if I just let it go. So, I do. I write whatever comes to my mind. No editing. Sometimes it's just nonsense, and sometimes the answer appears." He gets up and walks over to the desk, grabbing her a pad of paper and pen. "Try it. See if it helps."

Maddie takes the paper and pen from him. "Okay, I'll try anything to feel better."

"I'll give you a little space so you can let it out and sort it through."

"Okay, thanks," she says as she wipes her face with the back of her sleeve one last time.

Jordan leaves, and Maddie stares at her paper for a while. Then she starts writing. She doesn't edit a word; she just lets it flow like Jordan told her to do. She writes:

I can feel my soul pounding behind my chest. It cries out, "Why do you keep me trapped in here when I should be free?" I'm meant to dance in the wind, glide across the water, glisten in the sun, and be engulfed in love. "Let me out! Let me out! I have somewhere to be."

She continues to write:

I feel like my chest has been cut open, my muscles peeled back, exposing my heart and soul. My soul cowers behind my rib cage, too scared to escape, while longing to be free. It's been buried deep inside too long. My heart pounds, waiting for a hand to scoop it out and squash it beneath the pressure or heal it by gently holding it in their palm, repairing the fissures and cracks life has set upon it.

She reads what she wrote and scribbles some more:

The heart is in a constant battle with the mind. Is the mind the master, or does the heart concede, waiting for the right time to fulfill its desire?

A teardrop falls on her paper and smudges the last sentence. She thinks to herself, *Is now the time?* She writes one last sentence, answering her own question.

Brick by brick, memory by memory, all the feelings crush the wall. Crashing down so my heart can be free and my soul can live again.

She puts the pad of paper safely away in a drawer and heads to bed. She thinks about how unhappy she is and cries herself to sleep. That night, she dreams of Max again.

Maddie looks up from her book. Max is walking by, digging through his backpack looking for something. He hasn't noticed her yet. She sees him instantly, and a smile washes over her face. She waits for him to see her. She knows he will. He finds whatever it was he was looking for and pulls his hand out of his bag as he lets it fall behind him. He looks up to continue walking and meets her patient gaze. He stops dead in his tracks.

"Hi," she says softly.

He stands there, surprised to see her. He doesn't speak.

"Come here," she summons from her seat at the front of the auditorium. "Are you in this class?"

"Yes."

"What other classes do you have?"

"Why?"

"I'm just wondering if we have any other classes together."

He lists his classes off.

"Guess this is the only one we have together. Ironic, huh?"

"How so?" he says, still surprised to see her.

"We never had classes together when we were in high school, and now, here we are, as adults, in class."

"I've got to get to my next class."

Maddie holds her hand out toward him. "Don't leave," she says, asking more than telling.

He reaches his hand out toward hers. They are just far enough apart that only their fingertips can touch. His hand gently extends under hers, slowly dragging his fingers until they find her fingertips, and they grasp each other, holding softly but with incredible electricity.

He drops his bag and moves closer to her. She looks up from her chair, fingers still connected. He bends down and gives her a familiar kiss, like old lovers who've found themselves again. She touches his face gently, and it startles him. He pulls back and stares at her without saying a word. Both of their hearts are beating heavily in their chests.

"Come back to me," she says with intent.

"Okay," he says as he turns to go.

"Wait," she says, "do you have a girlfriend?"

"I do, but I'll break up with her."

"Okay," she says, believing him, and watches him leave. She knows this time they'll be together. She's at peace. She's happy. Then she realizes she's with someone too. She shakes her head, trying to shake the thought of her boyfriend away. She doesn't care. She's going to enjoy this moment and deal with that later.

Maddie wakes from her dream and sees Jordan. She knows she has a choice to make.

Chapter 36

Maddie meets up with some girlfriends at the dock bar outside of Bayside for drinks. It's a humid summer night and she orders a beer to cool off. As she's waiting for her drink to arrive, a couple of her old classmates walk by.

"Hey, Kyle!" Maddie says.

"Holy crap, Maddie! We were just talking about you," Kyle says.

"Me? Why?"

"We were just wondering if we'd see you here."

"Oh, why?"

The waitress walks up with her beer just as it starts to rain. Before Maddie can ask any more questions, everyone bolts indoors. Maddie sees a few other friends who had already grabbed a booth in the bar, she and her girlfriends join them. Everyone wipes the rain off their stuff and Maddie thinks to herself, *It's not supposed to rain on the lake*. Maddie is facing the door watching the crowd pour in from the patio. Surprisingly, she sees a number of her classmates come in.

"Hey Maddie!" Jake says as he walks over.

"Hey Jake! What's the occasion?" Maddie asks as she gestures to the other guys.

"I just took a new job as a ski coach and am leaving town soon," Jake says joyfully.

"Oh, wow, congratulations! You'll have to let me get you a drink later."

"Yeah, you and your friends should come join us."

"Sure, that'd be fun. Actually, we're waiting on a couple of others. We'll come join you when they get here."

The other girls show up a few minutes later, and Maddie and them head over to the group to say hi to everyone. As Maddie is saying hi to her classmates, she sees Max walk in with Tyler. She knows instantly now why Kyle was talking about her. She had heard from mutual friends that since the reunion, Max would occasionally talk about her if he had too much to drink. After decades, their secrets were coming out.

Maddie quickly looks away and grabs her phone to call McKenna.

"He's here!" Maddie says.

"Who? Where's here?" McKenna asks.

"Bayside and, you know who."

"Oh man. Don't talk to him."

"I know. I can't."

"I wish I was there."

"Me too."

"Are you going to leave?"

"I should, but I am having fun. A ton of people here tonight."

"Be careful. Let me know if anything happens."

"I will. Ugh."

"Proceed with caution."

Maddie and friends order another round of drinks and go back to her friends at the booth. The bar is packed, and it is easy to keep her distance. She has a few drinks and thinks to herself, *Therapy must be working. I'm not freaking out. I've got this. It's going to be fine.*

As people make their way to the bar and back, the crowd jostles around, letting people through. People move from conversation to conversation, saying hi as they see each other. Maddie moves to the side to get out of someone's way, and she finds herself looking directly at Max, who has two drinks in his hands. She assumes one, the red one, is for his wife. He looks past her, desperately searching for his wife so he can move away. Maddie can tell that he can't find her in the crowd.

"She's over there," Maddie says, having spotted Ashley earlier.

"Who?" Max responds, caught off guard.

"Your wife," Maddie says, nodding towards the red drink. "I assume that is for her. It matches her hair."

"Yeah," Max says. "Where is your fiancé?"

"He's at home."

"Why isn't he here?"

"I wore him out last night," Maddie replies with a mischievous tone.

Max smiles, obviously thinking about how Maddie could have worn her fiancé out. Then he spots his wife and starts to walk away.

Maddie thinks to herself, *Okay. That went well,* and drops her guard a little. She continues to talk with her friends and classmates. Someone hands her another drink, and the crowds continue to move. She finds herself towards the back of the bar area when Tyler appears.

"Hey Maddie," Tyler says in the tone that lets you know he's up to something.

"Hey Tyler," Maddie replies, looking around for anyone else to talk to.

"You know he still loves you."

"Who?"

"This guy," Tyler says as he grabs the back of Max's shirt and pulls him around to face them, just like he did at Fletcher's over a decade ago.

Same old tricks, Maddie thinks.

Max looks surprised to see them talking. "Hey," he says casually.

"Hey," Maddie says back casually.

"Remember the first time you two kissed at the band concert?" Tyler says, trying to stir things up.

"Yeah, I remember everything."

"Isn't it lucky to remember," Tyler asks.

"Speaking of Luck, he just had his seventh kid. Can you believe it? Lucky number seven." Maddie says, trying to change the subject.

"Good for him," Max says.

"He married an Ashley too," Maddie says.

"What's that supposed to mean?" Max says defensively, feeling bad that his old friend had seven kids and he had none.

Maddie is a little startled by the tone of his question and tries to defuse it.

"He married a girl named Ashley, just like you married a girl named Ashley. Did you know that Ashley means dream in Irish?"

"I should have married you," Max replies.

"See, I told you he still loves you," Tyler adds.

"Then why didn't you?" Maddie asks, shocked to hear the words come out of her mouth.

"You didn't come to my wedding," Max says.

"You didn't invite me," Maddie says, as if the conversation is perfectly normal.

"Yes, I did," Max says.

"Well, I never got the invitation," Maddie says, a little annoyed—thinking - he invited me to his wedding?

"Did you forget to put a stamp on it?"

"No, it had a stamp and an address," Max says matter-of-fact.

"I never got it," Maddie says.

"I know," Max says.

"He loves you," Tyler adds again.

"I never mailed it," Max explains.

"Why not?" Maddie asks curiously. "I probably would have come."

"I know. If you did, I would have had to marry you," Max says like it would have been an option to switch brides at the ceremony no problem.

"I would have married you," Maddie says, agreeing that would have been an option.

"I should have married you. My life would be so different," Max says longingly.

"You should have," Maddie says like it was a simple mistake. "It would have been different. More than you know."

They stare at each other for a minute. Tyler, wanting to say, "See, I told you," holds it in, not breaking the silence. The electricity between them is undeniable but not mentioned.

"I waited for you," Maddie says, looking deep into his blue eyes.

"I waited for you," Max says, returning the stare.

"Clearly you didn't," Maddie says, not flinching.

"Yes, I did," Max says, not flinching either.

"You're married, Max," Maddie reminds him.

"I'm still waiting for you, Maddie," Max says.

"I'm still waiting for you, Max," Maddie says. She puts her hand on his forearm and leans in toward him dangerously close. "Are you okay? I've had some dreams about you that weren't good."

Max looks stunned and says, "You still dream about me?"

"I can't stop them, no matter how hard I try," Maddie says.

Neither of them has broken their stare. People are beginning to notice. Tyler has a front row seat and can't wait to see what happens next.

Kyle walks up to the trio. "What's going on here?"

The moment is broken, and Maddie turns her head to answer him. She can see Max's wife about thirty feet behind them talking to Tyler's wife and pointing toward them. As she reenters reality, breaking from the trance she and Max were just in, she pulls her hand off of Max's arm and says without thinking, "Tyler is just telling me how much Max loves me."

"Is he?" Kyle says, looking at Tyler annoyed. "Do you mind if I steal Max for a minute?"

Maddie looks at Kyle, confused. Kyle nods his head toward Ashley and Sheila.

Maddie looks at the women and back at Kyle. "Sure, he's all yours," Maddie concedes, not wanting Max to go.

"Max, come with me," Kyle says to Max.

"No," Max says stubbornly.

"You should really come with me. Ashley is really upset," Kyle says.

It clicks in Maddie's brain when Kyle says that. She's upset that they are talking.

"I don't care," Max says. "She's always upset with me."

"Come with me, Max," Kyle insists.

"No!" Max says.

"Do you want to get divorced, Max?" Kyle says, dead seriously. "If not, you need to come with me this minute."

Maddie looks at Max. Max looks at Maddie. Maddie gives him a small smile, letting him know it's okay to go. Max desperately wants her to tell him to stay, but she doesn't. Max drops his eyes to the ground in defeat. Once again, he doesn't pick Maddie in the moment. Kyle puts his hand on his shoulder and turns him away from Maddie, and they start to walk toward the door.

"He really does love you," Tyler says as his wife Sheila walks up to them.

Maddie remembers Tyler's wife from the reunions and says hello.

"Should I go?" Maddie asks Sheila.

"No, it's okay," Sheila says.

"I don't want to cause any problems," Maddie says.

"She'll be fine," Sheila says. "They've been fighting a lot lately."

"Everything okay?" Maddie asks.

"Just a lot of stress at home," Sheila says.

"And he loves you, but can't talk to you," Tyler says.

"He's married, Tyler. He chose his life," Maddie says. "It didn't include me."

"I knew I liked you," Sheila says. "I told Ashley if she got to know you, she'd like you too."

"Why were you talking about me?" Maddie asks Sheila.

"She was asking me what I knew about you and Max," Sheila says.

Maddie flashes back to Ashley yelling at Max, "Who is she?!"

"Not much to know," Maddie says.

"That's not what Tyler says," Sheila responds, looking at Tyler.

"He loves you," Tyler says again.

"Stop saying that, Tyler. He's married," Sheila says.

Maddie changes the subject, not wanting to get sucked into Tyler's game. Some other friends join them. They all continue to drink and laugh about old times. Maddie occasionally scans the crowd to see if Max is still there but doesn't see him or Kyle. She notices that Ashley isn't around anymore either and assumes they left.

Sheila picks up on it and says, "They really have been fighting a lot. They can't have kids and that has been really hard." She starts to tell Maddie stories. Maddie says she doesn't need to hear it, but Sheila is drunk and insists on sharing. Maddie suggests they go outside so other people don't hear. Sheila, Tyler, and Maddie grab their drinks and go out on the patio. It's stopped raining, but most people stay inside or have gone home since it's almost bar close.

"I always liked you two together," Tyler says.

"We were never together," Maddie says.

"Yeah, you were. What really happened with you two?"

"We weren't ever together. That was the problem. He never wanted to date me. I don't know why he couldn't date me but wants to marry me—especially when he *is* married."

"I know," Tyler says triumphantly. "His dad wouldn't let him."

"Let him what?" Maddie asks. "Date me?"

"Date anyone," Tyler explains. "He wasn't allowed to date girls or do anything that was going to screw up his hockey career."

"How would a girlfriend screw up a hockey career? Plenty of hockey players, professional ones even, have girlfriends and wives," Maddie says, frustrated.

"Yeah, and so did his dad. Then he got his mom prego and he had to give up playing hockey to help raise Max's sister. His dad never got over that. He pushed Max to do what he didn't get to do, and that meant no girls."

"I didn't know. He never told me."

"His dad literally would have killed him if he knew what the two of you were up to back then," Tyler goes on to say. "Why do you think he became a cop?"

"How do you know what we were up to?" Maddie asks curiously, thinking about the cop statement.

"I always suspected, but he finally told me after the accident. Once he found out he wasn't going to be able to play Division One hockey, he was ready to tell his dad about you and finally date you. By then, you had Connor, and he felt like he missed his chance. He lost you and his hockey dreams our senior year. He's never really gotten over either," Tyler tells Maddie.

Maddie's head is spinning, swishing, full of alcohol and this new info about Max.

"Why didn't he ever tell me?"

"You ran away to Michigan and never came back. That especially hurt that you went to the school he was going to play hockey at, that is, until his accident."

"Well, that's ironic," Maddie says without a filter.

"What is?"

"Nothing, it was a long time ago."

"He thinks about you all the time."

"I'll have to let my therapist know I'm not crazy then."

"What?" Tyler and Sheila look at her confused.

"Like I told you at the first reunion. I still dream about him. It comes in waves. I assume it's when he's thinking about me. I told my therapist that, and she told me it was all in my head. She doesn't believe we have a dream connection." Maddie shares, as if having a dream connection is normal.

"What do you dream about?" Sheila asks curiously.

Before Maddie gets a chance to respond, Ashley walks through the door and is headed toward them. She looks angry and is moving fast, finger pointed at Maddie, red hair flowing behind her like she's on fire. Maddie thinks to herself, *I'm about to get punched*. Maddie's body responds before her brain can tell her to protect herself. Instead of getting ready to dodge a punch, she throws her arms wide open, and as Ashley gets close to her, Maddie gives her a big drunk hug. Maddie can feel the anger drop from Ashley's body. She doesn't retreat from the hug, maybe she was stunned or maybe she just needed a hug. Maddie did give good hugs.

When they pull apart from the hug, Maddie says, "I'm sorry, I didn't mean to upset you. I just want you and Max to be happy." Her hand still on Ashley's back.

"We are happy," Ashley says defensively.

"Good," Maddie says sweetly, meaning it, and pats her back.

Before there is time to say more, Kyle and Max come around the outside corner of the building and see them. Max's eyes dart from Ashley to Maddie to Ashley to Maddie. Maddie flashes him another small smile as if saying, good luck.

Kyle sees the group and thinks, *Oh shit. This isn't going to be a good ride home*. He says, "Time to go. Let's move." He puts his arm around Max and turns him away from Maddie for a second time that night. Tyler and Sheila grab Ashley and start to walk away. This time, Maddie just stands there, watching everyone leave. She waits for Max to look back at her. He doesn't.

Ashley suddenly turns and comes back to Maddie, pointing her finger wildly at her again. "I know who you are! I know who you are!" she says sternly, with a glare in her eye. Then, just as suddenly, she turns and walks away.

Maddie thinks to herself, *Who am I?* and wonders what Ashley thinks the story is because Maddie has no idea anymore.

Her friends find her moments later and tell her it's time to go too. Maddie calls McKenna.

"You are never going to believe what just happened. Queso tomorrow?"

"Yes. I am dying to hear."

Kyle, Tyler, Sheila, Ashley, and Max pile onto Kyle's boat. There is an awkward moment of silence until Max breaks it.

"What did you say to her?" Max asks Ashley.

"Nothing," Ashley says defiantly.

"You turned around and walked back to her. What did you say?" Max insists on knowing.

"I told her I know who she is," Ashley says, full of spite.

"You don't know who she is," Max says.

"Kids, settle down," Kyle says from the captain's chair.

"I know who she is," Tyler says, adding fuel to the fire.

"Tyler, you've done enough tonight," Kyle scolds. "Quiet!"

They all sit there quiet for a minute until Ashley breaks the silence.

"I saw the way she looked at you when we walked away. She was waiting for you to turn around. That's why I went back," Ashley tries to explain.

"You're making a big deal out of nothing," Max says.

"Yeah, Ashley. She said all that was a long time ago. Tyler kept trying to provoke her like he does, and I don't think you have anything to worry about." Sheila says, trying to smooth things over.

"What did he say to her?" Ashley asks.

"He was asking her about high school, and she said they were never together," Sheila answers. "You heard her. She even told you, she just wants you two to be happy."

"We are happy!" Ashley says again, angrily.

"Are we, Ashley?" Max asks. "It doesn't feel like it. All we do is fight."

"That's because you won't admit that you still have feelings for her," Ashley shouts back.

"Why would I do that? We are married. I want to stay married," Max says, frustrated.

"Do you?" Ashley pushes.

"Guys," Kyle says, trying to distract them.

"No, it's okay, Kyle. I want to know. We all saw the same thing tonight. There is no denying it. There is something between Maddie and Max, no matter what either of them says. It's electric. Even a blind person can see it," Ashley says exaggerating.

Max says nothing. There is nothing he can say.

Ashley turns to Tyler, "You're drunk enough to tell me."

"What?" Tyler asks.

Max knows what Ashley is about to say and shakes his head no at Tyler. Kyle does the same thing behind Max.

"Does Max love Maddie?" Ashley asks Tyler bluntly.

"Ashley that's crazy," Sheila says.

"Does he?!" Ashley stares at Tyler.

"Since the day he met her," Tyler says without hesitation.

Ashley looks at Max. A tear rolls down her face. Max pulls her in close, wanting to take the pain away. He wraps his arms around her and says, "I'm sorry."

Ashley cries on his shoulder for a moment. Everyone is silent. Kyle glares at Tyler. Tyler shrugs it off. Sheila slaps his chest, thinking the same thing Kyle is thinking, that she is going to kill Tyler when they get off the boat.

CHAPTER 37

Mckenna and Maddie meet up the next day at their favorite Mexican place.

"I'm dying to know what happened," McKenna says over a bowl of chips and queso, a tradition they started at Chi-Chi's back in their broke college days.

Maddie relays the whole night to McKenna.

"No, he didn't say all that. That didn't happen," McKenna says in disbelief.

"He did. What the hell do I do with that?" Maddie asks.

"You have to talk to him again, soon. Otherwise, it'll be like another decade before you run into each other. I can't wait that long," McKenna says as if she's waiting for a movie sequel. "I think we're due for another reunion, aren't we?"

"I'm not sure I can handle any more drama. I almost got my ass kicked last night but ended up throwing her off by hugging her. I do not need that to happen at a reunion. Pass!" Maddie says.

"Maddie, I'll be there to protect you. When would our next one be anyway?" McKenna counts in her head for a second. "Next year! It would be next year. Twenty years already!"

Maddie shakes her head no. "Listen, I now know why it was a secret all those years. He's married. He made his choice. I finally got my closure. It's time to let it go."

"But you're his lobster," McKenna says, pleading with Maddie.

"This isn't *Friends,* McKenna. I'm not Rachel and Max isn't Ross."

CHAPTER 38

Lizzy and Maddie are on a spring training run again. It's been seven months since Maddie and Max's last run-in at Bayside. Maddie is running with her friend Lizzy again on the old abandoned railroad tracks. They occasionally meet at Maynard's, which is adjacent to the tracks, so they can park and run and grab a drink or brunch afterward. They are training for a half marathon, and the tracks are about halfway between their homes.

"I had a very eerie dream last night," Maddie says to Lizzy.

"What was it?" Lizzy asks.

"It's going to sound really weird when I tell you, but I need help figuring it out."

"Shoot. I love deciphering your dreams," Lizzy says. Maddie has been sharing her dreams with Lizzy on their runs since she started therapy.

"This one felt really real. I can still feel/see the sensations I'm about to describe to you," Maddie says, warning her.

"Okay, this is going to be good, isn't it?" Lizzy asks.

"Yeah, here goes. I dreamt I was in Excelsior, like a normal day. Then I notice that my body is disintegrating. I look at my hands, and they look like there is black sand falling off my fingertips as I move them through the air. I wave my hands around. I'm in a trance, watching the tips of my fingers. Then my fingers float away as black specks drifting into the air. It's like little molecules are dying and floating off into the universe. As I fade, I start saying goodbye to as many people as I can. I begin to disintegrate faster. My forearms are nearly gone. I'm frantic, trying to get through people. I discover I can fly. I jet up into the air to see the world below me and then drop down into different parties, saying goodbye to different groups of people. I'm fading faster, and it is getting harder to breathe. I'm getting lighter and lighter. As I do, I can fly faster and higher. I know I only have a small amount of time left. I am desperate to find Max. The more I search for him, the more people I have to wade through to find him. There are too many people to say goodbye to. I fly up into the air and drop into a different location. Each time I land, I see there is less and less of me.

At my last stop, I find him. We instantly embrace. He wraps his arms around my body as the last of me is disintegrating, and I'm desperate to tell him I love him. I try to grab the sides of his head and scream over and over with the last bits of energy I have, but my arms are gone. 'I love you. I love you. I love you,' I shout, not being able to make a sound. He can't hear me.

I look down at my legs and watch them drip off of me like sand falling from a cliff. I look at my stomach and watch it disappear rapidly, like the last grains of sand falling in an hourglass. I know this is the last moment I have, and it's fleeting, and then I'm gone. I'm just a ball of energy, a pile of black molecules floating together in the air. Then I turn into powerful, unencumbered energy that floods the sky and shoots up into the atmosphere to be with the stars looking back down on Excelsior."

Lizzy contemplates this as she runs. Finally, she says, "It sounds like you are about to say goodbye to your old life and are ready for something new."

"I can still feel myself disintegrating. I look at my hands, and I can see them disappearing, just like in my dreams."

"Isn't this exactly what you've been working towards in therapy? Letting go of your past?"

"Yeah."

"I think that is your mind finally agreeing to let it all go. This is huge. We have to celebrate!"

"I am so glad you say that. I was thinking that too. I think I have finally had a breakthrough," Maddie says, relieved. "It was that, or I am about to die."

"Breakthrough!" Lizzy shouts. "Woo Hoo! Let's grab drinks after our run. We can call McKenna to join us."

"Do you really want to drink after running? Don't you want to go home and shower first?"

"No, this is too big. Plus, we've burned a ton of calories today. Let's enjoy it."

"Okay!" Maddie agrees happily. She's ready to move forward and mark the occasion. It's been a long time coming.

Lizzy and Maddie finish up their run.

"Let me call McKenna. I'll meet you at Maynard's." Maddie jogs over to her car, towels off quickly, and calls McKenna.

"Come to Maynard's. I had a breakthrough. Lizzy and I are grabbing drinks to celebrate."

"What? Okay. I'll be there as soon as I can. Putting Walter down for a nap now."

"We'll save you a seat. See you soon."

Maddie feels like a weight has been lifted off her shoulders as she walks over to meet Lizzy.

"That was a good run. I needed that. Thanks so much for listening. I know this story has to be old by now."

"No, I don't think it could ever get old. There is always a new twist or turn."

"I'm so happy for you!" Lizzy squeals and gives Maddie a big hug.

As they are hugging each other, a familiar voice calls out.

"Hey Lizzy, everything good with the ex?" Max shouts as he starts walking up to her.

Lizzy and Maddie turn, recognizing the voice.

"What are the chances?" Lizzy mumbles under her breath to Maddie as Max approaches them.

Max realizes who Lizzy is hugging as she lets go of her embrace, and he sees Maddie. He sees she is dressed in running clothes, just like when they first met. He wants to retreat, but he knows he can't turn back now and approaches them.

"Hey!" Lizzy says to Max. "The ex is back in jail, thank goodness. Thanks for your help with him."

"Yeah, no one deserves what he did. He can stay there until he learns his lesson." He turns to Maddie. "Funny running into you here again."

"It is," Maddie says, a little shy.

"What are you guys doing here? Looks like you just finished up a run."

"Ah yeah, we were going to grab a quick drink."

"After running?"

"Celebration drink," Lizzy blurts out.

"Oh yeah, what are you celebrating?"

"Umm," Lizzy looks at Maddie.

"Just something I've been working on for a long time that is finally wrapping up," Maddie says. "McKenna is going to join us. What are you doing here?" She asks, trying to change the direction of the conversation.

"Meeting Tyler. We're going to watch the hockey games."

"Oh yeah, who's playing?"

"Your old school, in fact."

"Which one?"

"UMD is playing tonight. If they win, they'll play the University of Michigan in the playoffs. Don't you follow hockey anymore?" Max asks, as if she should know.

"I haven't for a while."

"Why's that?"

"I didn't have a reason to watch anymore, I guess."

Lizzy stands there, not quite sure what to do. "Hey, seems like you have some catching up to do. I need to run to the bathroom. I'll be right back, okay?"

They both look at her and nod their heads yes. As she leaves, they turn back to each other.

"Hey, it's really good to see you. Tell Tyler I say hi," Maddie says, trying to wrap up the conversation.

"Do you want to join us?"

"I don't think that is the best idea."

"Why's that?"

"I don't want to cause any trouble between you and Ashley."

"You won't; it's fine."

"Yeah, she never seems happy when we talk, it's probably better if we just don't," Maddie says, trying to keep the door shut that she just closed.

"Don't you want to talk to me?"

"I can't talk to you. It's not good for me. It takes me a long time to get over our conversations. I can't do it again," Maddie says, trying to protect herself.

"What's that mean? It takes a long time to get over our conversations. What conversations? I've barely talked to you since we graduated."

"Yeah, but when we do, they're epic conversations, aren't they?"

"How so?" Max asks, knowing perfectly well what she means.

"You know how. You tell me you love me. You tell me you want to marry me. Then you ignore me. Then you tell me you should have married me. But it's all talk. It makes me feel crazy. I replay it over and over in my head, like a loop, trying to figure out where it all went wrong. I always come back to the same conclusion. It's just a game to you. You don't care about me."

"I do care about you! I've told you so many times that I love you, and you've never once said it back to me," Max says defensively.

"How can I? You don't let me love you! You open up and then disappear from my world literally for years. How am I supposed to love you if you're always running from me?"

"I'm not running. I'm waiting for you."

"Waiting for me? I have waited my whole life for you. I have spent years in therapy trying to get over you. What do you want from me? All you do is play with my heart," Maddie says, upset. "You and Tyler."

Max says defensively, "What's that mean? I'm not playing with your heart. I've apologized for everything."

"Have you, though? I've spent a lot of time and a lot of money thinking about this. Let's review, shall we? Where should I begin? How about Mexico? You tell me you love me for the first time and then you go and sleep with Kelly," Maddie says, peeling back the years of therapy work she has done.

"I didn't sleep with her!" Max says back, with a confused look on his face.

"Then why were you in her room the next morning, and she had a huge grin on her face?" Maddie yells, hurt and a little surprised.

"After I left you, after you rejected me and told me you didn't believe me that I loved you, I ran into her. We sat up most of the night talking about how to make you believe me. She had a big grin on her face because I confessed how much I loved you," Max says in his defense. "She knew our secret."

"Sure, that's why the next night we slept together, and you never talked to me the rest of the trip," Maddie pushes back.

"We didn't sleep together. I'm pretty sure I'm the only guy who didn't get laid on spring break but spent the night with multiple girls."

"What?!" Maddie demands, now really surprised.

"We made out in the hall, and then those guys helped us back to my hotel room. They pulled out the bed because we were too drunk to do it. They put us in it and left. We started making out again. You took off all your clothes and then started calling me 'Connor' while we were kissing. I'm pretty sure you were blacked out by then. I stopped kissing you, and we both passed out." Max explains.

"We didn't?"

"We didn't."

"Why'd you ignore me then?"

"I was trying to make the rumors die down that anything happened. I know how much you loved Connor, and although I wanted you, I didn't want it that way. You deserved to be happy. I missed my chance. I took you for granted."

"Well, what about that time before we left for college? You played Sammy Kershaw for me, and then asked me if I'd leave Connor for you. I said yes, but then you never asked me too."

"You never said yes. You just wanted me to ask you. You would never have left him. You were too in love."

"You don't know that!"

"Yes, I do."

"How?"

"How about that time I did take a chance, and I was going to drive hours to see you and you told me no?"

"You never came."

"You told me no."

"Your roommate said you were coming. You never showed up."

"We started to, but then I thought then what? You have a boyfriend. You don't want me there. And let's say I got past that hurdle. Then what? We're going to date long distance? I couldn't even keep you when we were nearby. So, we turned around."

"Your roommate said you never made it out of the parking lot. I called to check on you."

"We did. We turned around an hour into the drive."

"Bullshit. It's always about you. Like the time you fucked me on the tracks and then told me you had a girlfriend. Your now wife, I might remind you. I was heartbroken over breaking up with Connor, and you took advantage of it. I never felt so sad in my life. I didn't think I could feel any worse, but you showed me I could. You coaxed me out of my house, you fucked me, and then you acted drunk because you didn't have enough balls to tell me the truth," Maddie says, trying to prove a point.

"I did tell you the truth," Max says, hurt.

"Yeah, you had a girlfriend, and you married her!" Maddie says, equally hurt.

"You told me never to talk to you again."

"I wish you hadn't!"

Max looks like a dagger went through his heart.

"Who does that? I told you how sad I was. You took advantage of that," Maddie says. "You didn't even know the half of it. I wasn't just sad, I was devastated. My grandpa died that week too, and…"

"I didn't take advantage of you," Max says sadly. "Do you really think that? I thought you forgave me."

"I did forgive you, but it doesn't mean that it didn't hurt. If you weren't using me, then why did you do what you did?" Maddie asks, demanding the truth.

"I did miss you. Things weren't going well, and I just wanted to see you. You always made me feel better when we talked—just like old times. I never thought I'd actually get you to come out. I was beyond happy when you said yes. Then you showed up, and the moonlight hit your blonde hair just right, and you looked like an angel, just like the first night I met you. I wasn't thinking. I was just consumed by you. It happened so fast. I didn't know what to think. So, I freaked out and started acting drunk. But you made me tell you, and then you told me never to talk to you again. I've never seen you so angry and hurt. You literally ran away from me, and I didn't know what to do."

"You should have run after me. You should have called me the next day. You should have called me any day after that, and said you were sorry."

"I wanted to..."

"Then why didn't you?"

"I hated myself for what I did to you and what I did to my girlfriend. I hated my dad, and I was afraid I was about to become him. I couldn't run after you because I loved you."

"Is that why you said you had hope when I ran into you at Fletcher's?"

"Yes."

"But you were engaged."

"You never wanted to talk to me again."

"You were engaged, and you were telling me you wanted to marry me someday. Why didn't you end it with her and come after me?"

"Because I saw how bad my dad hurt my mom. I couldn't do that to her. I had just asked her to marry me. Plus, you didn't ever want to hear from me again, remember, especially after you found out I was engaged."

"But that's the thing. You say all these nice things to me and make me let down my guard, and then you hurt me. You say you want me but you never pick me."

"You've never given me the chance."

"Me? Okay, let's talk about our fifteen-year reunion. It was ten years since you told me you hoped to marry me someday. Ten years! I waited for you, and you ignored me. Like I never existed. Like I never mattered. I'm sorry, but you're complaining I never gave you a chance? I waited ten years to be able to get some closure with you, and you went out of your way to ignore me. And on top of it, I've got your buddy chasing me around, saying you really wanted to talk to me that night but you were afraid we'd run off and get married. You never gave me a chance."

"I couldn't talk to you. I wanted to, but he was right. I was afraid I would marry you."

"Well, you could have married me, but you ran away!"

"What?"

"I went to Haskell's right before I was supposed to get married. Apparently, you were toasting me, and then ran out of there when you saw me coming in. The bartender told me."

Max has no words.

"I was ready to get married. I wanted to get married, and then you snuck into my dreams again. The day of my wedding, I couldn't shake the feeling of you. McKenna and Samantha took me to Haskell's to get a drink and calm my nerves. I almost called off my wedding because of you that day."

"Did you call off your wedding, or are you still engaged?" Max asks, looking at her empty ring finger.

"Why did you run from me?" Maddie ignores the question.

"I didn't want to hurt you like I always hurt you, so I left before you could see me."

"But that did hurt me."

"But I didn't mean to; I didn't know you saw me. I was trying not to ruin your wedding day."

"It was ruined anyways…"

"I know, I'm so sorry about your dad."

"What about the reunion? You made me feel like I never existed, never mattered to you."

"I didn't know what to say," Max tries to explain. "We got off to a bad start, and I just didn't know what to do."

"You could have said, 'Hi, how are you doing, Maddie? What's new in the last ten years?' I would have told you my dad died, and you were the one who got me through it. You were the one I dreamt about every night when all I wanted to do was die. You were the one who brought me peace while I slept, so my heart could put itself back together. I was so fragile. You destroyed me—again. You burst the little bubble my brain built to keep me from falling apart as I grieved my dad and had to be strong for everyone else. I needed to share a simple moment with you acknowledging that we had something special, something real, a long time ago, and that memory, that innocence, was what protected me as my life shattered. But instead, you ignored me. You made me question if any of it was ever real or if I was just a naïve little girl you took advantage of when you were bored. You treated me like I never existed and that broke me," Maddie shouts at Max. "You broke the bubble I was living in, and it shattered in on me, and I was already in a million pieces just trying to hold it together."

"I wanted to talk to you so bad. My heart ached for you. I didn't even want to go, but I went to see you. I knew if I talked to you, I would spill my guts. I couldn't. I was married. We just had another failed round of IVF. My marriage was already on the rocks. I couldn't do what my dad did. I couldn't do that to Ashley. But when I looked at you—it all came back to me. Every thought and feeling I ever had about you. It was all there, and it was too much, and we were trapped on an island. I couldn't get away."

"You destroyed me. I grieved the loss of you, and I grieved the loss of my dad, I grieved the loss of…I grieved a lot. It took me so long to put myself back together. I was broken. Broken! I've been doing therapy since my dad died. It has taken me a really long time to process my grief, to let him go. To let you go. To let…never mind. That's what we were going to celebrate today. I finally made a breakthrough—I thought. Just when I am ready to move on with my life, the universe throws you in my path to test me."

Max, scared, has never seen Maddie actually cry over him. He puts his arms around her and just holds her as she lets it out.

When she's done sobbing, she looks up at him and says, "I can't. I just can't talk to you. It's too hard; I have to let you go…"

Lizzy walks up to them at that moment. "Is she okay?"

Max shakes his head no, pulls away from Maddie, and hands her off to Lizzy. He backs away feeling awful about what she just said to him. He stands there for a moment watching her cry on Lizzy's shoulder. He nods to her; Lizzy nods back that she'll take it from here. Max walks away with his head down and goes inside to meet Tyler and tells him what just happened.

"Hey, Chief! Over here," Tyler shouts from a table in the bar.

"Hey!" Max says as he walks up.

"Who ran over your dog?"

"What?"

"You look like someone ran over your dog. What's going on?"

"I just ran into Maddie in the parking lot."

"Oh yeah?"

"It did not go well. I really fucked up."

"What happened?"

"She just let it all out, how much I've hurt her over the years. She told me that she dreamt about me when her dad died."

"What? She dreamt about you, and you hurt her—in her dreams?"

"She said that when I ignored her at the reunion, it made her feel like she never mattered, and it broke the bubble she was living in since her dad died. She's been doing therapy ever since. She came here to celebrate with Lizzy and McKenna—

she said she is finally moving on from me. Then she started sobbing and said she couldn't talk to me."

"Ouch, not the best timing once again. What are you going to do?"

"Nothing. What can I do? It seems like every time I talk to her, I hurt her, or I hurt Ashley." Max pauses. "Tyler, she knew we were at Haskell's the day of her wedding. She almost called it off because of me, and then her dad went to the hospital, and she had to call it off anyway. I broke her heart, and then her dad's heart broke. What if it is all my fault? What if she channeled me not wanting her to get married, and it killed her dad?"

Tyler stares at Max in disbelief. After a moment, he says, "Dude, you didn't kill her dad. None of this is your fault. She loves you, and you love her. You always have, and she clearly always has. You two belong together. It's as simple as that. Go after her."

"But I can't become my dad. I can't forgive him for what he did to my mom."

"So, what are you going to do? Just love Maddie from afar and stay married to Ashley, even though she knows you love Maddie?"

"I'm not sure we are going to stay married, but I am sure I can't leave her for Maddie. I've spent the last fifteen years trying not to be my dad. I can't become him now. I can't do it."

"How's she doing, Ashley?"

"As you can imagine, that bomb you dropped on her didn't feel good. I've been pretty honest with my feelings but have also told her I love her too and am committed to our marriage.

I've made a promise I'll never do what my dad did to my mom, to her."

"What does she think about that?"

"She believes me, but she's not sure it's enough. She can't get past me hiding Maddie for all these years, and not being able to get pregnant isn't helping. I've told her whatever she wants to do, it's up to her. If she wants to stay married, we'll go to counseling; if she wants a divorce, I'll make it easy on her. She doesn't deserve to be unhappy because of me. She's been a good wife. I've tried my best to be a good husband. I've denied the one thing I've always wanted, for her."

"What do you think she will do?"

"We're going to keep trying to make it work while she decides, but if one more thing happens, I'm pretty sure it's over."

"Sorry, buddy."

"I don't know why I still talk to you. You're technically the root cause of all of this."

McKenna pulls up to see Maddie and Lizzy in the parking lot. She is ready to celebrate.

"Hey ladies! What are we celebrating?" McKenna shouts from her minivan.

"Celebration is off," Lizzy says.

"What, I just got here? I got out of my sweatpants for you two." She looks at Maddie. "Have you been crying?"

Maddie nods.

"Sorry, I should have told you not to come. We ran into Max on the way in. My breakthrough was short-lived."

"What happened?"

"I was trying to move on. You know, breakthrough and all. So, I tried to end the conversation, and he invited us to sit with him and Tyler. From there, it just spiraled, and I basically threw every time he hurt me at him."

"I went to the bathroom, and they were fine, and when I came back, she was in tears, and Max looked—well, scared? Hurt, maybe?" Lizzy explains.

"What are you apologizing for, Maddie? That is a breakthrough. You stood up for yourself. You told him how you felt after all these years. That is incredible."

"It doesn't feel that way."

"I think McKenna is right. I've been listening to your stories for years, and you always let him do the talking, and you never tell him what you feel. It was your turn. You needed that for real closure," Lizzy says, agreeing with McKenna.

"You think?" Maddie asks both of them.

"Yes! I know!" McKenna says.

"I agree. We should still celebrate," Lizzy says.

"Okay, but not today. I don't feel like it anymore."

"Okay, how about if we go away this weekend? We can go up to Duluth and get away from here. We've got tickets to the hockey game if UMD wins tonight, which they are expected to. They are playing Michigan if they do. It'll be fun," McKenna says.

"I heard. Okay, that sounds like a good idea," Maddie agrees.

"Bring Jordan. We'll make it a weekend. Lizzy, can you come?" McKenna asks.

"I can't this weekend, but I definitely want to celebrate. How about when you get back?" Lizzy suggests.

"Okay. Sounds like a plan. But not here!" Maddie says.

They all laugh.

♦ ♦ ♦

That night, Maddie has a dream. Maddie finds herself sitting across from Max on a couch. No one is around. Maddie sits up straight, looking directly into his eyes. Max moves a little closer. Maddie doesn't flinch. Then he leans in and gently presses his closed lips on hers. They linger for a moment, and then Maddie leans forward into the kiss, pressing her closed lips firmer against his. They slowly start to move their lips in a sweet kiss, like their very first one. Gradually, the kiss becomes more passionate, faster, and more intense. Maddie feels the desire growing inside of her, and when she can't contain it anymore, she forcefully grabs a handful of Max's shirt at his chest and pulls him closer to her, signaling to Max she wants more.

Before anything more can happen, Maddie senses they are no longer alone. She breaks from the kiss and turns her head, looking back over her right shoulder, seeing Jordan staring at her in shock. In a split second, the desire drains from her, and regret takes its place. She watches as the life they built together shatters in front of her as his shock melts into hurt, then hate.

She knows the damage is done, and her brain can't come up with a reason to explain it away. The decision to get up to try to salvage her relationship or go back to kissing Max flashes across her mind. Before she decides, she wakes up.

Maddie reaches out and touches Jordan, making sure he is still there. He is. Relieved, the guilt of the dream sets in, and she thanks God silently for the wonderful man lying next to her. Then she thinks, *Please make these dreams stop. Why are they starting again? I thought we were past this?*

CHAPTER 39

Maddie and Jordan join McKenna and Tommy for a weekend away in Duluth. They all settle into their seats just before the hockey lineup is announced. Each player's name is called, and they skate to the center line, their picture flashing on the scoreboard.

Maddie and McKenna are chatting through the lineup glancing at the pictures as they are presented. When number eighteen of the Michigan team is called and his picture flashes on the board, it stops McKenna in midsentence.

"Then we were headed—" McKenna stops what she is saying. "Maddie, look at him!" McKenna points to the board. Maddie looks up just as the picture drops from the screen.

"What?"

"I swear I just saw Max on the scoreboard."

"Oh God, please don't let him be here," Maddie says, glancing around.

"No, I mean college-age Max. It's what he looked like when we were freshmen."

"What are you talking about, McKenna?"

"Number eighteen on Michigan's team, spitting image of him. Same piercing blue eyes."

"I'm sure you're just seeing things."

"Yeah, you're right, right?" McKenna asks, trying to picture it in her mind again. The two go back to chatting. Jordan and Tommy were talking too and didn't pay attention to the board.

During the second period, number eighteen scores a goal against UMD. The announcer says, "Scoring for Michigan is number eighteen, Cody Banshee." His picture flashes on the scoreboard again next to his stats as "Sweet Child O'Mine" blasts from the speakers. McKenna makes a point to get a good look. When she sees the picture again, she grabs Maddie's arm and says, "See!" pointing at the board with her other arm. "Look at that black hair and those eyes. He's even the same height."

Tommy says, "Holy crap, that looks like Chief," and snaps a photo of the board.

"Who's Chief?" Jordan asks.

Tommy freezes for a second, looking at the girls. McKenna shakes her head no.

"A guy I played hockey with. The girls graduated with him," Tommy explains.

"Think that's his kid?" Jordan asks.

"Doubt it, different last names. Must be a nephew or something," Tommy says.

"Did Max have relatives in Michigan?" McKenna says, turning to Maddie.

"How would I know?" Maddie says defensively. "Just because I lived in Ann Arbor doesn't mean I know everyone there."

"It's just uncanny how much they look alike. If I didn't know better, I'd swear that is his kid," Tommy says again, looking at the picture.

Maddie stares straight ahead, watching the game. McKenna watches Maddie, unfazed. McKenna starts counting on her fingers, doing the math. She assumes number eighteen is a freshman, which means he would have been born their freshman or sophomore year of college.

"Let's get a drink, Maddie. Guys, you want anything?" McKenna asks, standing up.

"I'm good," Maddie says, remaining in her seat.

"Come with me anyway," McKenna urges her.

Maddie looks up at McKenna and hesitates for a second before saying, "Yeah, sure, whatever." She gets up and follows McKenna up the stairs to the concourse. They walk a bit in silence until McKenna can't stand it anymore.

"What's going on, Maddie?" McKenna asks accusingly.

"We're getting drinks," Maddie says, pretending she doesn't understand what McKenna means.

"You know what I mean," McKenna says firmly. "We just saw a picture of Max on the scoreboard and nothing? You don't have a single thought, reaction, gasp, anything?"

"I don't know the kid. Why would I have any sort of reaction? I mean, I'm glad he scored, but other than that?"

"What aren't you telling me? That kid would have been born the year you moved to Michigan."

"Nothing. What do you think there is to tell? That I moved to Michigan and had Max's baby and forgot to tell you?"

"Maddie, Max has a kid, playing hockey, at this game, and you have no thoughts on that?"

"I mean, yeah, there is a striking resemblance; it's a little creepy. Maybe he knocked a girl up while at hockey camp. I don't know. Frankly, I don't want to think about it. It's too painful. But like Tommy said, different last names. They are probably related somehow, a relative or something."

"If you say so," McKenna says, backing down. "Aren't you a tad bit curious?"

"Honestly, it scares me," Maddie says. "I had a really bad dream last night that Max came between Jordan and me. I don't want to think about him. Let's just grab drinks and drop it."

"Okay," McKenna says, letting it drop.

♦ ♦ ♦

Tyler and Max are sitting at the bar having drinks, the game is on in the background. Max's phone rings.

"You got a relative playing for MI tonight?" his buddy asks.

"No, why?"

"Kid just scored that looks just like you. Number eighteen, are you watching?"

"Must be a good-looking kid. I'll keep an eye out."

"Don't flatter yourself," his buddy says as he clicks off.

Max doesn't think much of it but pays a little more attention to the game. He gets a couple more calls asking the same thing.

Tyler asks, "Everything okay?"

"Yeah, I keep getting calls from friends that some kid on the Michigan team looks just like me," Max says, thinking that is strange.

"Hey, can you put the hockey game on that TV so we can see it better?" Tyler asks the bartender.

The bartender puts the game on the TV closest to them. They watch for a bit but can't really tell what the players look like under their helmets. The game goes into the third period tied up. Tyler and Max order another round of drinks and have almost forgotten about the kid until he scores the game-winning goal with seconds left. The buzzer sounds, and the game is over. The announcers are going wild.

"Number eighteen, Cody Banshee with the game-winning goal for Michigan!" the announcer shouts. "This kid just came out of nowhere. He's a walk-on freshman for Michigan with two goals in tonight's game. Watch out for this kid. He's going to sneak up on you."

The TV replays the game-winning goal a couple of times and then flashes Cody's picture on the screen. The picture looks exactly like Max when he was in college. It could have been his hockey picture.

Tyler looks at Max, "You forget to tell me something?"

"No!" Max says in disbelief.

"He looks exactly like you. I mean exactly."

"I know, good-looking kid," Max jokes again, still not believing what he is looking at.

"Do you know him? Relative, I hope?"

"Never seen or heard of him before."

The bartender overhears their conversation, "Looks like you've got a doppelgänger."

"It's that or a kid I don't know about," Max says with a laugh, trying to make light of the situation.

Max's phone rings again. He ignores it. More friends are calling asking about the kid. Max thinks, *Is everyone watching this game tonight?* Then he gets a call from his dad and ignores it.

His dad leaves a message, "Looks like you did the one thing I told you not to do, son. At least he was good enough to play for Michigan. Not like you."

Max shoves his phone back in his pocket after listening to his messages, and orders a shot of whiskey.

Tyler and Max stay at the bar after the game and meet some of their other friends. All the wives are out together tonight and are going to meet up with them later. Max is dreading seeing Ashley because it's going to cause more questions and more problems. Max orders the crew a round of shots to take his mind off it.

Later that night, Samantha shows up. She's in town for her mom's birthday. She didn't tell anyone she was coming to town as it was a quick in-and-out trip.

"Hey, Chief, what are you doing?" Samantha asks, walking up to the bar.

"Just having a good time, you?" Max says.

"Have you been sitting at the bar all night?"

"I have, watched some hockey too."

Samantha can tell he is very drunk. Max looks around again and then asks, "Where is she?"

"Where's who, Max? Your wife?" Samantha knows exactly who he's asking about.

"No, not her. She's over there," Max points toward a bunch of wives at a table.

"Then who are you asking about?" Samantha makes him say it.

"Maddie. Where is Maddie?" Max demands.

"I think she's in Duluth this weekend for the hockey game," Samantha says and doesn't give him any more explanation.

"Oh," Max says, defeated. He's trying hard to let her go, but it isn't working.

"How much have you had to drink tonight?"

"A lot!"

"Any reason why?"

"That stupid number eighteen looks like me."

Samantha saw the game and knows what he is talking about.

"Chieeeefffff!" yells a drunk guy at the bar. "Shots?"

Max looks at Samantha, "Come have one with us for old time's sake," he says. Then he walks over to the guy who called his name. Samantha follows him.

After finishing their shots, the drunk guy says to Max, "Everyone wants to know if that kid from Michigan is yours. Is he? He looks just like you."

"No, he's not mine. He's my dopple, dopplegerder, ganger...how do you say it, Sam?"

"You mean doppelgänger?"

"Yeah, that. He's my doppelgänger. Right, Sam, I don't have a kid I don't know about. I would know if I had a kid?"

"You would think unless you knocked someone up that you don't know about."

"You spent a lot of time in Michigan, didn't you, playing hockey? Kid's a pretty good hockey player like you from what I saw."

"He's better than me. You know, I was supposed to play for Michigan until my accident."

The drunk guy interrupts, "Did you get a lot of action in Michigan?"

Max laughs, "Only on the ice, big guy. Only on the ice."

"So, no chance you knocked a girl up in Michigan a couple of decades ago?" the drunk guy asks again.

"Nope, never slept with a girl in Michigan. There was only one girl for me, and she was in Minnesota."

"That's right," Ashley says as she walks up to the bar to check on Max. "I scooped him up, and I can tell you for certain he hasn't been back to Michigan since his accident, and we all know I haven't had a kid."

"You sure you didn't sneak off to Michigan behind your lovely wife's back for a one-night stand? You know it is totally possible he could be yours if you did," the drunk argues.

"Like I said, he hasn't been back to Michigan since his accident, so I don't know how his swimmers would have got there without him," his wife says as simple as possible to the drunk guy to put the question to bed.

Samantha watches Max's face while Ashley intercepts the line of questioning from the drunk. She can tell Max is pondering how that could happen without his knowledge. In a moment of clarity, his brain makes the connection how: Maddie transferred to Michigan after freshman year.

Max looks at Samantha, "It's not possible?"

Samantha doesn't say a word.

"What?" Ashley says, turning toward her husband.

"What?" Max says back.

"You said it's not possible," Ashley repeats.

"Right, it's not possible," Max repeats more confidently. "I wasn't in Michigan, like you said. Doppelgänger. Can I get another shot?"

"No, let's get you home. You've had enough," Ashley says.

"Yeah, Max, you should probably go home," Samantha says, supporting Ashley.

"It's not possible," Max says to Samantha before getting up and putting his arm around his wife. "It's not possible."

♦ ♦ ♦

The next day, after the game, Max is very hungover.

"How are you feeling today?" Ashley asks Max.

"Terrible, what time did we come home?" Max asks.

"About three shots later than we should have. You were hitting it pretty hard last night."

"Feels like it," Max says, trying to recall the end of the night.

"Glad that's over."

"What do you mean?"

"All those questions about that Cody kid last night were getting old. That's all anyone wanted to know last night. I don't know how many people I had to tell you haven't been back to Michigan since the accident."

Max starts to recall the conversation in his mind. He remembers making the connection between Maddie moving to Michigan and their last night together on the tracks.

"Yeah, thanks for doing that. That was really cool of you."

"He does look a lot like you, though," Ashley says, handing him a glass of water and a couple of aspirin. "Take this, should help."

"Thanks," Max says, popping them in his mouth. "Have you looked him up?"

"Of course. Did you know in Ireland a Banshee means death is coming?"

"That's creepy. Does his dad look like me?"

"Don't know. He's adopted. Maybe your dad has a secret love child you don't know about, and he's your brother."

Max laughs. "I wouldn't put it past him. Probably was cheating on my mom while I was in the hospital in Michigan."

Ashley does the math quickly. "No, that's too early. It would have had to be our freshman year of college. But that makes sense, it's the year your parents split, right?"

"You know his birthday?" Max asks.

"Yeah, he was born January 18, 1996. Nine months before that would be April-ish, which is a couple of months after we met."

"Yeah, and right around the time I was moving my mom out of the house," Max says, thinking again about the night he and Maddie met up on the tracks.

"You don't think he really did, do you?" Ashley asks.

"What?" Max asks, not paying attention.

"Your dad? Have a secret kid we don't know about?" Ashley repeats.

"When you say it like that, it sounds like a talk show. Nah. I'm sure we're not related. He's just my doppelgänger. I need some breakfast," Max says, changing the subject.

As Max recovers from his hangover, he spends time thinking about Cody. He tries to figure out how he might be related, thinking about his cousins and where they are all now. He asks his sister if she knows if any of them spent time in Michigan. His sister says she's already gone down that path because she's getting the questions too.

Ashley takes note of how much time he is spending thinking about the kid and wonders why. Later that night, she brings it up again.

"You've been a little obsessed with Cody today."

"Oh, me? No, just killing time as I nurse this hangover."

"Why were you drinking so much last night?"

"I just got caught up in the game."

"Is that all?"

"Yeah, just having a good time with the guys. Did you have a good time with the wives?"

"Yeah, it was nice, except for that part about people asking if you have a kid. That hurt a little. You sure it's not possible he's yours? I'm not sure I could handle you having a kid after us not being able to have kids."

"It's just not possible," Max says, wanting wholeheartedly for that to be true. "I'll ask my dad if he knows anything."

"But you haven't talked to him in years," Ashley says.

"I've got his number. I'll call him," Max says. "Maybe we can get some closure."

Later that night, Max calls his dad against his better judgment.

"What were you trying to say to me with that message last night?" Max asks his dad when he answers.

"It looks like you've got a kid playing hockey where you should have played. Pretty straightforward, isn't it?"

"Funny. I thought maybe he was yours."

"I take responsibility for my mistakes."

"Like you did with the accident?"

His dad doesn't respond. Max thinks it doesn't matter; he got his answer, and hangs up.

Max walks into the living room where Ashley is sitting.

"It's not my dad's," he says.

She looks at him and says, "Are you sure it's not possible?"

"It can't be possible," he says, with a question in his voice.

"Max, be honest with me. When was the last time you were with Maddie?"

Max thinks, takes a deep breath, and says, "About nine months before that kid was born."

"Do you think?"

Max shuts his eyes and sees the kid in his mind. He shakes his head no. "It's not possible," he says again.

"You know we can't survive this?"

"I know. I'm sorry. I didn't know. I don't know." Max says, unsure of what he is saying.

"But you do. You just have to admit it."

"It's not possible…"

"Congratulations, Max. You're a dad. And you did what your dad couldn't do. You've got a kid playing college hockey," Ashley says as she gets up and walks away, tears streaming down her face.

Max doesn't go after her. He knows it is over, and there is nothing he can say to fix it.

♦ ♦ ♦

Samantha calls Maddie from the airport that morning. "Did you have fun at the game?"

"Yeah, it was fun. Sorry, I missed you. When are you coming back again?"

"Not sure. You should come for a visit."

"I would love that. Wouldn't mind getting away for a bit."

"Like you did back in college?"

"What do you mean?"

"When you visited me in Chicago?"

"Sure?"

"I saw the hockey game last night."

"Okay?"

"I saw him. Everyone did!"

"Who?"

"Number eighteen"

"Not you, too!"

"I saw Max last night at the bar. He saw the game."

"Doesn't surprise me."

"And?"

"And what?"

"Maddie, I was there. I know your secret."

"Are you implying I have a secret kid?"

"Yes."

"Do you really think I'd keep that from you?"

"No, but you did move to Michigan, and none of us saw you for a year."

"Let it go. McKenna already grilled me."

"The whole bar grilled Max."

"Glad I wasn't there for that. How'd he handle it?"

"He thinks he has a doppelgänger."

"He does."

"Right up until a drunk guy asked him if he had a one-night stand with anyone in Michigan."

"Who asks that?"

"I saw the look on his face when that thought clicked. He thinks you had a kid."

"Are you serious? Oh God."

"The math works out. Thought you should know."

"Thanks for the heads-up. You didn't say anything did you?"

"Your secret is safe with me."

Before Maddie goes to bed that night, she writes in her notepad:

How can I let you go when you were never mine? How can I say goodbye when you won't say hello? How do I find peace in sleep when you haunt my dreams? How do I wait patiently when I know you're not coming?

When she's done, she flips through her notepad and looks at the pages upon pages of notes, dreams, thoughts, and poems she's written. She thinks Jordan was right. Writing has really helped her.

Part 4

Memory Plays With The Heart

CHAPTER 40

The next day, Jordan asks Maddie if she thinks they are ever going to get married.

"I guess I haven't really thought about it," Maddie says.

"Do you want to get married?"

"Well yeah, of course."

"To me?"

"Why would you ask that?"

"I didn't mean to, but I found your notepad. I was looking for something and there it was. I didn't read it, but I did see the top page."

Maddie tries to think about the last thing she wrote. "And?"

"It just seems there might be someone else on your mind. I'm not sure if that was about your dad or about someone else."

"Does it matter? It's just where I write what comes to mind, like you said," Maddie says, not hiding or denying anything.

"Do you love me?"

"Of course, I do. I'll marry you right now if you want."

"Is that what you want?"

"I just said I would."

"I know, but is that what you want? If that is really what you wanted, why haven't we got married yet?"

"You know why, Jordan. I just couldn't after my dad. I've been dealing with that."

"It's been years, Maddie. I've been patient with you. I get it. We're not having kids, so I'm not in a rush. It just seems like you're waiting for something. Waiting for something that isn't coming. Then I see your note, and it kind of confirms it."

"What do you think I am waiting for?"

"I don't know, but it's not me. Maddie, I love you, but you have to be honest with me and yourself."

"Okay."

"Okay, what?"

"Okay, I'll be honest with you. I just need a little more time to work things out in my head so I can be honest with myself."

"Okay, but it needs to be soon. I need to know if we are moving forward or not. Deal?" Jordan says as though he's negotiating a contract.

"Deal," Maddie says like she is too.

Jordan kisses her on the forehead and walks out of the room. Maddie lets out a big exhale and thinks, *I guess it is finally time.* Maddie changes into her running clothes. She walks into the living room and kisses Jordan on the cheek. "I'm going for a long run. Clear my head. Okay?"

"Okay, I'll be here," Jordan says and kisses her cheek softly goodbye. "I love you."

"I love you too," Maddie says as she walks out the front door. She looks both ways down the road, not knowing which way she will go, and slips on her headphones. "Hells Bells" plays as she starts running. She runs a mile, then another, then another. She's not paying attention to where she is running. After six miles, she finds herself running through her parent's neighborhood, and then, on a familiar path. She cuts through the woods and across the railroad tracks and ends up in Max's old neighborhood. She turns and runs to the church.

She is exhausted when she gets there and plops down on the hill. The one where she and Max used to spend many afternoons. The second she stops moving, tears start to stream down her face. She lets them go until she is all out of tears.

Maddie managed not to think while she was running, but sitting on the hill now, it all comes flooding back to her. "Be honest," she says aloud. "Be honest?" she says again. "How can I be honest when I don't know the truth?"

She thinks about Max while she plucks grass out of the ground where she is sitting. She thinks, *Did he really love me? Could we have had a future together? Do I tell him about being pregnant back in college? What about Jordan? He's been so good to me, but he seems like he already knows the truth. He didn't even have any emotion over it. It was as if he needed to know if he should file the marriage license or not, as if it was a fact, not a major life decision.* "Be honest," Maddie says again. "Okay, if I am honest, I know I can be happy with Jordan. He's a good partner. But if I am really honest…" she can't bring herself to say it. She tries again, "But if I am really honest, I could wait the rest of my life for Max and not regret a day." Maddie lets out a big long, "Fuck!" Then she yells, "Let me go, Max. Let me go!"

Maddie takes a deep breath and releases a long exhale. She knows what she has to do. She's known for a long time but hasn't wanted to admit it. Maddie gets up and brushes herself off. She takes a last look around and laughs inside, remembering the time the pastor caught them there. She brushed herself off and raced home that day, she fondly remembers. She presses play and hears "Edge of Seventeen" start as she jogs across the parking lot and cuts to the street. While running away, she turns her head and looks back one last time. Just then, she sees a police car driving in. She smiles and thinks about the time they got caught by the cop. Then she sees the cop get out and sit where she was just sitting and she realizes who it is.

Maddie keeps running and looks back again. Max is looking at her. She can't tell if he knows it is her. Then she trips on the cement that has heaved up from the winter's freeze and thaw. She goes down hard, putting her hands out as she falls, just like in her dream. Only this time, she doesn't wake up from a dream. She hits her head hard on the sidewalk.

♦ ♦ ♦

Max drives, thinking about Maddie and the possibility that she may have had his baby. He doesn't know where to go either and finds himself driving to the church. His marriage ended last night, and today, he lets himself go down memory lane, thinking about their last night together on the tracks.

He parks and gets out of his police car and sits on the hill where Maddie had just been. He notices a bunch of grass has been pulled and left on the ground. He wonders for a second and looks around to see if anyone else is there. He sees a woman across the parking lot running away from the church. She looks back for a second and then turns. When she does, he sees her long blonde ponytail. *Couldn't be,* he thinks to himself. *What are the odds?* Then she turns again, and he thinks, *Could it be?* As the thought crosses his mind, he sees her fall. She doesn't move or make a sound. He gets up and sprints toward her.

Before he gets to her, Maddie gets up and stumbles with her first few steps. She turns, sees Max running toward her, and instinctively runs away from him. Still shaken from the fall, she stumbles into the street.

"Maddie, stop!" Max shouts as she runs into the intersection.

Maddie looks back at him. They lock eyes and she slows down but doesn't stop. On her next step, she's clipped by a car. Her body is thrown across the intersection, and she violently lands on the curb. The car doesn't stop.

As Max gets closer, he can see the pool of blood forming around her head. She's still not moving. He clicks the radio on his shoulder and calls for an ambulance. In the distance, sirens kick on, and cars start to pull over on the street by them.

"Maddie! Maddie, can you hear me?" Max shouts as he drops down onto his knees next to her. He puts two fingers on her throat, looking for a pulse. There is a faint one.

"Maddie! Maddie, wake up! I'm here," Max shouts at her. He wants to shake her, but he knows he can't move her. He gently puts his hand on her to let her know he's there and to check for breathing.

Maddie's eyes begin to flutter open.

"Maddie, stay with me. Don't go. You have to stay with me."

Maddie fades in and out, blood streaming down her face.

"You're going to be okay. Stay with me!"

Maddie's eyes slowly open. Max stops shouting. He lays down on the ground, placing his face in front of hers. He slides his hand from her back to her face, brushing her blood-stained blonde hair out of her eyes. As he does, their eyes lock in a stare just as they used to do. A small smile washes over Maddie's face, and Max smiles back, getting lost in the delicate moment.

"Help is on the way. Can you hear the sirens? Those are for you. You just have to stay with me, okay? Can you do that? Can you stay with me?" Max pleads with her, looking for a response.

Maddie smiles really big, like when they first met. "I've waited my whole life for you to stop me from running away," Maddie says faintly. "You never chase after me. You always let me go."

Max stares at her in silence, not knowing what to say. He knows it is true. Then a look of sadness comes over Maddie's face, and she says, "I have to go. My dad is waiting for me."

"No, no, no, Maddie. Stay with me," Max pleads.

"My dad needs me to come home," Maddie says as she starts to fade.

"Maddie, your dad can wait. I need you! Stay with me. You belong with me."

"I have to do what my dad says. I miss him so much."

"No, Maddie! Stay with me."

"I have to go."

"I love you, Maddie. Don't leave me. You can't leave me!"

"I love you."

Max doesn't know if she is talking to him or her dad. "Maddie! Please, stay with me, Maddie. I can't lose you again. Stay with me!"

"Dad?"

"No, Maddie, it's me, Max."

"Did you want to be a dad?"

"Yeah, Maddie, very much. Did you want to be a mom?" Max says, trying to keep her talking.

"Yes," Maddie says faintly.

Max hesitates before saying, "Maddie, did we have a baby?"

"Yes," Maddie says. A moment later, she says really softly, "Twins."

"Twins?" Max repeats, not sure he heard her clearly.

"They tried to kill me," Maddie says as her eyes close.

"Wake up, Maddie," Max shouts. "Tell me what happened, Maddie."

"I lost everything."

"Maddie, stay with me."

"A part of me died that day," Maddie says, barely conscious. "There he is. I can see him. He's with my dad."

"Maddie, look at me. Don't look at them," Max tries to get her to open her eyes. "Maddie, look at me!"

"I have to go." Maddie pauses, out of energy.

"I love you, Maddie! Don't leave me. You can't leave me!"

Maddie turns her head away from Max. "I love you," she says faintly.

Max doesn't know if she is talking to him or to her dad.

"Maddie! Please, stay with me, Maddie. I can't lose you again. Stay with me!"

Maddie draws a deep breath and, as she lets it out, she quietly says, "Find me in my dreams."

Her body slumps heavily in his hands. "Maddie!" Maddie, no, you have to stay with me! Don't go!"

Maddie doesn't move.

"Maddie!" Max's heart shatters.

CHAPTER 41

Max debated whether he should go to Maddie's funeral, not sure he could handle it. He blames himself for chasing Maddie. If he hadn't, would she be alive today? He can't shake her words. All she ever wanted was for him to chase after her. He did, and it killed her. No matter what he did, he always ended up hurting her. This time he can't take it back.

He waits until the funeral starts and slips into the back so no one sees him. McKenna is giving a eulogy and spots him. She gives him a nod when she's done. After the service is over, she sees him slipping out. She breaks from the guests, runs up to him, catching him in the parking lot.

"Max! Wait!" McKenna shouts after him.

He turns, his eyes filled with tears.

"I have something for you. I was hoping you'd come."

"For me? What?"

"She wrote to you."

"To me?"

"She had a lot of things she wanted to say to you but couldn't."

"Why couldn't she say them to me?"

"She never stopped dreaming about you. She tried but couldn't. She said it was like you had a whole life together in her dreams. She always wondered if you were actually thinking the things she was dreaming or if it was just her mind playing tricks on her. So, she captured them on paper in case she ever got the chance to ask you. You'll have to let me know."

"How much did she write?"

"Hundreds of pages. It's full," McKenna shares as she hands him the notebook.

Max takes it and looks at her in disbelief.

"She would have loved you so deeply if you had let her. You know she died at your church."

"I know. I was there. She gave me a big smile before she closed her eyes and it felt like the first time I met her. I finally asked her to stay, but her dad was calling her home," Max says, choking back tears.

McKenna had no idea he was the cop who found her. She looks at Max with heartbreak as tears flow down both their faces.

Later, Max drives to their church, parks, and grabs the notebook from the passenger seat. He walks up to a new bench on their hill. He sits down under the tree, opens the notebook, takes a deep breath, and begins.

As he's reading, he hears a voice. He looks up and sees Maddie dressed in running clothes like the ones she wore the first day she ran to his house. "Do you like it? It's a memorial bench. Read the plaque. I wrote it for you."

Max reads the inscription:

Dream tethers souls while circumstance conspires to part

And the universe waits patiently, while memory plays with the heart

"That's beautiful, Maddie."

"I waited as long as I could in this life. You have to find me in the next one and never let me go, okay?"

"But we're together now."

"For a moment. Read to me."

Max reads from her letters, *"What could have been haunts my dreams, staying with me in the day and eluding me in reality. So, I run from you. Your memory clings to my mind and I can't escape. No matter how fast I run or how many miles I put between us, thoughts of you tap me on my shoulder and catch me by surprise. Today, I miss you, and tomorrow I will too. I'll miss you until the day I die."*

"Do you like it?"

"Yes, Maddie, but you're not dead. It's time to stop running and come back to me."

"I'm sorry, Max. I had to go."

"No, Maddie, it's time to be with me," Max says, reaching for her hand.

"I told you, find me in my dreams."

"I know, Maddie. I'm here. I'm here in your dreams. I came to wake you up so we could be together. It's time to wake up. Wake up, Maddie. You have to wake up!" Max says, squeezing her hand tightly in his.

CHAPTER 42

Maddie squeezes Max's hand back.

"She squeezed my hand," Max says. "Maddie, wake up! I'm here Maddie!"

Samantha, McKenna, and Tommy gather around Maddie and say, "Maddie, we're here too! Maddie, wake up!"

"I'll get the doctor," Samantha says as she leaves the hospital room.

Max strokes her forehead, brushing her hair out of her face. "Maddie, please open your eyes."

Maddie's eyes start to flutter open. She sees Max. Then they close again.

"Stay with me Maddie. Open your eyes. Look at me!"

Maddie tries to open her eyes again. She sees Max. Max smiles at her. Slowly, a smile comes across her face. Max keeps smiling, not breaking his stare, not wanting to lose her again.

"Maddie, I'm here. It's time for you to wake up and be with me. It's time for us to be together. But you have to wake up, okay?"

"Okay," Maddie says weakly.

"Maddie, I'm here too," McKenna says. "It's time to wake up."

"Where are we?" Maddie asks.

"You're in the hospital, in Chicago. You had emergency surgery, and there were some complications," McKenna says. "Samantha went to get your doctor."

"Samantha married the doctor," Maddie says.

Samantha laughs as she walks into the room with Maddie's doctor and Griffith, whom they met at the club.

"Not yet, Maddie. I thought I told you to keep that a secret," Samantha says, blushing a little in front of Griffith.

Maddie's eyes open. She looks around the room, still unsure of what is happening. She sees Samantha, McKenna, Tommy, and Max.

"I don't understand. What's happening?"

"You came to visit me in Chicago. We went out to the clubs last night, and you got really sick. Griffith took us to the ER because he thought you might be miscarrying."

"Miscarrying? Like a baby?" Maddie asks, looking at the doctor.

"Yes, Maddie. Do you remember talking to me? You were pregnant with twins, but one was ectopic and caused your fallopian tube to rupture," the doctor explains. "You lost the babies."

"No, I had Cody. Cody is all grown up now. You saw him, McKenna, at the hockey game, remember?"

"I'm sorry, Maddie. We did save the baby with your first surgery. But there were complications while you were in recovery. You ended up losing your second baby too. We almost lost you."

"What do you mean, 'lost me'? It's been decades since I've been here. Why am I here? Why are we all here? How do you look so young?"

"I called McKenna when you went into surgery so she could get a hold of your parents and let them know what was happening," Samantha explains.

"When Sam told me what was happening, I called your parents. Your dad is making his way back to the states and then he and your mom are coming straight here to see you."

"My dad died. His heart stopped when they gave him morphine."

"Actually, you almost died when we gave you morphine," the doctor says. "You were recovering from surgery, and we gave you some for your pain, and you had a severe reaction. You stopped breathing and then your heart stopped, and we almost didn't get you back. Eventually, we were able to revive you, but the shock to your body was too much. We had to do another surgery for your heart. You lost the second baby during it. I'm sorry."

"My dad is alive?" Maddie asks.

"Yes, Maddie, your dad is alive and on his way back from Germany. He's been calling and checking on you every time he switches flights," McKenna says.

Maddie starts crying. "Oh, thank God! It felt so real. I wanted it to be a dream so badly, but I was at his funeral and was completely devastated. The only thing that made me feel better was…"

Maddie looks at Max. "You. It was you."

Max smiles at Maddie.

"Why are you here?"

"McKenna called me and told me what happened. I hopped in my Bronco the second I heard, raced to Duluth to get her and Tommy, and we drove through the night to be here. We were here when you were waking up from your first surgery."

"But you're married."

Max lets out a nervous laugh. "I'm not married, Maddie."

"I met her. You married your girlfriend you had when we… you know."

"Actually, I went back to school, told her what happened between us, and broke it off. It wasn't fair to her or to you. I've been trying to figure out what I could possibly say or do so you'd talk to me again. I'm so sorry. I should have chased after you that night and told you."

"Told me what?"

"Told you that I love you. That I've loved you since the first day we met. That a day doesn't go by that you don't cross my mind."

"Then why didn't you?"

"Because I didn't think I deserved you. You're this bright cheery light, and whenever we are together, I feel like I put that light out in you. I don't know how not to hurt you. I mean, look at where you are—because of me."

"Why because of you?"

"Because we got pregnant that night on the tracks, and here you are in the hospital because of me. I'm always hurting you, and I never mean to."

"You only hurt me when you're not with me. But I had the baby. He plays hockey at Michigan. Just like you were going to do. You'd be so proud of him."

"Maddie," the doctor interrupts. "You're on a lot of pain meds, you're coming off of anesthesia, and for a period of time you weren't getting any oxygen to the brain. I imagine you've had some pretty intense dreams. It might take a while for your brain to sort it out, but you've only been here for twenty-four hours. It hasn't been twenty years."

Maddie looks at her hands. Then she looks around at her friends. Studies their faces.

"So, you two didn't get married?" Maddie asks as she points at Griffith and Sam.

"Nope, we just met last night. He may have saved your life, so I'd consider going on a date with him, but marriage is out of the question - right now."

Looking at McKenna and Tommy, "And you two? Are you married? Did you have Walter yet?"

"Not yet. We have to graduate college first. But I like the name Walter."

"And my dad, is he really alive?"

"Yes, Maddie. He's coming home for you now. He knows you need him. He said everyone else can wait," McKenna says.

"And I just got to Chicago?"

"Yes," Sam says.

"And I was pregnant with twins, but now I am not?"

"Yes," the doctor says.

"And they were yours?"

Max nods his head yes.

"And you drove through the night to be with me?"

Max nods his head yes again.

"Why?"

"Because it's you, Maddie. It's always been you."

"But it hasn't always been me. In fact, it's never been me. Why now?"

"Maddie, you don't have to believe me. I haven't done a great job of showing you how much I care for you. But I can tell you, without a doubt, I don't want to spend another day without you in my life. I can't lose you again."

"When did you lose me before? You mean because I'm with Jordan now?"

"Who's Jordan? You mean your nurse Jordan?" McKenna asks.

Maddie looks at the nurse in the room. He looks just like her fiancé, Jordan. He waves, "Hi, I'm Jordan."

"So, I'm guessing were not engaged?"

"I'm afraid not, but you've been a great patient right up until you crashed on me."

"Maddie, we got here right as that was happening. I was by your side when your heart stopped. Mine stopped too in that moment. When they got you back, I knew I had to be brave for once in my life," Max continues.

"What does that mean?"

"That means, I haven't been brave enough to tell you, or anyone else, how much I love you and how much I want to be with you. So, here I am, telling you now. I want to be with you, and only you, from this day forward."

"Does that mean you finally want to be my boyfriend?"

"Not exactly."

"What?! Are you serious?" McKenna demands.

"Yes," Max answers McKenna. Then to Maddie he says, "I don't want to be your boyfriend. I want to be your everything. I don't want to be scared to love you out loud anymore. And I don't ever want you to run away from me again."

Max takes Maddie's hand, gets down on one knee, and pulls out a promise ring, "Maddie, will you stop running from me? It's time to come on home and eat onion rings."

"Dude, when did you have time to get a ring?" Tommy asks.

McKenna elbows Tommy in the ribs, "Don't spoil this."

"It was my grandma's. She and my grandpa loved each other very much. My mom gave it to me during spring break when I was home helping her move. I told her about you. About us. She saw how upset I was after you ran away from me, Maddie. She told me to stop being scared to love you just because her and my dad didn't work out. We had a long talk about how their marriage was one of obligation, nothing more. She told me that I deserved better. That I deserved you, if you could forgive me. So, can you forgive me? I promise to try to get it right this time."

"I always forgive you, Max."

"So, will you promise to never run away from me again? I know I won't get everything right, but I promise to at least tell you what's going on in my head."

"This is so overwhelming. I mean, I swear I just lived the last twenty years. During those twenty years, I drove Sam and McKenna nuts waiting for you, dreaming of you, and trying to figure out why we couldn't be together. I still don't know why we didn't work out before. I only know what Tyler told me. I expect you'll tell me I dreamt that too."

"What did Tyler tell you?"

"That your dad wouldn't let you date and that he'd probably kill you if he found out about me."

"Yeah, well, your dreams got that part right. My dad blamed my mom for ending his hockey career and forced me to make his dreams come true. That all ended when he crashed the car on the way home from Michigan. He almost killed me. Do you know why we crashed?"

Maddie shakes her head no.

"We were fighting about me going to Juniors because I didn't want to leave before I fixed things with you. He wasn't paying attention to the road because he was too busy bullying my mom. Then we crashed, and he ended my hockey career. When Michigan told me they didn't want me anymore, I figured you wouldn't want me either."

"Oh, Max, I didn't care about hockey. I cared about you. I was so hurt when you ignored me."

"I worked really hard to get better because I didn't think I had anything to offer you without hockey. I had to stay focused. I wasn't trying to ignore you. I was trying to concentrate, to be something for you I didn't mean to hurt you. Then you met Connor. I missed my chance. I waited for you two to break up when we went to college, but you seemed so happy together. I tried to move on. I was shocked when you told me you broke up."

"Connor told me not to go back to you. You're bad for me."

"He's probably right but I'd like to try to prove him wrong."

"And you think we could be happy—after everything?"

"If you give me that chance, I'll do everything I can to make that dream come true."

"That's your dream? Not going pro?"

"Going pro was never my dream. That was my dad's. Loving you was always my dream."

"That's been my dream too."

"So, will you?"

"What?"

"Come home with me and eat onion rings?"

Maddie looks around the room at everyone anxiously waiting for her answer. She thinks about it for a minute and smiles just like the first day she met Max.

"Yes, that can be our first official date."

"And will you come to my hockey games and cheer me on?"

"What games?"

"Maddie, I did it. I worked alongside the Bemidji hockey team and with my trainers last year. Over Christmas break the USHL let me try out and I made Juniors. I played the rest of the season with them and really developed my skills and my speed. Michigan kept a close eye on my progress and invited me to join their team."

"Oh, Max, I'm so proud of you! I can't believe it."

"I haven't accepted yet. I'm not going unless you go with me. I never wanted to be there without you and this time I'm doing it on my terms. My dad doesn't even know."

"McKenna did you apply for me to transfer to Michigan?"

"How did you know I did that?" McKenna asks.

"I dreamt it." Maddie laughs. "Out of curiosity why did you pick that school?"

"Well because they have a great journalism program and I know that is what you want to do."

"And?"

"And because Tommy told me Max made Juniors and was doing really well. I figured it was only a matter of time before he ended up there too. If you were going to run away, I thought I should at least point you in the right direction. I've always known you two belong together."

"Thank you," Maddie smiles at McKenna. To Max, she says, "Assuming I get accepted, I would love to go with you and cheer you on at your games, like a real girlfriend."

"Good, because Samantha's aunt is wrong. The heart shouldn't have to endure love alone. We belong together. Maddie + Max."

THE END

Book Club Questions

Character questions

1. What characters did you relate to or empathize with the most and why?
2. What character did you dislike the most and why?
3. Do you think Tyler and McKenna helped Maddie & Max or should they have pushed them to move on instead of fanning the flames?
4. What do you think happens to Maddie & Max after the story ends?
5. Did you know people like Maddie, Max, McKenna, Tyler, or Samantha when you went to school?

Story questions

1. How would you describe this book in one sentence?
2. How would you describe Maddie's & Max's relationship?
3. What are the main themes of the book? How do you think those influenced Maddie & Max thought process? How relatable are those themes from the 90's in today's world?

4. Do you believe Maddie & Max are soulmates or are they too young to know any better?
5. Do you agree with Samantha or McKenna when it comes to Samantha's aunt take on love – sometimes the heart has to endure love alone.

Book reaction questions

1. How did this book make you feel? Did it evoke any emotions from your past? Were there any parts that made you want to throw it across the room?
2. What surprised you most about this book?
3. What was the most satisfying or disappointing part of the book?
4. How did you feel about the ending?
5. If you could ask the author one question, what would it be?

ACKNOWLEDGEMENTS

Thank you to all my friends and family that supported and encouraged me as I wrote Maddie + Max. I sat down to write a leadership book to honor my dad and out popped this book about love, loss, and letting go. Grief has a funny way of appearing when you least expect and it gives you so many gifts if you embrace it instead of running away.

Angie, this story is as much yours as it is mine. Thank you for the countless conversations we've shared discussing Maddie and Max and helping me bring the story to life. My dad loved you like a daughter and would be proud to know that you and Sophie helped me.

Sophie, you gave me such joy watching you read the first few chapters of this book. I have no doubt you'll publish stories of your own and I can't wait to return the favor. Thanks for your insight, it was a pleasure to share with you.

Krista, thank you for being the very first to read Maddie + Max cover to cover and for your encouragement to publish when I doubted myself. I know my dad would appreciate you giving me the kick in the pants to keep going. I'm sure our dads are looking down on us with smiles.

Teresa, you inspire me to write and live in a world I didn't think was possible. Thank you for always challenging me to stretch my creative bounds. Reading and writing fills me up and you reintroduced me to it when I needed it the most. I can't wait to see my book on the shelves at your store, Village Books.

Laurie & Corinne, I truly appreciate the feedback you shared and the endless questions you answered as I worked through my drafts. Your connection to storylines helped me understand how stories can create meaning for readers. I loved hearing who you related to most and why.

To my wonderful husband Gary, I know I drive you crazy. Thank you for loving me anyways and supporting my endless endeavors even when I write a "loveless love story". I am forever grateful for you taking the time to read the final draft and challenging me to make the story stronger. That's one of the things I love about you the most, you push me to be better when I just want to be done. I love you!

Printed in the USA
CPSIA information can be obtained
at www.ICGtesting.com
LVHW021941221124
797277LV00001B/160

* 9 7 8 1 9 5 5 5 4 1 3 3 6 *